COMMUNION

COMMUNION

Jon Doyle

Atlantic Books
London

First published in hardback in Great Britain in 2026 by
Atlantic Books, an imprint of Atlantic Books Ltd.

1   3   5   7   9   8   6   4   2

A CIP catalogue record for this book is available from the British Library.

Hardback ISBN: 9781805465133
Trade paperback ISBN: 9781805465140

Printed and bound by CPI (UK) Ltd, Croydon CR0 4YY

Atlantic Books
An Imprint of Atlantic Books Ltd
Ormond House
26–27 Boswell Street
London
WC1N 3JZ

www.atlantic-books.co.uk

Product safety EU representative: Authorised Rep Compliance Ltd., Ground Floor,
71 Lower Baggot Street, Dublin, D02 P593, Ireland. www.arccompliance.com

The weak walls
Of the world fall
And heaven, in floods, comes pouring in

Thomas Merton, 'After the Night Office,
Gethsemani Abbey'

PART ONE

Laborare Est Orare

I

His father answered for him when they first asked the question. Words flat and weighted like pebbles dropped to the bottom of a pond. No, no, he's not into that sort of thing. Mack didn't correct the statement. Just wiped at his nose, sipped at his drink. Sat with his face lowered as the men stared in his direction.

That's fair enough, Curly said, waving away the idea. Bald Curly from down the sinter plant, sorry now he'd ever asked. Just thought it might've been up his street.

Mack looked towards his father, Jackie. Made a stupid joke the men didn't catch. It was noisy in the club. Fellers laughing, fellers shouting, fellers coughing into fists. The bone-pile clink of glasses stacked, the rumble of pool balls released from the machine. Mack considered saying the joke again but didn't like to repeat himself. There were only so many times a man could speak without being heard.

Jackie had seemed surprised when he'd asked to meet him after work. Pleased but quiet with it. Composed in his delight. Mack had never been much of a drinker but felt compelled to do something with his father. He was home now, likely for good. It was time to set things straight.

His father's group always sat at the same table. Jackie and Curly and Peggy and Bryn. They'd pinched an extra chair and stuck Mack on the end. Cautious with him, like he was a victim before them, a failed suicide returned. A mood Mack wished to dispel but couldn't quite shift. He was thirty now, but did not feel it. As though on stepping into the club, the line of time had bent back upon itself. The present him no different despite everything. The same quiet kid sitting with his dad.

A hollow thud sounded from the dartboard. A cheer rose from the back wall. The club bustled with a Sunday crowd. Fellers in tattered blazers and hard-bottomed shoes. Custom pool cues and tucked-in polo tops. The hardcore all-dayers and sleepy-eyed regulars, old boys shuffling in shoes fastened with Velcro, their cheeks red and noses too, suits worn shiny at the knees.

The men supped their drinks in awkward silence. Eventually, someone spoke.

We're all doing it, though? Why not him?

The question was addressed to Jackie this time. Mack's father merely shrugged.

He don't have to if he don't want to.

I don't want to either, but it's important, innit? A sort of duty, like.

Bryn Davies. Bryn the Welder. Ears like dishrags, skin hard and dark as unburnished brass. Started in the steelworks with Jackie in the seventies and took voluntary redundancy with him four decades later. A year last February. The older men had felt obliged. If they hadn't gone, it would have been someone else. A lad with a young family. They had a fuss made of them in any case. The foreman played the Last Post on a trumpet at the end of their final shift.

Mack reached for his drink to busy himself. Gulped and made to put the glass down but instead took another swallow. A rushed action. Something to do with his hands. The fizz brought water to his eyes and he blinked against it. He only drank soda and lime these days. Soda and lime or Pepsi Max. No lemon, no ice. That way they really filled up the glass.

He'll only have to take off his shoes and socks, Bryn offered, as though to change his mind. There's nothing to be embarrassed about.

They were calling the Passion an immersive perform-ance. Thursday to Sunday. The Easter story front to back. A spectacle that would unfold in real time across four days, the town itself the stage. Professional actors would play Christ and Pontius Pilate, Joe Public everything else. Hundreds of roles big and small had been divvied up among the commu-nity. The production was organised by a theatre group from out Cardiff way, but they wanted local people at its heart. A chance for the town to come together, they said. An oppor-tunity the steelworkers had snatched with both hands.

Industrial action had been brewing for years. The Steel Company had neglected the plant, a managed decline in a changing world. Negotiations had gotten the unions nowhere, and they'd long lost hope in the government or the ballot box. How better to make a statement than walk out when all eyes were on the town? The stage set, the spotlights on? The performance was already getting attention in the regional news. There were rumours of big names attached.

Pending a final vote, a strike would be called in line with the play. The workers would down tools on the evening of Maundy Thursday and not return until after Sunday's resurrection. A period during which even the blast furnaces would be suspended. An unprecedented pause for every hour their Saviour was dead. It would cost the company millions.

The whole town was excited. It was all anyone talked about.

The theatre company had embraced this new dimension. Cast twelve steelmen past and present as the apostles, arranged to host the Last Supper right there in the club. The men would wear their work uniforms as costumes. Had already been in rehearsals for weeks. Foot-washing. Bread-breaking. Christ the Body and the Blood. Only now Dai Francis had dropped out and they wanted Mack to fill the space. A role for which he didn't feel qualified. He'd only worked a handful of shifts since coming home and wasn't exactly a steelworker at that. But Bryn didn't seem bothered by such details. Mack worked in the plant now. The logo on his jumper was proof.

There's only a handful of scenes you'd need to be there for, Bryn said, brandishing the programme across the table. Last Supper in here next Thursday evening. The Saviour's arrest in the gardens down the beach—

Mack's father exhaled through his nose. Like I said, if he don't want to—

Can't he speak for himself or what?

A ripple passed through the men. A few glances towards Jackie. The convenient sup of a drink. Bryn's gaze settled on Mack, eyes bobbing like bubbles in a spirit level over the froth of his pint.

Mack took the schedule. He'd never been in a play before, barefoot or otherwise. Had no intention of starting now.

But I haven't rehearsed? he pointed out as he flicked through the pages. I wouldn't know what to do.

Don't worry about that, mun, it's easy. You just keep an eye on us. Follow our lead.

Mack studied the order of events. After the betrayal and arrest, the Saviour would be tried Friday noon in the town square, then paraded through the streets and eventually crucified before the entrance of the works at sundown. Saturday was listed as an intermission of sorts, a day of rest and contemplation, while details for the final day were scant. The programme just asked that people gather first thing Easter morning in the centre of town. They should wear their Sunday best, it suggested. Prepare themselves for a celebration.

If I wanted to play dress-up, he said, repeating his earlier joke, I'd have stayed up there in the seminary.

The men heard him this time. Mack tried not to look too pleased when they laughed. A sudden release. Withheld permission granted. All of them laughing but Jackie, though Mack could do little about that.

He made to drink but found it empty. Saw a chance to capitalise.

You know what? he said above the commotion. I think it's my round.

I'll give you a hand, boy, his father said gruffly, already on his feet.

They said little as they waited. Mack stood at the bar, Jackie at his shoulder. Terry Thomas the barman busied himself with a rag. When Terry finally came over, Mack realised he didn't know what the men were drinking. Found himself turning again to his father.

The usual, Jackie said, stepping forward. Terry got to it without a word.

Mack retrieved his wallet and started counting. Terry lined up the pints, paused a moment, then looked to Jackie again.

And the boy? he asked. Another pop?

I think I'm all right, Mack said. There's only so much soda water you can drink. Jackie studied his son a moment before turning back to the bar to repeat it. Terry said nothing. Made no difference to him.

Tell you what, Jackie said, he'll have a bag of nuts.

Terry moved down the bar a way then came back, put two flavours on the counter.

Do he want salted or dry roasted?

Jackie turned back to Mack.

His father had laughed when he first told him about the seminary. Mack had had to say it again. The three of them at the kitchen table, food half eaten, forks in hand. The television talking through the wall. Mack seventeen and tight-voiced, looking to his mother as though she might explain it better. Like she could see inside of him, had known this would be the way of things all along.

Dad, he had said, I'm going to become a priest.

He remembered the quiet, remembered his father's chewing. The nose breath, mouth sounds. Remembered the bead of sweat tracing the line of his ribs, the static catch of his mother's tights as her legs squirmed beneath the tabletop. Remembered his mother starting to speak, his father not waiting to hear it. *Jesus Christ* was all Jackie said, seizing his plate as he stood. Mack remembered watching as his father moved heavy-footed across the room. Remembered the silence. The opening of a cupboard. The rustle of the bag in the bin. The glint of fork against china, and what remained of his tea falling with the dull thud of a dead weight.

Listen, Mack said, stepping to the bar again. Changed my mind. Think I will have a pint after all.

Terry took the nuts back to their boxes without a word and reached for a glass from the rack. He wiped the rim with his rag, then looked up, face expressionless, and said: Stella, issit, like your dad?

The men were all looking at him when he got back to the table. Eyes on his face, waiting for the reaction. All but Bryn, who was sat with his palms pressed together, eyes closed, a folded napkin threaded through the collar of his shirt. A joke they'd planned together.

Mack put the pints down, slid one to Curly and one to Peg, but on reaching to give the last to Bryn he pretended to fumble it, sending the glass and its contents over the lip of the table and onto Bryn's faux-leather shoes.

He raised his palms in hasty apology. Bryn leapt from his chair. *Fuck*, he yelped, the rest of the men in stitches. They fetched a towel and a fresh pint free of charge. Terry Thomas on his hands and knees, casual around broken glass. Mack knelt too, held the pan so Terry could sweep. Bryn pulled off his sodden shoes and socks and rolled his trousers to the calf.

You'll regret this, boy, he said, arms folded, eyes hooded in warning. I'd sleep with one eye open if I was you . . .

Got feet like tree stumps, ain't he? Curly said to the others. Like Nelly the fucking Elephant.

Do us a favour, Bryn, chuck a towel over 'em or something, will you? Putting me off my crisps.

Whoever's playing Jesus has gotta touch 'em next week. He'll be out in a hazmat suit.

Peggy tapped a fag from a pack and balanced it between his lips. Told you who's playing Jesus, didn't I? S'all secret like . . .

The men rolled their eyes. Peggy was prone to tall tales. Lied not so much to convince anyone of the truth as to maintain something he'd started. For the perseverance of the lie itself. Irritated plenty but his mates had grown fond of him. Listened for the entertainment value if nothing else. Like how Peggy claimed to have gone on *Gladiators*, sometime in his golden youth. Tore up the competition, he reckoned. Pissed all over Shadow and Wolf and Jet. Set a new record on the Eliminator, a time previously thought impossible. But the episode was scheduled for the Saturday after Diana died. They never aired it out of respect.

His name was Colin really, but they called him Peggy for reasons lost to time. Peg had a nasal drawl with a bit of Swansea blood in it. Bit of Townhill.

Hasn't Jesus appeared in rehearsals? Mack asked.

Beneath him, that is, Bryn said. Been practising with a stand-in.

A tennis ball on a stick.

He's busy, I heard.

That's 'cos he's famous, Peggy teased. Real special like . . .

Fucking hell, Peg, we're not playing charades. Spit it out, mun.

Peggy took the cigarette from his lips and put it behind his ear. Leaned over the table, voice set low.

I'll give you a clue, he said. Think A-list. Think Hollywood.

Fuck off, Curly laughed.

Peggy raised his eyebrows. It's what I've heard, swear down.

There was only one candidate. The current pride of the town. The latest in an exclusive group of locals who had ascended to the silver screen. The actor had come into school once. A special guest for the play they were putting on, not that Mack had been in it. He'd volunteered as a stage-hand to avoid having to get up before the audience.

This changing your mind, boy? Curly grinned. Some star appeal?

Oh yeah, Mack said, deadpan.

Oi, don't knock him. The awards and stuff he's won.

Peggy also reckons Elizabeth Taylor's playing Mary, though, so take it with a pinch of salt.

Fuck off, Peggy said. You'll see.

So who is playing who exactly? Mack asked. Which apostle are you, Dad?

Jackie seemed confused. We haven't really gone into specifics, he said. We're just the apostles.

Peter I am, Curly announced. He's the sidekick, ain't he? The second in command?

Jackie scratched his head. Simon Peter?

I don't know none of 'em from Adam, Bryn said.

Adam was the feller with the snake.

Think there's a couple of Jameses. A couple of Johns.

There's only one John, Mack said.

John the Baptist.

John the Baptist wasn't—

There's an Andrew and a Bart.

Fuck off there's a Bart, Bryn laughed.

Serious, Curly said. Bartholomew. Looked 'em all up.

A *Bart* in the Bible? Bryn shook his head, eyes landing on Mack. Not pulling my leg, are they, boy?

No, Mack said brightly. There was an apostle named Bartholomew. The son of the furrows. They skinned him alive with a knife.

Couldn't get a knife through them soles, Curly laughed, gesturing towards Bryn's feet again. Have to bring a chisel.

What about you? Bryn pressed, ignoring the comment to eyeball Mack once more. Which apostle do you want to be?

Mack moved his pint and leaned forward too. The tabletop was tacky, so he tried not to put his elbows down.

I told you, he said. I'm not doing it.

Aw, come on, I thought you'd come round!

Goes against my beliefs, Mack said, sarcastic again. Having your feet washed by a false prophet? That's blasphemy.

They'd done the foot-washing every year at mass. One of his first memories of church. The Thursday before Easter, stools lined up on the altar. The smell of polished wood and prayer books, incense and Old Spice. Twelve of the congregation invited forward. Elderly men bending to remove their socks. Brylcreemed hair and signet rings and the rolled-up legs of rayon slacks. The monsignor so old he needed help to kneel, help to rise again, visiting each of the twelve men in turn. He remembered the gentle splash of water. An intimate, private sound.

You're allowed to be blasphemous now, mun, Curly laughed. That's the benefit of packing it in.

And there's nothing false about him, Peggy said. He's Hollywood.

Mack shook his head, resolute, though before the men could protest, they were interrupted by the withdrawn disciple himself. Dai Francis, a feller with only half an ear on one side. He'd lost it playing rugby as a youngster and become something of a local legend. A bloke bit him in the scrum, he reckoned. Swallowed the ear right there in the mud. No one believed the part about the swallowing, but they'd never found the ear. Made do with one and a half for the rest of his life. They took to calling him Dai Eighteen Months.

Sorry, Dai, only apostles at this table, Curly said.

Not too busy for a pint, though, is he?

Dai ignored the comments. Fucking heads up, boys, he said, thumbing over his shoulder. There's a telly crew coming in. Apparently wanna speak with us.

The men turned towards the doors as the team entered. A camerawoman, a sound person, a couple of fellers with lights. People seemingly fascinated by the scene into which they had wandered. Enthralled by the shutters over the bar, the polished wood floor. The plaster ceiling tiles white no longer, jaundiced by years of smoke or rising ghosts. The wall by the entrance held posters demanding justice for the workers, a fair future for steel. In the corner, above the door, hung a small scrap of tinsel. A glitter in the uneven light. Some vestigial Christmas thing.

There was a reporter too. A woman around Mack's age, tall and bony, pretty in a severe kind of way. Dark mascara, hair blonder at the ends than the roots. She wasted no time in venturing into the room. Knelt beside patrons to speak to them on their level. This woman dressed like a foreign correspondent trapped in her hotel. Scarf around her neck, hair tied back with elastic. Jeans, boots, fleece.

The men watched openly as she moved to and fro. Hoped she'd come closer, choose to talk to them.

No tits to speak of, Dai murmured as he squeezed himself into a seat next to Mack, but not half bad.

Oi, love, Curly called out, chancing his arm as she passed. D'you know if there's a Bart in the Bible?

The woman turned, bright smile on her face.

Do I know if there's a what, sorry? she asked, her accent English or posh enough to pass.

A Bart in the Bible, Curly repeated. In the Gospels like?

You don't know she's even Christian, Bryn pointed out, sizing up the woman before them. Could be one of those whatchamacallits.

Buddhists?

I was thinking them kooky ones. The kind who worship trees and stones.

Actually, I'm a humanist, the woman said, voice demure in playful conspiracy. I believe in rational things. Science, individual will.

Curly raised his eyebrows. Didn't miss a beat.

Issit your individual will to have a drink by here or what?

He slid to one half of his seat in invitation. Looked up at the woman and grinned. She narrowed her eyes. Retrieved the pencil from behind her ear and placed it between her teeth.

Mack enjoyed watching the woman. The way she blushed through the men's attention. Refused to be daunted no matter how outnumbered or overwhelmed. He felt better now he had a pint in him. Warmer, loose. Sitting there with the works logo on his chest. Just another one of the boys.

I don't drink on duty, the woman said, holding up a bottle of water. But I'd like a chat if that's all right?

She was interested in the strike and the performance. How the two had become entwined. It was big news. The broadsheets were coming. The arts and culture mags. Crews from Channel 4 and the BBC, though this particular team were more independent. Cool online journalism, as the woman put it. Dispatches with a gonzo edge. Her team planned a big editorial but would film stuff too. A pivot to video. It was the twenty-first century.

The men made further comments. The woman gave as good as she got. She kept looking at Mack and smiling, so he sipped his drink and smiled back.

His earlier reticence was a smudge in the rear-view mirror now. The drink went down easier with every gulp. When he'd left the seminary, he felt he'd been cast out into nothing. A small branch cut from the only tree he knew. But there among the men, he came to see he'd been mistaken. The scales on his eyes had shaken loose. He was a part of something. A larger tree, stretched out in every direction. The men around the table, Terry the barman too. Even the faces in the pictures on the walls, champion teams posed stiff in their jerseys, hollow-eyed in browned monochrome. The more Mack drank, the more embedded he felt. As though he grew bigger with every sip.

The journalist's eyes fell upon Bryn's bare feet beneath the table. She glanced at Bryn, then back at his toes.

Bunions, Curly said. Fucking horrible, innit?

Don't listen to him. Bryn shook his head in apology. Some knobhead spilled beer on my shoes.

The woman seemed keen for a diversion. Turned to the programme.

Have you all signed up?

Most of us, aye.

Bryn glared at Mack.

You're not taking part?

The woman lowered the sheet.

Dai's not taking part either, Mack pointed out.

Wish I could, Dai said, but I've got important stuff on next weekend.

Important like what?

Like important family stuff. Like none of your fucking business.

Well I might have shifts, Mack said. That's important too.

His words came out different now. Consonants sanded down like glass in the tide. The journalist, at least, seemed happy with the excuse.

I guess someone has to keep an eye on the place. I'll make sure to mention you in the—

Hang on? Dai asked, leaning forward with a pained expression. What do you mean, *shifts*? The whole place is shutting down. We're going on fucking strike.

The woman studied them.

Mack worked evenings in security. Something Jackie had sorted out. Security guards had once been employed by the Steel Company, but now a private contractor handled the service. He'd only been in work a week, was yet to join a union. Wasn't entirely sure where he stood.

We've asked our bosses, he said. We're waiting for them to get back to us.

The men eyed him suspiciously. He was determined not to look towards his father.

We explained the situation, he insisted. I'm sure they'll understand.

But Bryn wasn't listening.

Our Mack's *different*, see, he explained to the journalist. Thinks he's above shit like this.

She considered Mack like a puzzle she wasn't sure how to start.

But everyone else is doing it?

He started to explain, but Bryn spoke over him.

Forget it, he said. We've tried. Bryn squared himself in his chair, seizing the woman's attention. I'll answer any questions you've got.

He extended a meaty hand across the table and the woman took it. She wore pink nail varnish but no ring.

Bryn Davies. Retired steelworker, proud apostle.

He spoke with extra lilt, enunciated every word.

I would've taken on a bigger role if I could have. I thought it was a Catholic thing.

It *is* a Catholic thing, Jackie countered. The Passion's the Easter story. Jesus on the cross?

And we're the fucking disciples! Curly laughed. What bigger role did you have in mind?

There was a sense of performance in the way the men spoke to one another, as though their potential audience was already sat before them. Mack wished they would be quiet. He wanted the woman to talk to him.

Don't see what Catholic has to do with anything, Bryn

said. Don't care if it's about Easter or Hanukkah or fucking Ramadan so long as it brings people together. That's what this is about, see? Community.

The journalist turned the page of her notebook. Introduced herself by name. Said she was interested in this idea of community. Mack nodded to show he was paying attention but had forgotten her name already. He enjoyed listening to the woman speak.

Will there be singing? she asked suddenly.

Singing?

You know, male choir?

In the Passion?

No singing, Bryn said. Not that we've been told.

Oh. The woman was put out. I figured there might be singing. I thought you were into that kind of thing.

A man in a green sports coat emerged from the bathrooms across the hall. Must've been nearing ninety. Stick in hand, comb-over dyed jet black, skin like poured cement. He made for the row of fruit machines blinking patterns along the nearest wall. Went to his pocket for change but the game malfunctioned. Its light show gone haywire. A nasal thrum emanated from the workings inside.

The drone filled the silence. The men took a communal sip of drink. They doubted there'd be singing but they didn't know for sure. The director of the production had stressed how she liked to empower her performers. Claimed the true beauty of theatre existed within unforeseen energies on the night.

And what about the star lead? the journalist asked. What's he like?

What's who like? Bryn asked, narrowing his eyes. It's a secret, innit?

The woman hesitated. Yes, she said, I just assumed—

You know who it is?

Me?

She was flipping through her notes now, pink in her cheeks again.

She does.

I don't. Not for certain. I've only heard . . .

Heard?

I've heard rumours.

She leaned close, hand to her mouth to whisper.

I know it's someone famous.

Uproar at the table. Peggy beamed like he'd won a prize. Mack put his drink down and picked it up again. Looked at his father and found him flushed in the face. To his left, the man in the sports coat thumped the broken bandit, trying to get his money back. The machine whined high and needling. A nest of winged beings. The noise seemed to get under Dai's skin, jumpy next to Mack now, knees jouncing against the table's underside. Mack edged sidewards to put a little distance between them. He could smell old smoke coming off Dai's clothes as he moved.

That fucking bandit's doing my head in, Dai muttered. Gonna put my foot through it if it carries on.

Bryn! the journalist said brightly, slapping both palms on the table. Can I call you Bryn? Let's get back to what you were saying earlier. The stuff about community.

Mack could smell her perfume. A floral warmth across the table. The slightest hint of spice. When she said community, it sounded italicised.

Bryn drained his glass and put it down decisively, foam lining the sides like a caul.

Community, aye. What you wanna know?

Why not start with the situation with the steelworks?

She spoke with a voice as clean and crisp as a new twenty-pound note. Every so often pulled the elastic from her ponytail and shook her hair loose over her shoulders. Gathered her hair in her hands and put the elastic back in.

Well, it's a long story, Bryn said, but basically the Steel Company don't want to stump up the cash any longer, so they're ripping the heart out of the plant under the guise of going green. They say they're going to switch from proper furnaces and virgin steel to electric arcs, which would essentially make us a recycling depot. Only a fraction of the workforce would survive. Tensions have been simmering for donkey's years but things are boiling over. They're being disingenuous, see? Offering lump sums for voluntary redundancy but only if you're good and docile. No protests, no bargaining, no organised action. You'll jump before you're pushed, they're telling us. And you'll jump fucking quietly.

And how does the production figure in this? the woman pressed. Countering the prevailing image of the town? Because it has a reputation, right? A picture projected by people who don't know it as well as you?

The men quieted, suddenly cautious.

We did surveys, she said, licking her thumb to flip back through her notes. Asked people from around the country for their impressions of the place. A failing town. A dirty town. A town existing under a cloud.

I see you've read the brochures.

Mack sipped his pint to hide his smile. The woman examined him across the table. Her earrings twinkling, swinging pearls.

When he glanced up, she caught him looking. She smiled before he could avert his gaze.

The play's an opportunity, Bryn said. In more ways than one. Our protest will have more impact when people like you are here to report on it, but it's also a chance to show the outside world who we really are. There's more to the town than meets the eye, see? And we've always punched above our weight in acting.

The journalist wrote with a quick hand. Kept glancing at Mack as if to confirm it all true. The warmth in his limbs was taking on a new dimension. The smug rush felt by locals in the presence of tourists, able to amaze with the simplest of things.

Performance is a big part of this community, Curly said. Acting and that is in our blood.

Even the Passion play's a tradition, Jackie added. Happened every year when I was a nipper. Open air in Margam Park. Families with picnics, kids running around. That was the idea behind this play originally. Resurrecting the good old days. I keep thinking what my old man would say if he was here to see it now.

Someone at a nearby table hitched a chair across the floor. Mack felt the vibration through the soles of his shoes.

He'd be chuffed, mun, Bryn said, clamping Jackie on the back. We're gonna do him proud.

Mack watched his father nod slowly, face shadowed in its downward tilt.

Grampa O'Brien had died back in the summer. A month to the day after Gran. A shock for everyone, but maybe for the best. Gran always said she'd come back to haunt him if he didn't look after the garden when she'd gone. Mack came home for the funerals. Two Mondays, four weeks apart. Jackie delivered one eulogy, then the other. Endured the wakes then carried on like nothing had happened. Even their house remained untouched.

Roman soldier one year he was, Jackie said. Quiet now, talking towards the tabletop. Helmet, sword, sandals. One of them skirts they had. I remember how big he seemed in the hall. Looked like Richard Burton in an old Bible epic. People were tooting their horns as we made our way to the park. Felt like the whole town was there. Kids today haven't had anything like that.

The woman smiled at Jackie the way a doctor might. A nursery teacher on her knees in the yard. The fruit machine blinked in the corner. Mack could see the coloured light on her teeth.

Well now you can all be a part of it, she said. Your kids, your grandchildren . . . Do you have grandchildren?

The men eyed Mack, saying nothing.

Bit of a complicated one, old Mack, Bryn chuckled. I would say he was enjoying his freedom, but—

No grandchildren, Jackie clarified, like a man before a judge. Not yet.

The journalist looked towards Mack again. Eyes narrowed, almost playful, a faint smile on her lips. The noise of the room had softened. The edges rounded. Like insulation wrapped around metal pipes. Mack drained what remained of his drink with a flourish and set the glass down. Shrugged at the woman as if to say, what can you do?

Anyway, he said, getting to his feet. It's my round.

Still got half of mine left, Curly laughed, raising his glass to eye level.

And you've only just been up. Peggy hasn't got out of his seat all evening.

Dai hasn't got out of his seat all *year*.

Mack's making up for lost time, ain't he? Bryn said.

Lost time where? the journalist wanted to know.

Mack didn't reply, unsure whether he was savouring the mystery of the lingering question or worrying what she'd think of the answer.

I'm not keeping score, he said. Think of it as my treat.

He's been at the seminary, Bryn interrupted. Wanted to be a priest.

The journalist chewed her pen as she measured Mack, face a cartoon of scepticism.

You're teasing me.

We're not, mun. On my mother's life.

He's not a priest.

He is!

A Catholic priest?

The men were laughing now. Mack's ears burned.

Well, I'm not actually a—

Prove it, she demanded.

A fresh wave of laughter. How's he meant to do that?

I don't know. Do something. Perform a miracle.

She looked at him. Mack wiped his mouth with the back of his hand.

Tell you what, he said, gesturing towards the bottle beside her. I'll turn that water into wine, how about that?

Mack's ears were ringing when he got to the bar. He felt so good it seemed he was floating three inches from the ground. The way the men had laughed when he delivered his punchline. The journalist's expression as she held her water out. He couldn't recall the last time he'd made a person laugh before this evening, let alone a crowd of them. Wanted nothing more than to feel the giddy rush again.

The rector had questioned his motivations for joining the seminary. Suggested he was moved by a desire to be good, rather than any authentic call. The criticism had stung and confused him in equal measure, but he was coming to see the funny side. Him, a priest? A teenage decision. A kid in a man's clothes. For the first time he saw it through his father's eyes. But rather than embarrassment, he felt the bright glow of epiphany. He wasn't a priest. He didn't need to save the world. He was home, among friends, and free to imagine the future he'd thought could never be his.

Two men stood ahead, pints already in hand. Mack nodded along with their conversation, affection blooming inside him. The town suddenly full of buddies. He didn't know what wine the woman wanted but didn't go back and ask. He felt he'd never make another mistake in his life.

The shorter of the men told the other: What's the worst that could happen? A put-on accent, American. He said it again and laughed.

There's a journalist over there, Mack interrupted, half whispering, a secret to keep under wraps. She wants to hear our story.

The men turned to face him, rustling with the nylon of their coats.

We've been served, mind, the taller one said, stepping aside. A beanpole feller with the kind of glasses found in the glovebox of a serial killer's transit van.

Right you are, Mack said, frisking for his wallet. He was

using phrases he'd never uttered in his life. Felt as big as he'd ever done. Himself and a half.

Terry Thomas eyed him from behind the pumps. The bar just a hatch in the wall.

I'll be with you in a sec, Ter, Mack said, still patting for his wallet. A new wave of satisfaction came over him. He kept remembering everything he'd figured out.

It called for a celebration, he decided. Brandies, whiskies, something to toast with the old man. He'd be sure to get the seat next to Jackie so they could share the moment. A little reconciliation, just the two of them.

As he ordered, he spotted a pile of napkins on the bar top. Added to the plan in his head. He tore a napkin in half and folded it lengthways. Rested it on the counter and folded it again. He hitched his jumper down to thread the napkin through his collar, just like Bryn had done.

He could see himself marching towards them. Father Cormac O'Brien, returned with the good news.

Is this straight? he asked, turning back to the bar.

Terry stared unimpressed.

I'll use the mirror in the bogs, Mack laughed, already setting off. Get us a round of whiskies and a glass of your best red.

But as he exited the bar and turned into the corridor, he almost walked headlong into someone coming the other way.

The surprise of it made him flinch. Avert his head and close his eyes.

I'm sorry, he said, laughter quick to fill the gap panic had vacated. Are you all right?

The woman made to speak but stopped abruptly. Offered nothing but a surprised syllable. It was only then he really looked at her. Gears turned sluggish in his head but she was more nimble in her recovery.

Hello, stranger.

She observed him with her eyebrows raised, arms folded across her chest. Her hair dark and knotted in a practical bun though strands escaped around her face. A jacket folded over her arm, a knit jumper with a neck high on her throat. Freckles on her nose, blood in her cheeks, a small pendant on a fine gold chain. She smelled clean, cold, the outside brought in. The chain was barely thicker than a spider's web.

Ever since she was a girl, a crease had marked Siwan's forehead when she concentrated. She was concentrating on him.

Mack looked over his shoulder, as though to check whether anyone else saw her too.

What are you doing here?

What am *I* doing here?

She looked into his face. He stood there numbly, rubbed the back of his neck.

I've just come for a shandy, she said. That's all right, isn't it? Or have they got my picture up behind the bar?

Her eyes slid to the napkin in his collar. He snatched at it and closed his fist.

Is that all right?

Mack tried to meet her eye but felt his chin was wired to the floor. The works logo on his breast suddenly felt conspicuous.

It's just temporary, he started, looking down at his jumper. Security. Things haven't quite gone to plan.

An old cigarette machine was nailed to the wall behind her. A line of coats strung on hooks like the skins of dead animals. A frigid draught fell down the corridor, the night finding its way inside.

Are they setting up a camera? she asked, standing on her toes to view the room back down the hall. Who knew a little play would attract so much attention?

Mack noticed she was holding a programme. He coughed to clear his throat, reluctant to share an opinion on the Passion without knowing where she stood.

A quiet settled between them, each waiting for the other to go first. Dark lines under her eyes betrayed a certain fatigue. He couldn't believe how much she looked like her mother. The same thought had struck him when he'd last seen her, standing on the cobbled path outside the seminary. Siwan fiddling with the hair at the back of her neck. The sun dipping. Blackbirds singing softly in the trees.

They'd rung up to his dorm. A visitor, no name. He found her waiting in the half-dark. He wasn't allowed guests to his room, so they'd gone to the library. One of the private cubbyholes. Sat facing one another. A jail visit, only this time it was the visitor with a confession to make.

Do you want a drink?

Siwan held his eye after the question, daring him to explain why not.

Mack didn't answer. He was cold now. Skin gooseflesh under his clothes. He wasn't sure whether he was suddenly sober or if the drink was really sinking in. His earlier confidence had vanished. In its wake was not much of anything.

She stood and looked at him, learning plenty despite his silence. He kept glancing around, afraid of who might see them there.

Forget it, she said. I'll go.

He reached for her arm, but a door banged in the bathroom behind them. They waited like guilty schoolchildren for someone to emerge. Instead, the hand dryer sounded.

I didn't know you were home, Mack said.

He started to shiver. Sweat grabbed at his shirt as a nausea stirred.

Why don't we get coffee sometime? he suggested.

Coffee sometime, Siwan repeated. Right.

She unfolded her jacket and put it on, one arm then the other. Mack stood and watched.

Do you want my number? she asked.

Your number?

To put in your phone?

Oh, he said, scratching at his neck again. I haven't got a phone.

She smiled at that. Of course you haven't.

Why did you come here, Siwan?

She considered the question, but instead of answering just brushed the creases from her jacket. As she turned to leave, she stopped.

Mack . . . she said.

A dread crept over him as he looked into her face. He felt tired all of a sudden. Like the life had drained out of him. It was an effort just standing straight.

Are you all right?

Her head tilted sidewards. The crease back on her forehead.

Mack said he was fine, but he wasn't. He felt dizzy and sick.

Whoa, Siwan said, stepping to take his arm. How much have you had to drink?

I haven't— Mack started, but he couldn't finish. He smelled the fruit scent of her hair as she took hold of him. Felt the heat beneath the chill of her clothes. Smelled another fragrance too, something deep and blood-warm and living.

She felt sturdy against him. Able to bear his weight. He might have stayed in her grasp forever, but then the door to the toilet banged open and she stepped away.

Drink plenty of water, she called over her shoulder as she headed for the exit. And don't forget that coffee.

Mack watched her go, then pushed into the men's. The old man in the sports coat was stood at the only urinal, studying the wall ahead with a resigned patience, pissing like a kinked hose. He wore trainers, this feller. Miracle white with laces in long loops.

Mack ducked into the cubicle and locked it. Considered getting to his knees before the bowl but didn't trust the floor. The bathroom dripped like a limestone cave, smelled of piss and sweat and bleach. The old man's belt buckle clinked. Mack put the lid down and sat on the toilet. Felt the blood rush through the smallest vessels of his head.

He closed his eyes and tried to calm himself, old rhythms returning.

Lamb of God, you take away the sins of the world. Have mercy on us.

Lamb of God, you take away the sins of the world. Have mercy on us.

Lamb of God, you take away the sins of the world. Grant us peace.

When the nausea passed, he opened the cubicle door. The old feller was still there, shifting his weight from one foot to the next in a slow and cautious dance.

Bless me, Father, for I have sinned, that's what Siwan had said at the seminary. The library silent but for distant footfall. The latent quiet of a held breath. Ceiling lights on motion sensors blinking off around them. A heaviness to the air. The dormant weight of books.

Mack in a sweater, slacks and shoes. All black, symbolic. Death to the world and to the self.

He'd sat dumb before her, suddenly self-conscious. A child in fancy dress. It had felt impossible she was there, or rather there felt impossible in her company. The past returned to mock the present. Mack woken to find himself wearing the clothes of a dream.

His thirtieth birthday had been two days away. At first, against all reason, he'd thought she'd come for that.

I've yet to be ordained, he had told her. I'm a student. A lay person studying theology.

She'd watched him across the table. Face blank, hands in her lap. She said: It has been too long since my last confession.

He'd laughed then. Waited for her to laugh too. Siwan, he said, you're going to get me excommunicated. I'll get a letter from the Vatican.

But she hadn't laughed. Only raised her eyes to his.
Humour me, Mack.
He shook his head. I'm not a priest. I couldn't—
Please?
Mack had fallen quiet. There were things he wished to tell her too. How his life seemed to be unravelling. His character questioned, his suitability for the priesthood doubted by those with the power to decide his fate. He'd had a meeting with the rector of the seminary on the subject. One to one

in a plush office with cheap biscuits and lukewarm coffee. A reasonable man up to a point.

Siwan, I can listen as a friend but—

I didn't come to see a friend, she had said. I came to see a priest.

He'd hesitated then. Would it hurt to play along? After all, wasn't he about to leave?

Okay. All right. Why don't we take it from the top?

She had straightened in her chair. Closed her eyes and crossed herself. But before she continued, she raised her head, one eye open towards him.

Just so we're clear, she had said, I know the rules of this. What I say cannot be repeated. Not to anyone.

The men were stood at the bar when he returned. A silent congress, whiskies held but not yet sipped. Jackie with one in each hand, waiting for his son. The broken fruit machine whined above everything.

Only Bryn remained at their table. Sat now before a camera on a tripod and a light angled so shadows exaggerated his face. Everyone in the room was listening. Bryn looked straight down the lens as he spoke.

First you have to understand the *context*, he said. The town's *history*.

The journalist lingered out of shot with her notebook raised. Bryn paused in thought, chin thrust upwards, eyes towards the ceiling. A man sombre before his audience, ready to provide the theatre they craved.

But the droning bandit spoilt the image. Bryn couldn't help but look.

We can edit that out, the journalist said, nodding in

encouragement. Please continue.

Bryn apologised. Said it wasn't just the immediate jobs they were worried about. It was the supporting industries. The engineers, the IT boys, the local barbers and caffs. If the works went under, the town went under. Might as well cut out its heart.

A smile broke over Jackie's face as Mack sidled over. He extended a glass towards his son. A double whisky, a toast.

Mack felt he'd been gone hours. Kept thinking of things he should've said to Siwan. The men grinned in his direction, bobbed their drinks to him in thanks. He thought of the joke with the collar. He couldn't remember what he'd been thinking with the drinks. The plan of a man who'd since upped and left. He'd returned himself and nothing more, and he'd brought the draught in with him. The cold air lifted the bunting behind the till. A slow rise and fall, a sleeping creature breathing.

He took the whisky from his father, touched his glass against his. Jackie, saying nothing, stepped forward and pulled him into an embrace.

Mack could smell the beer on him. The same old aftershave. Thanks so much, boy, his father said, a handful of Mack's jumper balled in his fist. It means a ton to me.

Mack wasn't sure what meant a ton but didn't have the chance to ask as Bryn's monologue continued across the room.

There was a time when things were good, he said, voice raised above the bandit. When a feller wouldn't work anywhere else. You couldn't find a painter in town. Men threw down their aprons in the bakeries. And with the jobs came pubs, cinemas, playing fields. The brand-new lido down the beach. Treasure Island, they called it. A gold rush with no one having to kill each other for the prize.

But then along came the eighties. A change of focus. You Know Who.

Bet she's looking up at us now, Curly called out, glass aloft above his head.

The gathered crowd cheered. Jackie eased his grip.

I've been thinking, he said, hands on Mack's shoulders, barely able to meet his eye. It's time we cleared Gran and Grampa's house, don't you reckon?

His father's voice was small, his eyes wet, his face set and solid, a mask he was trapped inside. Mack didn't know what to say to him. He said okay, all right.

Jackie drained his liquor and slapped the glass on the bar. Bryn had paused, drawing energy from the crowd.

But we've fought till now, he said eventually, voice slow and loaded. And we'll keep on fighting. For the future. For the very town itself. More cheers. Bryn out of his seat. They might have been the underdogs, but they had each other. They had a friend in fucking Hollywood. So what if the government had forgotten them? If corporations saw nothing more than mules to work to death? They'd stand their ground until the very last moment. Even if it meant making a noise about it. Even if it meant walking out.

The men surged forward to meet their spokesman. The journalist and crew retreated with grins on their faces. Thumbs up. Job done. Mack stayed with his back pressed to the bar as nausea slithered over him again. He thought once more of Siwan. That evening at the seminary. Appearing after the best part of a decade with a simple question.

Could he take her seriously?

A sheet of paper lay on the counter beside him. A page crumpled and wet with a ring of a drink. *The Apostles*, the title read. A list of names. Jackie and Curly, Peggy and Bryn, every one of their mates. And at the bottom, in handwriting Mack didn't recognise: *Father Cormac O'Brien*, the twelfth name on the list.

He sensed a warm body beside him. A floral smell. Breath in his ear saying, did you bless it yet?

For a second, he expected Siwan. The journalist held the wine in two hands, offered out to him.

A toast, Jackie shouted in the middle of the room, a toast for our family. But before he could speak further, the fruit machine spluttered, gurgled its gears, started wailing.

Mack felt dread return like fog rising from the ground. He looked around in desperation.

I've had enough of this fucking thing . . .

Dai before the bandit. A darts trophy raised in both hands above his head.

The journalist inhaled sharply. The room suddenly in slow motion. An underwater scene. You'll pay for any damage, Terry Thomas warned, but it was too late for Dai now.

The screen collapsed under the weight of the trophy's base, the cracked glass threading outwards. The machine wheezed, sparked once, twice; then, with the briefest hesitation, its screen extinguished and with it every bulb in the club.

II

The night brought hail. God's bluntest message, hammering dull across every surface. A downpour that built towards a promised climax yet eased as quickly as it had begun. Mack climbed from his bed to see it peter out. Found the road covered white as though a snow had fallen. The street dripping and muted as if shell-shocked.

He'd been dreaming, though the specifics had receded. He stood barefoot and childlike at the window, watched the hail turn translucent as it melted under street lamps. It seemed it was his dream from which the street was recovering. The world itself rattled by the pictures in his head. He remembered standing on a beach, remembered the crab claws and gutweed and bladderwrack, a looming sky and a salt-heat and a sound. But the dream was also becoming meltwater now. Impossible to hold onto, running thin through his grasp.

He stalked the hall and pissed, then washed his face in the sink. Returned to bed and lay there. An alarm sounded from the works. A warning not a mile away. He gave up and went downstairs, taking the blanket from the bed.

The sofa was not comfortable, but it was a change at least.

The clock on the VCR flashed phosphorescent. The television screen stood like a basalt block. Behind the clock on the mantel was balanced a palm cross from mass the previous morning. There was a dampness to the linen at that hour. A dew to the dark. He pulled the blanket around himself, knees bent halfway to his chest, and when sleep did arrive it came shy and drifting. A state that never quite descended.

The yelling television roused him. Mack heard it before he opened his eyes. Felt a brief disorientation. A spun penny settling flat. He was on the settee in the living room, only it was light now and the sparrows chattered outside.

When he opened his eyes, he found his mother on the opposite sofa. Her lips moving. The hood of her dressing gown pulled up. A familiar scene played on the television. Early morning, real life. A documentary taped from one of the channels between the regionals and the news.

The top of a building was on fire. The girl filming yelled down a phone. It's on fire, she said, it's on fire. The picture was low definition and shaky but the girl had a pretty good handle on the zoom. In and out, in and out, the adjacent windows glinting like fish scales, the sky a shocking sweep of blue.

Something was happening. Something serious. History as it unfolded outside her window.

We're freaking videotaping it, the girl said. We're getting it all.

Mack watched with one eye creased shut, afraid that to move was to betray his consciousness.

The TV showed black smoke billowing up and leftwards, a plume like a great hand reaching down. Paper suspended in the air, blown from windows and gathering like a flock of seabirds.

The girl zoomed closer. The picture swayed and rocked.

You should watch the news, someone said off camera. It's all over the news.

Mack shifted his body, felt a chill as he disturbed his own heat from the cushions. His mother was watching the television and praying but stopped abruptly as he moved.

Cormac? she called, crossing herself quickly. Her voice hushed, half whispered. Testing the depth of his sleep.

He shut his eyes and didn't answer. Felt he'd walked in on an act of intimacy. Better to pretend he hadn't seen. Feign slumber for them both.

A reporter's voice joined the commentary. Said something about a plane. The reporter said: I just saw flames inside. He said: You can see the smoke coming out. A reporter shouting at the top of his voice, shouting as though afraid of stopping, as if any second of dead air might bring the whole thing to the ground.

We have no idea, the reporter concluded. We have no clue what's going on.

Mack cracked his eyes. A covert viewing through eyelash fuzz. He watched fire engines approach. Sirens front and back. Something was falling from the building at irregular intervals. The camera zoomed, trying to catch them. Zoomed so close everything became a blur.

A flash on the left. A truncated gasp. A terrific arc of steel and fire and concrete and glass.

Oh my God.

Oh my God!

Oh my God.

Oh my *God*.

Oh my God!

Clara paused the television. Crossed herself again. Rewound to the second crash. The spray of debris, an orange-black bloom. An eye suddenly opened then closed again, reverted to a depthless black.

His mother's lips began to move.

Eternal rest grant unto them, oh Lord . . .

She had seen the clip before, and others just like it. A thousand syndicated angles of a single event. She had seen the clip before but still took it upon herself to pray for them.

The smoke, the towers, the gasping orange flash. The people jumping not by choice but because of the fire at their backs.

Let perpetual light shine upon them.

Clara was always praying for the dead. A custom passed down the maternal line. Her mother's mother and her mother before that. Women who believed so devoutly they risked straying towards some occultist other side. A proper Catholic was how Nanna Caitríona had described herself, though Jackie had called his mother-in-law a witch behind her back. A woman who claimed to hear disembodied voices and animal growling, swore she'd seen candlesticks dance down the mantelpiece as a child. Clara had laughed it off until her own experiences started. A persistent presence behind her. The occasion her bedclothes were snatched back by an unseen hand.

The dead! Nanna Caitríona had exclaimed when she learned of it. Trapped souls asking for your help.

Clara had started praying that night. At first in hope as much as belief. Twenty-something and forward-thinking, wishing to be free from such antiquities. Yet terror was a convincing thing. And with conviction came habit, with habit, compulsion. With compulsion, the sense of balancing the world. For generations her forebears had prayed for the souls they knew, tracing relatives along vast oral genealogies, but Clara did not limit herself. The family was a lot smaller by the time they buried her mother, but by then there were different connections. Poor souls on every screen.

The dead needed looking after, as Nanna Caitríona had put it. They were trapped in purgatory. You could offer up your prayers or offer up your pain. If you were suffering, they need not. What the Lord taketh, he giveth away.

Amen, Mack's mother murmured towards the television. She crossed herself like putting down the phone. Mack stirred as though woken by the end of the programme. Felt his mother turn and look.

Heavy night?

I didn't drink, Mack said, propped on one elbow.

His mother made a face.

He got off the sofa and went to the window. Stretched his back as he parted the blinds. Found a day clouded and glaring. Morning traffic on the street. Water standing on the flat roof opposite but no rain in the air. The last of the relic hail like frogspawn in the gutters. A sinter plant stack loomed above the opposite terrace, a great cigarette balanced on end.

The previous night kept returning. Conversations in fragments. The things he'd said, things said to him. He felt a vague shame recalling his bravado around the journalist.

Felt worse remembering the encounter with Siwan in the hall. Like he'd been caught trying to be a different person entirely, some part of his soul attempting to pull his body in a new direction, or else the other way around. His ears were muffled, still full of the hum of the fruit machine, the blustering voices, the rain. He'd left the club under the cover of darkness once the power had cut, without a word to anyone. This morning his head felt lighter than the rest of him. A helium balloon on a string.

I drank a bit, he clarified. Just to get the men off my back.

His mother shifted towards the edge of her seat, expression betraying nothing.

Nanna always said your father was a bad influence.

Mack never saw Nanna Caitríona outside of her own living room. Small and bony, propped upright in her chair. Like a one-man tent collapsed and stuffed into a bag. It was always unbearably hot in her house. The gas fire hissing blue flames in a nest of ceramic logs. She saw out her days listening to the wireless and imparting wisdom to anyone who came close enough.

Negative attracts negative, she told him once, talon finger thrust in his direction. The pessimist brings tragedy to life.

Nanna Caitríona had subscribed to such things without nuance. If you dwelt on darkness, you became dark yourself. Why do you think all those horror films were cursed? Entire sets gone up in flames. Healthy actors dropping dead. One time Jackie snuck Clara in underage to see *The Exorcist*, and on finding out the old woman had berated them with such anger it seemed she herself was possessed.

Talking of bad influence, Dad said you've put your name down?

His mother was standing now, a forced nonchalance to her voice. A fresh wave of regret came over him.

I thought he was messing about. You? *Acting?*

I didn't—

Suppose you got used to it. Standing in front of a crowd. You know, up in the . . .

She trailed off but didn't leave, sizing his prone figure on the couch. His mother had trouble talking about the seminary. Like she didn't want to hear his reasoning for leaving, or else didn't know where to begin.

I've been meaning to say, she started again, her tone back to feigned indifference, Dad put that box of books up the attic.

Mack felt cold. Pulled the blanket closer to his chin. What books?

The ones Canon Sylvester dropped off? I told you on the phone.

The television was still on but no picture was showing. He didn't know anything about any books.

I know you probably aren't interested now, his mother said, but—

But you're telling me anyway?

He was asking after you outside mass yesterday. He always asks after you.

Clara paused. Looked towards her slippers on the carpet.

You should come along sometime. He'd love to see you before—

Mam, he said.

His mother flinched as though he'd shouted. For a moment he thought she was going to cry. He wasn't sure if it was his ignoble return that bothered her or its unoriginality. A young man losing his faith. How disappointing. How clichéd. That, after everything, he wished for no more than his father or his father before him. A pint in his hand, steady work, a woman with whom to share a bed.

Well, she said eventually, the books are up the attic anyway.

Mack had spent much time walking the streets since returning from the seminary. Beset by restlessness, a desire to move. As though to stay in one place was to risk being located. Backed into a corner and made to explain himself. He walked head down, collar high, thinking he might have known every person he passed. Faces he remembered but couldn't place. People who did not greet him nor he them. He wasn't sure which was worse: to be recognised or taken for a stranger. After all, he'd left to become a different man and come back more or less the same.

Father O'Brien had never materialised. He was stuck just being Mack.

The roil of the works disturbed the air. The power plant with its boilers and blowers. The vacuum degassers. The sinter stack and its rising rusty plume. He headed down Connaught Street and the bottom of Tan-y-Groes, past the telephone exchange and sorting office and onto the main road by the lights. The Plaza stood on the corner there, the old cinema ruined now beyond its art deco facade and faded Pepsi sign. The front boarded up, a triptych of heads spray-painted on the plywood sheets. Three famous actors who'd left the town for Hollywood over the years. Their holy trinity.

The Plaza had closed before Mack left adolescence, though its interior persisted in his head. Something almost Ancient Egyptian in its splendour. A temple with the wind of old glamour still blowing through. The walls under the canopy painted black so the artwork stood out. The stairs leading into the foyer shimmering with glittered tiles. The auditorium had red velvet curtains, a choice between the upper and lower tier. The popcorn machine possessed a dense amber glow.

He and Siwan had gone to the Plaza together as children. A cryptic arrangement decided by their parents above their heads. Kid Mack sensed it an attempt to distract her. Get her out of the house for a while. A couple of hours in the dark with bottles of pop and peanut M&Ms. He could picture the first time now, waiting in the car as his mother knocked the front door, craning his neck for a glimpse inside. He understood Siwan's mam had something wrong with her, but he didn't know what and didn't want to. The woman he saw in church didn't look poorly, but mothers were good at hiding things.

He remembered Siwan at the door, still in her school uniform. Remembered the pair of them awkward on the back seat. Her lips thin, hair pinned with clips, sat with her hands in her lap and her back straight, like she didn't want to put a crease in her clothes. He let her choose the film. An abstract gesture of sympathy. They took seats halfway up on the left. Mack in the middle between his mother and Siwan. The latter said little to him, nor he to her. When their hands met on the armrest, Mack ceded the ground. But when the lights went down and the curtains parted and the screen came to life, they might have been somewhere else entirely.

He felt her leg press against his and he pressed back, her body warm in the dark.

Heat rose to Mack's face as he recalled the previous evening again. Him in his works jumper, lager on his tongue. Siwan suddenly before him. He wished to explain himself better. Clarify or apologise. Ask the one question that had burned in his chest ever since her visit to the seminary.

She hadn't really meant what she'd said, had she?

He crossed the railway line at the train station and took the new road back towards Taibach. His pace charged with a sense of direction. A small tightness in his chest. Road signs warned of traffic disruption in the coming days. Crews in hi-vis vests set out crowd control barriers along the road-side. He didn't know if Siwan still lived where she used to live, but there was only one way of finding out. He would walk up to her front door, he decided. He would raise his hand and knock.

The road cut right up to the boundary of the works. Close enough for anyone to stand beneath the towers and the stacks. A group of workers were erecting a scaffold on the roundabout before the blast furnaces. They called instructions to one another. Single words, gestures with hands. Whether they were part of the strike or the play was not entirely clear. The furnaces growled behind them, those dull metal bodies hiding ferocious pressure and heat.

The blasts stopped at nothing. Smelted iron ore every hour of the day and exhaled clouds into the sky. When Mack first moved away, he'd felt something had been taken from him. The world too quiet all of a sudden. A silence too much for sleep. But on occasion he would wake in the dead hours of the night and feel the vibration in his marrow. You could not escape the song of the furnaces quite so easily.

He'd buy her breakfast, he told himself. A café where they served pancakes with butter and syrup. A place with red check tablecloths and sugar in a shaker. A waitress who came over every so often to refill the coffee. But they only did that in America or on television and he was spooked by the idea of seeing someone he knew. A school friend, a boy he'd played football with once upon a time. A feller he hadn't seen in forever with questions about how he had spent the blank years in between.

He went into the supermarket instead. The small one on the road with parking at the back. They had Easter chocolate on offer, lined up near the entrance. They had toy rabbits, yellow chicks, baskets of painted eggs. He couldn't remember what Siwan liked, or rather came to realise he'd never known. He stood in the bakery aisle and assessed his options. The doughnuts looked a little sorry for themselves. The cherry pie had a crater in the middle like someone had dropped it on the floor.

After some deliberation, he slid two pastries into a paper bag with the plastic tongs provided. The tongs were looped on a wire and tied to the shelf as if they feared someone might pinch them. He poured her a coffee from the machine and added two sugars. Wanted to get himself a coffee too but there was only so much he could carry with two hands.

Outside, a man in a boiler suit climbed a ladder to attach a new poster to the billboard on the side of the library. He pasted the glue with a brush and slowly unrolled the sheet from the top. Old displays were visible on the back mount, images disintegrated into ribbons, the strata of years superimposed. As the new poster unfurled, its subject revealed itself. *HE IS COMING*, the message read. *OPENING THURSDAY. TICKETS STILL AVAILABLE.*

A distant rumble caused the man to turn, and Mack turned with him. The sound suddenly not so distant. An approaching freight train on the line, loaded with steel coils. They stood and watched the wagons pass for what felt like minutes, the train's two-tone skip across the rails like a dropped ball that kept on bouncing, its momentum a miraculous trick.

Siwan's road looked different to how he remembered. They'd done up the fronts of the houses. Identical pebble-dash, a council grant. Her front door held the same stained-glass panel but had been painted a different colour. White grab rails now screwed to the wall on either side. The old-model Corsa outside had a For Sale sign in the window and a coat on the back seat. He recognised the jacket as the one she had worn the previous evening.

He hesitated on the other side of the road. Walked some way up the street and back again. Made a point of looking at his watch. He wished he had worn his wool coat, a garment smart and heavy and black. But he didn't have his wool coat. He had a windbreaker that rustled when he walked. He had two pastries and a half-cold coffee. He had lint in his pockets and feeling in his stomach like a plughole sucking at a shallow bath. A curtain twitched in a window above and he instinctively glanced in its direction. The street was empty, but he couldn't shake the sense he was being watched.

They'd continued to meet at the cinema without his mother's supervision, though neither ever acknowledged the trips in the passage of ordinary life. After mass, they would study the floor while their mothers chatted in the foyer, mortified for reasons they couldn't quite name. At school, they blanked one another in the corridor as though total strangers, looked away should the other ever catch their eye. One time a teacher had asked them to work together, practise their Welsh or French, and though the noisy classroom offered a semblance of privacy, they'd had nothing to say to one another, not in any language they might have been taught.

There had been reality and there had been the Plaza. Those were the rules of their game.

Mack looked both ways. The breeze sent a can dancing down the road. He could not quite bring himself to cross.

At home, they kept a pole on the landing with a hook on the end. It took practice to unlock the attic hatch. Mack worked in silence, knowing that to be heard was to be offered help. He grasped upwards, a quiet action, humbled by the weightless frustration of doing something so intricate at such remove. When the hook slipped a second time it made a louder sound and he paused to let it pass. He lowered the pole and wiped his palms against the legs of his trousers. Half humiliated, half determined. A fairground punter, a burglar breaking in.

The eventual release startled him. The ladder screeched down on rollers as the hatch tipped away. The temperature dropped as he climbed. He pulled the light cord and crawled onto the rocking baseboards. Cobwebs hung from the rafters. A thick dust coated everything. The nearest box had his name felt-tipped on the side and he cut its tape with his keys. He felt the boards wobble beneath him. His knees and palms were black.

The first book in the box was titled *The Cloud of Unknowing*. Dated sometime in the fourteenth century. Canon Sylvester had written his own name on the inside cover, as though to aid its return should it ever be misplaced. Mack read the first page, the canon's voice in his head:

I CHARGE and beg you, with all the strength and power that love can bring to bear, that whoever you may be who possess carrying it, this book (perhaps you own it, or are keeping it, or borrowing it) you should, quite freely and of set purpose, neither read, write, or mention it to anyone, nor allow it to be read, written, or mentioned by anyone unless that person is in your judgement really and wholly determined to follow Christ perfectly. And to follow him not only in the active life, but to the utmost height of the contemplative life that is possible for a perfect soul in a mortal body to attain by the grace of God. And he should be, in your estimation, one who has for a long time been doing all that he can to come to the contemplative life by virtue of his active life. Otherwise the book will mean nothing to him.

He closed the box, killed the light and climbed down. Folded the ladder back into the hatch and repeated the trick with the pole. His father was in the hall when he went downstairs, standing in his baseball cap and paint-flecked overalls below a framed print of the Sacred Heart. Christ long-haired, bearded, robed and haloed, His exposed heart aflame and wrapped in thorns. The picture had always hung there. A wedding gift from his grandparents to his parents. What more could the happy couple want?

Both faces looked at him. Jackie wrung a rag in his hands. Heading out? Mack asked.

His father looked sheepish. He spent a lot of time in the shed since his redundancy. An endless cycle of odd jobs. He set his alarm in the mornings. Sometimes worked a full nine-to-five, came in for tea, then went back out again. Jackie enjoyed woodwork, carpentry, anything he could do with his hands.

You didn't have to, you know? he said, suddenly interested in something on the nearest door frame. Sign up, I mean. The boys could have found someone else.

I didn't— Mack started, but then noticed the smile warming his father's face.

It'll be good, though, I reckon. Jackie wiped at the door frame with a rag, words tempered into indifference. I know Grampa would be proud.

His voice cracked slightly. He cleared his throat and coughed.

Say, he said. You got an hour spare?

Mack looked him up and down. Now?

Jackie wrung the rag, looking everywhere but at his son. Yeah, he said.

But I've got work in a bit.

Won't take long. Was just gonna have a look in Gran and Grampa's.

Today?

Jackie was interested in the door frame once more. Was just going to see what needs doing, that's all.

But he knew what needed doing. It was the reason he'd

put it off. Wardrobes of clothes, cases of ornaments. Stuff likely worthless but impossible to chuck. Stacks of familiar plates and dishes, the cutlery he remembered using as a kid. Even the mess of the garage carried a nostalgic fondness. The spilled oil and rusted tools, half-empty paint tins stacked into precarious pyramids.

I've got work, Mack repeated.

Jackie said nothing, busy wiping at the jamb. When Mack looked down at his hands, he found his palms black with dust.

What about later in the week? he tried.

The play starts later in the week.

Jackie lowered the rag. Took a step back to examine his work. His overalls were navy, torn in places, splattered with white paint and cotton paint and beige, the odd dash of robin's-egg blue.

Like I said, he started slowly, eyes on the door frame. You don't have to be an apostle. I'm sure one of the other boys will—

I'll do it, Mack said.

His tone sounded short even to him and he quickly grasped for a way to apologise.

But the play doesn't start until Thursday evening, does it? We'd have time to do Gran and Grampa's that morning.

His father's eye was still on the door.

You haven't got work?

We'll be on strike by then.

Last I heard you weren't sure you were joining in.

Why wouldn't I join in?

You didn't know yesterday. With the different union and all?

Well I'm hardly going to cross the picket line, am I?

Jackie turned and met his eye. Made to put the rag in his pocket, only to hesitate as he noticed the dust on Mack's hands. He shook the rag out and offered it to his son.

Before I forget, he said. Bryn rang earlier. They've called the final vote tomorrow morning. In the school hall, bright and early.

Mack took the rag and wiped his palms.

You should come, Jackie continued, if you're taking part now. You can have a lift with me.

III

Mack wouldn't have said he enjoyed the job, but he appreciated its steady rhythm. He'd long been a man of routine. They clocked in. Read the notes left by the previous shift. Ensured the CCTV was set and operational. They patrolled the plant at regular intervals, locking the office behind them and getting into the van. They looked around, ensuring every door was secured, every lock fastened. They had the route printed out on a sheet.

So what did you do up in priest school then? Denzil asked. Mostly just pray and that, issit?

They stood on the access road off Longlands Lane, just east of the coke ovens, as the first signs of dark pulled over the mountain. Gas flares burned blue in the distance, flames flickering like serpent tongues. The sky was inscrutable in its clouded depth, the ground scrubby and blackened and constellated with broken glass. Mack tested the padlock on the gate with a firm tug. Unlocked it and locked it again, just to be sure. Denzil was in charge of the keys, wore them clipped to his belt on a chain, though he handed them to

Mack on occasion to make him feel involved. Gotta keep you out of trouble, as he liked to say.

Mack worked like he prayed. With great concentration, a kind of anxious effort. Never able to lose himself in the action as though at any moment he might slip and reveal the charlatan he really was. It took commitment to balance such an illusion. He fought to keep it going the way a nervous flyer kept a plane in the sky. Mack didn't have keys clipped to his belt but he had plenty of other things. A walkie-talkie, a pen torch, a gas monitor that beeped to warn of hazardous conditions. Low oxygen environments, combustible atmospheres, the silent seep of noxious air.

That's pretty much priest school, he said, voice raised over the steam hiss of the cooling towers behind them. Praying and studying.

The perimeter fencing shivered in the evening wind. Pre-galvanised steel, powder-coated, crowned with twists of barbed wire.

Why did you want to be a priest anyway?

The question caught him off guard. One he always feared but was rarely asked.

I suppose I just wanted to be taken seriously, he said. It was become a priest or kill someone.

Denzil laughed at that. Not counting the previous week, Mack hadn't seen Denzil McCarthy since comp. Denzil lived down Sandfields way. They'd done work experience together at the plant during their GCSEs. Part of a group of boys on a week-long placement intended to give a better understanding of what went on inside. The men gave them hell the minute they walked through the doors, and on the Friday the boys made a pact to never return. Spat on their palms in the car park and shook hands in a circle. It was supposed to be binding. Something they'd seen once in a film.

Mack remembered schoolboy Denzil as always laughing and always fighting. In any order, or both simultaneously. Denzil had favoured the headbutt by way of introduction. A sudden bucking motion. His opponent's teeth bouncing off the lean meat of his scalp. He'd stand with the boys when it was over, simmering like a neglected stove as they narrated the encounter back to him. His breath steadying, heart slowing, trails of blood threading through the close crop of his skull.

Mack had always been jealous of boys like that. Those who knew what they wanted and weren't afraid to act. Every class had one. The nutter, the headcase, the clown. The type willing to risk trouble in order to be themselves. Who took punishment as a necessary tax on their preferred way of being. Eventually Denzil spent eighteen months in a young offender institute for stealing cars. Seven in total. All burned out behind the playing fields in Margam for the simple pleasure of witnessing something bright.

I used to pray for a Gameboy Advance when I was a kid, Denzil said, climbing back into the van. A Volkswagen two-seater, white but for the sores of rust. Then Mam told me God don't work like that, so I stole one from the girl next door and prayed for forgiveness instead.

Back at the office, Mack hung his jacket on the hook and sat at the desk. Flicked the mouse of the computer to knock the screensaver off. The room had CCTV screens on one wall and safety posters on the other. Small windows caged with wire and glazed with blast-proof glass.

Do you not believe in all that now then? Denzil asked.

Mack rolled the sleeves of his jumper. Believe in all what?

You know, church stuff.

Mack took the clipboard from the shelf on the wall to tick off the patrol. Wrote the date, the time, a scribbled approximation of his name. The pen was attached to the wall with string. The stubby little kind they used in Argos or the bookie's.

Depends what you mean by church stuff.

Denzil nodded slowly as though some sage wisdom had been imparted. Anyway, he said, I'm dying for a slash.

The office had a motionless ceiling fan. A flip calendar branded with company logos. A landline telephone, a computer tower in a locked box. A fire extinguisher filled with foam and an old broom in the corner. Mack decided to sweep the floor, just to pass the time.

Denzil returned from the bathroom with a waft of body spray. The kind they sold on the lower shelf of the super-market, targeted at pubescent kids.

Stop it, you edda, he laughed, seeing Mack sweeping. You're making me look bad.

Mack shrugged, blood rushing to his face.

Bet they had you sweeping the floors up there and all? Denzil took a seat and put his boots up on the desk. Hard labour as part of becoming a priest?

You didn't go to the seminary to become a priest, the rector had explained on their first morning. You went to learn what God was asking of you. A tall man. Shoulders like he'd left the hanger in his jacket. Hair the colour of days-old snow on the roadside. Mack had withered before him, sat knee to knee with his fellow novitiates. Three years out of school and feeling like he'd somehow wandered back in.

He was never quite sure he was the sort of man to become a priest in any case. Feared he lacked the depth of mind. Prayed right enough but never thought to expect an answer. Catholicism was more like a cadence running through his head. But there was attraction in that way of living. The shelter of a life portioned up according to ancient rites. And nothing was ever set in stone, as Canon Sylvester always reminded him. He could follow the path with curiosity and wait for God to provide a sign.

In the months before he left, he read everything the canon gave him. Made diligent notes regardless of how much he understood. He did this alone and with great seriousness. Organised his days into blocks of time in his room with nothing but paper and a pen. He prayed every night. Hail Marys, Glory Bes. The Lord's Prayer and a period of silent contemplation. Devotion as a state of quietness. An open receptivity.

By their second morning, the rector had changed his tune. Suggested they not visit home. Limit their use of technology. He said a man could hone himself down to the sharpest edge without distraction. They were at the seminary to become instruments, after all. Hollowed-out instruments of God.

Mack was glad to be sweeping. Felt a constant need to make conversation but couldn't think of anything to say. He considered asking Denzil more about the job, its oddities, the curious things he'd seen at night, but he didn't want to know what else might be lurking off in the dark. Had too many ideas in his head already.

They'd shown him an induction video on his first day. In order to be a security guard, you had to think like a security guard, that's what the video said. Become aware of the potential for risk and threat. Vandalism. Trespass. Burglary and theft. Hazards concerning fire and combustion. Toxic substances. Moving parts. High-voltage electricity.

You'd likely never experience danger in forty years of work, but you had to see it everywhere. Envision the worst if only to ensure it never happened. The best security guards were imaginative.

He wasn't sure how long he'd last. There were licences you could get but he didn't have one. There were hierarchies of responsibility. You could progress in the job, climb the ladder. You could apply the key skills to a whole host of different industries. Denzil had started on the doors of clubs but the vibe didn't suit him. Said there were too many drunks, too many upper drugs. He'd once seen a bouncer paralyse a man with a single punch to the temple. He'd seen a man glassed so bad his eye hung against his cheek from a cord. Work nights too long and your skin went translucent, that's what Denzil reckoned. But then again, there were worse things than showing your insides off.

Say, Denzil said, spinning circles in the office chair and thumbing through a magazine left by the previous shift. Remember that girl in school?

There was more than one, I think.

You know, mun. Her mam ended up topping herself.

Oh, Mack said. Siwan?

Siwan, Denzil repeated, testing the feel of it on his tongue. Siwan Roderick.

When she'd first arrived in school, she'd taught the class how to say it. Shoo-an, Shoo-an, mouth slow and deliberate so they might copy its shape.

That's the girl, Denzil continued. Swear I saw her in Tesco's the other day.

Mack kept his head down and swept.

Thought she'd moved away?

Maybe, Mack said. No idea.

He heard the croak of the chair as it came to a stop. Felt Denzil's gaze burn the back of his head.

You used to like her, didn't you?

Mack kept sweeping, back stooped over the broom.

It was obvious like. You should've said something, mun.

I don't know what you're on about.

All right, Denzil said, grinning.

I don't.

Okay. Denzil held his palms aloft in mock surrender. Whatever you say, boss.

Mack swept from wall to wall and back again. Brought forth a grey fur of dust, human hair, the little paper circles from the hole punch. His father had found the job for him. He took the interview over the phone. They rang back an hour later, almost ironic in their congratulations, asking when he was able to start.

Her mother was mental, mind. Denzil spoke through a yawn, chair straining as he stretched his back. What was her name again? Began with a J, didn't it? Jess? Jazz?

Jasmine, Mack corrected in his head, though he didn't say anything. Her name was Jasmine.

Remember them leaflets she printed? Denzil continued. The Earth something or other. What did they call themselves again?

Mack could feel eyes on him, waiting for an answer.

Earth Liberation Front, he said. The ELF.

That's it! Denzil laughed. My old man was tamping. He fucking hates tree-huggers and hippies and all them soppy buggers. Some people are so soft it's dangerous, that's what he always says. Wouldn't know an honest day's work if it poked them in the eye. I weren't even allowed to talk to Siwan in school after that. Blacklisted, she was. All thanks to her mam.

Mack recalled a similar conversation with his father. Something he hadn't understood but knew better than to question. He hadn't really spoken to Siwan anyway. Not outside of the dark of the Plaza screens. What his mother thought of the matter she never said, but her own contact with the Rodericks also diminished. Siwan's family had once sat a few rows ahead of them at mass but soon stopped attending altogether.

He shared none of this. Pretended to be busy with the broom. When he eventually looked up, Denzil had turned to the monitors. A grid of four columns and four rows, the pictures bluish black and white, feeds changing at fifteen-second intervals. Every corner of the works going round on a loop. The footage was stored on a hard drive they changed on alternating months. They sent the tapes abroad to be analysed, Denzil reckoned. People paid pennies an hour. Warehouses of children on the subcontinent.

Nothing ever happened on the screens, but you could lose hours in their dormant quiet. As though you were only ever seconds away from an unexpected event. Denzil let them wash over him, those near-static images strangely sad and greyscale and mute.

Mack had swept the entire floor but didn't sit down. He wasn't quite sure how to act in Denzil's company, what version of himself he wished to project. The longer he spent with him, the more he felt the pull of a younger self. The person he'd been as a child. As if the years in between had made no lasting impression. That it wasn't God he wished to find, but a friend. Sometimes he caught himself thinking he knew Denzil better than he did. Imagined they'd been pals back in the day, rather than just classmates. That their bond went beyond a shared recognition of names. Remember Mr Bassini? Denzil would say. Remember Molly Murphy from the year above? Mack remembered Mr Bassini and Molly Murphy. Remembered the smell of the urinal cakes in the toilets, the sound of a handbell ringing around the yard. Sometimes Denzil spoke of things Mack could not recall as if certain he had been there. Yeah, Mack would say, I remember. He nodded his head and grinned.

Denzil kept glancing at him. Cleared his throat as if to speak but swallowed whatever thought had occurred to him. There was a tautness to the silence Mack didn't enjoy, but he wasn't going to be the one to break it.

She probably had a point in fairness, Denzil conceded eventually. Siwan's mam, I mean. Now I look back on it like.

He smiled, but not his usual smile. His voice cast meek in atonement.

Think about it, he said. All that muck we're breathing in.

He looked at his hands as he spoke. Cracked the joints of his fingers. One by one, methodical. When he finally looked up at Mack, his face was soft in appeal.

Do the blinds go all black down with you?

The blinds go black, Mack confirmed.

Denzil seemed buoyed by the response. Something in common again.

If the wind's blowing right, he said, my old man's lawn gets coated in orange dust. Funny, innit? What you put up with?

He cracked the fingers down his opposite hand. He seemed to want an answer.

Ever seen a bird covered in oil? Mack asked.

The question landed awkwardly. Denzil laughed but looked confused.

A bird?

You know, a seagull or something. After an oil spill.

Well yeah, Denzil said. On the telly like.

You know when they show the volunteers cleaning them? With their soapy water and toothbrushes? Little towels to wrap them in?

Denzil's face was wary now, but he didn't interrupt.

Someone told me only one per cent survive, Mack continued. Once the chemicals get inside them, there's nothing you can do.

Denzil paused as if to pay respect to the unfortunate fact, then rose with a chain-mail clink. Time for a fag, I reckon, he said, marching across the room. At the door, he peered back at Mack with what might have been curiosity or concern. Mack forced a smile. Told Denzil to have a fag for him.

He waited for the door to close before leaning the broom against the wall and taking a seat behind the desk. He enjoyed Denzil's smoke breaks as much as Denzil himself. A scrap of solitude where stillness descended. The computer, the furniture, the cold glow of the screens. Everything suspended. Oddly outside of time. Mack got to thinking differently in those stolen minutes. Found himself contemplating things he would not normally countenance.

The phone was on the desk in front of him. A dumb lump of plastic that at any minute might sing.

Bless me, Father, for I have sinned, that's what she had said. Only to scrunch her eyes, start again.

Bless me, Father, for I am *about* to sin.

He slid the phone closer and lifted the receiver from its cradle. A satisfying weight in his hand. He looped the coiled wire around his finger. Paused a second, listened for Denzil outside, then raised the handset to his ear and met a flat tone with no beginning or end.

He let the sound fill his head before punching in the number. A sequence he'd memorised from his mother's address book as a child but never put to use. He paused before pressing the sixth digit, reconsidering a moment. Her number might have changed, but what if it hadn't? What if she was now just a single button away?

The ringing felt like a shaft he might fall inside. He felt a turn in his stomach.

She said hello like a question. Mack dropped the receiver and killed the call with his hand.

Denzil was already speaking as he shouldered back into the office.

The bossman got back to me, by the way.

Mack was on his feet again, evasive, caught in a shameful act.

He offered us time and a half.

Denzil picked at his nose, waiting for Mack to set the next direction. Only Mack couldn't see they had any choice.

We can't cross the picket line, though, can we? he said.

Denzil nodded quickly in agreement. That's what I was thinking.

They stood there looking at the floor.

It can't be true what they're saying about the lump sums anyway, can it? Laying off staff with no payout must be against the law?

Denzil spoke as though to himself. A statement that came out as a question.

Could we just take leave all weekend? Mack suggested. My father's roped me into this play thing anyway.

My old man's a miserable old bugger, Denzil laughed. If they did the play at the bottom of the garden he'd pull the blinds. Not that he don't agree with the sentiment like. He's just old school. Thinks a strike should be placards and lobbing bricks at the police.

Denzil's father had been a steelworker too. Took early retirement for ill health. A dropped spanner hit him square in the chest and he was never the same again. A couple of years later he got caught up in a pension scam after British Steel closed their scheme and lost tens of thousands. Still found the energy to rag his son about getting a job in there. Like his own service hadn't quite been enough and he owed the place one last thing.

Forget about burying or cremating me, that's what Denzil's father said. Drop me in the molten slag.

All their fathers were the same. Started in the furnaces at fifteen. Cycled in every day on a pushbike, stupid o'clock in the morning, just them and the gulls. Helmets on their heads, the taste of hot porridge in their mouths, all wrapped up in goldfish-orange coats with reflective silver stripes. Mornings and nights. Four on, four off. Eighteen-hour shifts, doubling back. Hated every day but loved it too. Would do it all over if they could. Because if they hadn't loved it, why had they done it in the first place? All their lives, for what?

Don't get him started on shutting off the blasts, though, Denzil warned. Step too far, that. They'll never put 'em back on again, he reckons. Playing into the enemy's hands.

Before Denzil could continue, the door opened. Dai Eighteen Months.

What the fuck do you want now? Denzil asked.

Dai grinned. He brought the smell of diesel with him. Wore a woolly hat and the company fleece. Stubble on his face like a cartoon drunk. He'd stopped by on occasion the previous week too, though with no obvious reason. A social call from a man at a loose end.

New, are you? Dai said, putting both palms flat on the desk as he sized Mack up.

What you on about, mun? Denzil laughed. He was here last week. You shook his hand.

Aw, sorry, butt, Dai laughed, shaking Mack's hand again. No good with faces me.

Faces or women, Denzil said.

Faces, women and drink.

Dai laughed again. He still held Mack by the hand. If he remembered the previous evening, he made no mention of it. Denzil asked him how the boys were doing and he said they were doing all right.

The boys ran all day long now, Dai revealed. Drove the missus up the wall. But the thing was, if you stopped them running in the daytime, they ran at night instead.

Got a photo if you want to see 'em, he said, reaching for his phone.

A picture of two rodents. Sand-blonde and beady-eyed.

How long have you kept hamsters? Mack asked politely.

Hamsters? Dai laughed. They're not hamsters. They're gerbils!

The clock above the desk only made a sound on every other tick. When Dai left the office, he came straight back in again.

Lemme guess, Denzil said. You forgot where you parked the car?

Meant to ask. You boys striking or what?

Denzil snorted through his nose.

Contractors we are, mun. Different thing altogether. Nothing to do with us.

Scab bastards.

Apparently they're giving us double time and all. Little bonus like.

Fuck off.

Course we're fucking striking, you edda, Denzil said, taking Dai by the shoulders and shaking him. You think I'm gonna miss a long weekend?

The men looked at one another.

Well . . . Denzil said. Mack has to check a few things. He hasn't joined the union yet.

Why's that? Dai asked, face deadpan. New, are you?

He held Mack's eye, then broke into a grin. Mack grinned back, aware of every muscle in his face. The office smelled like computer manuals and cleaning fluid. The screens hummed like power lines. Every so often air thudded down the vents in the ceiling. Out in the corridor, the Coke machine gurgled like a drowning man.

Leave him alone, mun, Denzil said dismissively.

Denzil had intervened every time someone tried to pull

Mack's leg in his first week. Protective of his new partner, or else fearing he couldn't take a joke. Mack had been appreciative at first, though was growing uneasy. As though Denzil's concern said something he didn't want to admit to himself.

Dai was still smirking. It still wasn't clear he knew who he was looking at. I'm the man who stepped in when you let everyone down, Mack wished to say. The answer to your prayers. The apostle you should have been.

Oi, Denz, got time for a quick fag? Dai asked, turning his back.

Sorry, butt, only just been out.

Aw, come on, mun, no one's gonna tell.

I'm trying to cut back.

You're not gonna make me smoke on my own?

Dai held Denzil's eye like a challenge, an arm wrestle conducted via telepathy. The struggle lasted a moment but there was only one winner. Denzil looked down and that was all it took. Both men peered over their shoulder before departing as though afraid of who might spot them. The pair of them skulking, quiet, united in conspiracy. When the door opened, the cool of the night came in, and then it closed again, leaving Mack alone with nothing but the monitors glowing strange beside him and the telephone at his elbow. A silent thing, waiting.

IV

Mack woke before his alarm and watched the light inch across the bare paint of his bedroom wall. He always woke early now. Head still trapped in an old routine. Trained in the panic of oversleeping. To live a secular life, he was finding out, was to feel like a hand grasping for something it could never quite reach. For your body to twitch as though in attempt to move a phantom limb. Wasn't it time, it asked, to be dragged downstairs to the chapel for the Holy Hour? For adoration and the Office of Readings, morning prayer and benediction?

Mack found his parents in the kitchen. His mother fixing his father's collar in front of the sink. Jackie with coffee in hand, Clara telling him to keep still. He watched them from the doorway. They sounded different when he wasn't in the room. His mother stepped to the side to check the back of his father's collar. Tucked in the label at his neck. Jackie sipped his coffee with a crooked arm, eyes on the opposite wall. The washing machine was on. A slop of water. A slow, reluctant turn.

His parents separated when he entered, bashful. They'd first met when drinking with friends at the Vivian, so the story went. Started courting soon after. Jackie took her to see Simple Minds at the Troubadour for their first date. They got married in Our Lady of Margam and had the do in the Jersey Beach Hotel. A week away for their honeymoon. Majorca, all inclusive.

Mack went to the cupboard for a bowl but opened the wrong door. Pipes clanked inside the walls as the heating roused itself.

Thought we didn't have to be there until nine? he said.

He'd forgotten about the meeting but pretended otherwise. His father looked at his watch. Jackie was dressed in his best clothes, shoes and all. Hair still wet from the shower and combed through like a newly harrowed field.

Yeah, his father said, looking at his wrist again. But you don't know what the traffic's gonna be like.

Mack fixed himself cereal and went to the fridge for milk. Sat at the table with his back to his father but saw him reflected in the microwave door. Jackie looked to his watch, looked to Mack, fiddled impatiently with his keys. Mack's mother came to sit at the other side of the table and started to fill out the crossword in the TV magazine.

You can eat in the car if you want? his father said.

Mack took another spoonful of cereal. Didn't even turn around. His father's shoes clopped across the lino in irritation, turned on their heel and paced back to the sink.

Why did the canon bring books? Mack asked his mother.

Her face brightened at mention of the canon, though she didn't take her eyes from the crossword. Acting casual, as though a timid prayer had been answered but she was afraid of upsetting its tenuous hold.

I suppose he thought you might still be interested.

Yeah, Mack said, but why now?

Clara put her biro down and stared at him over her glasses.

Well, he can't take them all with him. You've seen the shelves in the rectory.

Mack dipped his spoon in the bowl. Raised it halfway to his mouth.

Can't take them where?

What do you mean where? I told you he's leaving.

Mack nodded, pretending it had all come back to him. His Weetabix had gone soggy and he had to choke it down. It seemed the washing machine had stopped, but then it lurched to life again. The kitchen smelled of washing powder, fabric softener, Nescafé Gold Blend.

When did you say he was going? Mack ventured.

Holy Week's his last week, his mother said. Voice firm and pointed, ensuring this time the information sank in.

Right, Mack said. Yeah.

You should go and see him before he leaves.

He nodded slowly, spoon still in hand.

I know he'd like that. He always asks after you.

Mack thought back to the book in the box. *The Cloud of Unknowing*. Its charges and begs. A text only to be read by those willing to follow Christ in perfection. Mack heard the words as the canon's voice in his head.

Do you know why he chose now in particular? he asked, only his father interrupted.

Listen, boy, Jackie said. I don't mean to rush you but they're expecting a crowd and—

Mack rose from his seat and drank the remaining milk from the edge of his bowl. Rinsed the bowl in the sink and dried his hands on the tea towel over the handle of the oven door. The digital clock on the cooker was an hour out, somehow still set to summer time, but when he reached for the buttons to put it right, his mother stood to intervene.

Don't, she said. You'll have me all confused.

Mack stepped back. But it's wrong?

I know, she said. But it's always wrong. If you change it, I won't know where I am.

Mack looked at the clock again, the middle colon blinking. He got a banana from the bowl on the counter. A snack for later on. His mother hovered near the cooker, guarding it.

He's all right, though, isn't he? Mack asked. The canon, I mean?

His mother hesitated.

He'd love to see you, she repeated.

He didn't close the door properly when he got in the car. Had to open it and slam it again. His father with his seat belt already fastened, face like a smacked arse, the pine-tree air freshener swinging under the mirror from the force of the door. The engine turned over before it caught and started. The keys in the ignition tapped against the underside of the dashboard with a censer's rhythmic beat. Jackie put the radio on but there were only adverts playing. Birds flew low in the morning sky. Gulls, screaming.

Sleep all right? Jackie asked, still gruff with the hour. The concern caught Mack out.

It's only now I realise how loud the works are at night, he said. Takes a bit of getting used to.

His father kept his silence. Changed gear, checked the mirrors. Tried the radio again. He wore the aftershave he kept for special occasions. For some reason, Mack felt sorry for him.

Did I say I've met this actor before? he asked, just to say something. He's all right. Seemed down to earth.

Met him where?

He came to school once. For a play.

Jackie nodded slowly, unconvinced.

To be honest, Mack said. Back then, I had no idea who he was.

A silence settled as they broached the flyover into town. The bus in front kept hitting its brakes. It felt weird to do such a familiar drive again, the school run complete with a cranked pressure as the minutes ticked on by. Mack watched from the passenger window. The police station was a block of flats now. The health centre converted into offices. But what really caught his eye were newer developments still. The crowd-control barriers for the play multiplying along main roads. Crews with hard hats and two-way radios erecting an assortment of signs and lights. The scale of the infrastructure went far beyond his expectations. The magnitude of the event began to dawn. He turned to his father, unsure just what they were stepping into, but if Jackie shared any of his misgivings, he kept them to himself.

They hit more traffic near the school. Pulled up behind a three-door Clio the colour of a Cadbury's bar. Children pressed their noses to the back window, pulling faces against the glass.

Trouble at that age, Jackie said, smiling now. One was bad enough.

Mack nodded as if he could only imagine. The car had a bumper sticker. *I Don't Know About You, But I'm Sticking to the Speed Limit.*

Magic, mind, Jackie added, smile fading but not entirely, a handprint on fogged glass. Can't beat it, mun.

The kids waved. Mack couldn't bring himself to wave back.

So what's your plan? his father asked.

My plan?

You know, mid to long term? Jackie shifted in his seat, made an adjustment to the sun visor. Where d'you see yourself in five years? What sort of man do you want to be?

The boys in the car beat their fists against the window. Mack pretended they weren't there. Jackie cleaned his ear with a finger, eyes set forward.

I mean, he said, are you really going to spend your whole life in the works?

There was an edge to his words. A serration of worry or scorn. Mack had never quite understood what it was his father wished of him. Seemed to have spent half his life warning against ending up where he himself had landed, yet lived the other half in mortal fear his son might do something different. He was quick to criticise the works yet fiercely protective. He'd hated his job, he loved it. Such things could coexist.

I'm working on it, Mack said.

His father flicked the indicator, leaned into a turn.

Working on what?

My plan, he said. Deciding the sort of man I want to be.

The school was yet to close for Easter. The Catholics always stayed until the bitter end. With no room in the car park,

Jackie pulled up in a side street and they walked in together. The place looked more or less the same, right down to the sign at the gates.

St Joseph's Comprehensive. Laborare est orare. To work is to pray.

The school had a special needs department, a hall for concerts and mass. A barn for five-a-side and playing fields with rusted goals and rugby posts, crossbars sagging and tagged with multicoloured tape. No lines marked out on the field, no grass in the goal mouth, just boggy patches and dog shit and mud. The place was overlooked by the hills they called mountains and boxed in by the housing estate and the motorway and the railway line. The younger kids would run towards the fence when they heard a train approach, wave maniacally without knowing if anyone was waving back.

Crowds had gathered near the entrance. Organised men with placards and badges. Some belonged to political parties and some to the unions. Some demanded climate justice. Others were kitted out ready for work that instant, proud in their overalls and visors and steel-toed boots. When cars drove by and sounded their horns, the gathered men cheered.

A beaming woman greeted the O'Briens at reception. Part of the theatre company, perhaps, or else a union rep. The meeting was open to all union members, she said, but they invited the apostles down the front. A special guest wanted to meet them before the vote. To lend his support to what was happening at the works. Introduce himself. She led them inside, down old corridors peculiar in scale. A dream in which everything was three-quarter-sized.

They had to wait for assembly to finish before they could use the hall, so the woman led them to the staff room for refreshments. The other apostles, already helping them-selves, were too busy scoffing to notice their arrival. Coffee in paper cups, plates of Jammie Dodgers, little sachets of sugar and Splenda and UHT milk. Mack had never been in the staff room before. Couldn't help but nose around. Found a mess of coffee mugs and abandoned coats. Lip balms, hand creams, Post-it notes complete with esoteric messages. He opened a drawer and found a collection of elastic bands, balls of Blu Tack, a book of raffle tickets. The fridge in the corner murmured oddly and he opened that too. A lonely box of coleslaw. A pint of semi-skimmed.

The men paired off and made conversation. Mack broke his biscuit in half and turned to the window instead. The staff room looked out towards the hall. A line of cherry blossoms ran across the grass there, already in full bloom. A sight he had forgotten until that moment. Prettier than he allowed the memories in his head. The pink-white shimmer of them. The way the petals drifted across the ground like snow.

Over his shoulder, Peggy was telling someone that he used to work at the wildlife park in Penscynor. Remember Penscynor? he asked. I used to feed the tigers there.

Kids began to emerge from assembly. Their ties the same green, red and gold but their jumpers changed. Blazers now with the emblem embroidered on the breast pocket.

You all right there, boy? Bryn asked clamping Mack on the back as he passed. Got a face like Goytre Hill.

Yeah, Mack said, not bothering to turn around. I'm all right.

The actor was waiting on the door when they arrived at the hall. The men hooted and hollered at the sight of him, lined up to shake his hand. He asked their names then repeated them back as though to drill them into his memory. When Mack said they'd met before, he laughed like he'd told a joke.

The school play, Mack pressed. Remember?

The actor seemed confused.

The play?

An Inspector Calls?

The actor brought a hand to his face in contemplation.

An Inspector Calls, he repeated. I think I remember. Who was in it?

Mack didn't know what to say. It had been a school play. Who did he think would have been in it?

Well, he started. Siwan was in it. Siwan Roderick.

He blushed to say her name. Wanted to say it again.

Siwan who? the actor asked. Was she the lead?

Mack shook his head quickly. Lots of kids were in it. Must have been half the school.

And who did you play?

The question stopped him. The teachers had asked everyone to audition but Mack had never liked that sort of thing. They made him a stagehand instead. The person tasked with opening and closing the curtains. A way to get near to the action without stepping onto the stage. An easy job, all told. You stood in the shadows and waited for a cue.

The actor appeared to want an answer. Mack just shook his hand again and stepped inside the hall. An audience of chairs had been arranged like back in the old days. He couldn't count how many hours he'd spent in there. Assemblies and summer exams, masses on holy days of obligation. The one space in the school that still seemed as large as the pictures in his head.

A man in the crowd outside had a bell. A chanted slogan. A horn blared in passing. The microphone on the stage whined every so often, the sound of it a lethal thing swinging by. The crowd filtered in through the doors at the back. Mack looked for Denzil among them. Someone he knew to talk to. Make him feel he belonged. In the end, he settled for a seat between Peggy and his father. The plastic chairs hadn't changed at all.

Exciting, innit? Peggy said. This sense of action? You can almost smell it on the air.

Mack couldn't smell anything but agreed nonetheless.

Peggy said he knew about action. Had been in the navy back in the day. Nineteen eighty-two. Thatcher. Galtieri. Fighting for something bigger than yourself could make a man feel alive. And talking of fighting, he'd been the champion boxer on deck if Mack would believe it. Welterweight, he was, though he'd put on a few pounds since back then.

Do you know what an Exocet missile sounds like? he asked. Whistling past your bonce?

Mack shook his head no. He didn't.

A stirring in the audience cut Peggy off. The actor had climbed to the stage and people were starting to notice. Would you be so kind as to allow me a moment before the meeting begins? he asked. Once the excited applause died down, he spoke of the event.

I know you're here for more important things, he started. But I wanted to say a few words. Perhaps you've heard of the production we've organised for this weekend? Maybe you're wondering how it fits in with everything else?

The actor gestured to the room, the gathered men.

The thing is, he said, we've always viewed the Passion as

a narrative woven into the town itself. Certain scenes are ticketed for health and safety reasons, but the majority are open to anyone. We want the town to shape the play as much as the other way around.

Applause rolled through the room again. The actor waited for it to finish.

That's why I was heartened, he continued, a roguish grin dawning over his features, to get wind of the potential hijacking. The theatre company might have organised the play, but it was always intended as something we could make our own.

The applause returned twice as spirited. The actor leaned closer to the mic.

After all, the play is but a minor scene within a bigger production. I myself am no more than a background figure compared to most characters in this event. Consider my apostles. Working men, past and present. Individuals taking a stand for the better future we deserve. The script might have them as devotees to my mission, but in real life, it's me who is in awe of them.

He indicated for the twelve men to stand. Clapped down the microphone and the audience joined in. The journalist was back, skirting the edges of the room with her camera person and notebook. Mack looked down the line at his fellow disciples. The men awkward at first but soon warming to the attention.

I want you to know, the actor concluded, that whatever you decide today has my full support. This performance can serve whatever purpose you wish. We'll make sure the spotlights are bright and shining.

The ovation that followed seemed to last minutes. When Mack sat down, Peggy dragged him to his feet again. The actor paused before them, drinking in the moment, then bowed in modesty and exited stage left.

The union shop steward had the misfortune to be up next. Awkward in the wake of his predecessor. Shuffling papers, promising to keep it short. A suit from the Steel Company was due next. The local MP watched sheepishly on.

Before we vote, the steward said, we thought it would be proper you hear from both sides. I'll go first, the Steel Company will respond. That way, every man can make up his mind for himself.

He rearranged his papers again. The audience patient with him, a little protective.

I've worked in steel since leaving school, he read from his sheet, just like so many others. On the first day of my apprenticeship, every bloke on shift came up to shake my hand. Well done, butt, they said. Bagged yourself a job for life. But then I watched the dominoes begin to fall. Ebbw Vale, the heavy end of Llanwern. Whiteheads. Newport. Teesside. Scunthorpe. Ravenscraig. Redcar. Rotherham. Communities left behind with no support or second thought.

Mack could see the journalist from the corner of his eye, writing something in her notebook. The shake dropped out of the shop steward's voice as his speech found momentum. He was reading no longer, clenched a fist as he spoke.

No one wants to walk out on the job they love. Least of all people as proud as us. But how are we meant to look after the interests of the town if the Steel Company won't even come to the table? Our every attempt at polite dialogue has been blanked, so it seems we'll have to be more drastic. It's not even that we disagree with their environmentally friendly ambitions. We just want any transition to be fair.

More applause. Hands in the air. The workers eager to add their two penn'orth.

Half the world's burning coal like there's no tomorrow, Curly called out.

S'only us silly buggers playing by the rules.

The interjectors brought laughs from the crowd. Daring schoolkids playing chicken.

Politics has shifted, someone reckoned. The green fad has come to an end.

I heard the company's dismantling the blasts and shipping the parts back to India. They're building their own furnaces out there.

They've got us by the short and curlies, mun.

They're taking the piss.

I mean, come on like, the Chinese own *British* Steel!

The last quip was delivered as a punchline and the audience reacted. The journalist made a note in her book. When the shop steward raised his palms to quell the laughter, he got too close to the microphone. Feedback shrieked high and quick.

You'll have heard by now, he shouted over the racket, the union feels it has no choice but to recommend the workers vote in favour of planned strike action, as outlined in the correspondence already sent out. The strike will commence Thursday evening and last through the weekend. Any man in work at seven p.m. on Thursday is to down tools and walk off site. Anyone whose shift is due to start later is not to report to work. Correct protocols will be followed to allow a complete halt in production and an efficient restart on Sunday evening. And suffice to say, the union wants to go on record in stating we will not be bullied with baseless threats.

The speech got the audience to their feet again. Their whistles and cheers still rang around the hall as the Steel Company rep made his way up to respond. A feller in a pinstripe suit and horn-rimmed glasses, tie turned skew-whiff to reveal the label on the back. The lanyard around his neck read *VISITOR* and the look on his face the same.

First of all, he said, voice scrubbed of accent, thank you for the invitation today, and for giving us this opportunity to share our exciting vision for this town.

The audience hushed once more. Eager to give the man his fair chance before ripping him apart, or else hoping an open stage was rope enough he might finish the job himself.

If we've learned anything in the years since taking over the site, it is the value and strength of community. This feels like home to us now. We've enjoyed good times together, endured the bad, worked in unison to make it the best place it could possibly be.

Well, if it ain't broke, a merry voice called out, unable to help himself.

The rep grinned too readily at the comment. A politician's habit.

Unfortunately, he said, pausing to remove his glasses, there's a new obstacle in our way. But we've overcome obstacles before. I have no doubt the good people of this town are ready to grasp the challenge. To claim our place on the cutting edge of a new industrial revolution.

The look on the rep's face suggested he'd hoped for applause of his own. He licked his finger, turned the page of his script, put his glasses back on.

We hear everything you are saying, he continued. We

admire your passion, we truly do. But we'd hate for that passion to prove counterproductive. To get in the way of our partnership just as a fresh era dawns. We can train you in the skills of this new age. Make your children the envy of the world. I understand feelings are running high, but please don't get swept up in the excitement. A bit of loyalty goes a long way. A family can only look after one another when they stick close together.

Mack felt the mood shift around him. A line crossed, patience worn through. The air suddenly as pregnant as the seconds before a thunderclap. Dense, dark, electric.

I'll tell you something for nothing before you go threatening us, a man called out with venom. People turned to see him. A skinhead feller halfway down on the right. Heavyset, half-inch of neck, head so big it might have had its own orbiting moon. There's no green revolution without steel. What do you think they're gonna build their fucking windmills out of? Their hydro-'lectric dams? Life as you know it can't continue without what we produce.

The man jabbed his finger in time with his words. So angry he could barely get them out.

There's really no need for bad language, the rep started. We can all be civil and—

That low-grade shit from electric arcs won't cut it, another voice yelled.

Plus the scrap they melt will have to come from somewhere.

Which means shipping it in from abroad.

Shipping it halfway across the *world*.

Where's the green logic in that?

Mack found it difficult to watch the company man stutter

under the barrage. The way he smiled as though in concert with his inquisitors. The buzzwords he clung to in the swell.

Offshoring, he started, is something we're working to—

The logic's green all right, Bryn piped up from the front row. The dirty green of a dollar bill.

Can you guarantee a supply of old steel? someone else wanted to know.

And what if it runs out? Have you thought about that?

Thought about it? Bryn laughed, turning to locate the man behind him. It's what they want to happen, mun! Them Indians haven't invested properly in ten years. Only took us over to see how we do it. Got all the secrets now so they're fucking off home to build a hundred plants of their own.

That's not true, the steel rep countered. As I've explained, we intend to train our workforce here in—

They sold the miners that reskilling bollocks too. How do you think that went in the end?

Okay, okay, the shop steward called from the side of the stage, hands raised in appeal for order. You can't expect the man to answer every one of you. He's only got one head, after all.

Two faces, though, someone shouted. The steward shook his head but couldn't help but smile.

Let's just boil things down to the fundamentals here, issit? Bryn asked, out of his seat to seize the moment. A simple question for our guest. Yes or no will do. Has the company committed to reducing emissions globally? Or issit just round here?

The company is part of the green vanguard, the steel rep started. For example, we're pioneering technology to suck carbon from—

Then why didn't you fetch half a dozen of those doodads with you today?

Each heckler triggered twenty more. The meeting descending into chaos. People shouted over one another. Argued amongst themselves.

But what if we're all wrong?

Mack barely remembered getting to his feet. The journalist was across the room but he did not look at her. Beside him, his father peered up with the strangest expression. Something between hope and distress. His son a called coin he'd just flipped.

Bryn's right, he started. They're only looking after their bottom line, just like they always have. But the Steel Company are correct about one thing. We shouldn't let our personal grievances cloud the fact. Just because they're exploiting the environmental situation doesn't mean it isn't real. We can't just go on living the way we always—

Applause broke out near the back. A sound that brought Mack the briefest flash of validation before he understood it was not intended for him. Because others were also speaking now. He stopped mid-sentence and the clapping continued. His voice had been lost in the crowd.

Or almost lost. For the journalist still looked his way. When Mack met her eye, the awkward dimensions of his body asserted themselves. When he sat back down, his chair gave slightly and for a moment he felt he was falling.

His father also studied him. Swivelled in his seat, the intensity of his stare like the heat off a bulb. But rather than judgement or rage, Jackie's expression was not all that different from that of the journalist. Sometimes his father looked at him like he had no idea who he was.

At the end of the meeting, the steward returned to the stage and called the final vote. One last check before a decision was made. Speak now or forever hold your peace. Every person who rejected the exploitative green transition was to raise his hand in the air. Every one willing to take industrial action. Every man ready to fight.

The sound of arms raising passed through the hall like wind through a field of wheat. Mack hesitated, unsure if he was such a person, but an elbow in his ribs helped make up his mind.

He could sense his father behind him as they made their way from the hall. Felt a hand at his elbow. A voice in his ear. But it was not Jackie's cologne that leaned close but the floral scent he'd met in the club. The journalist wondering if he had a minute.

Outside, the crowd was rowdy. They'd emerged from the meeting galvanised. Banners were raised on poles. Someone had found a drum. An unintelligible chant moved the air in the distance. The school windows were filled with the heads of curious kids.

I promise it won't take long, she said. It's just I didn't quite catch what you said in the hall.

Mack didn't break his stride.

It wasn't important, he said.

I think it's important.

She tugged him by the arm. He turned and found her eyes pleading, her frown laced with the smallest dash of mischief.

Pretty please?

He opened his mouth to protest, but something about

her expression stopped him. He felt warm all of a sudden. Realised he was grinning.

The others are waiting for me, he said, gesturing over his shoulder. They don't leave me alone.

It doesn't have to be here. We can get a coffee or something? Some place more relaxed?

Her eye contact pinned him down, demanded submission. Her hand was still on his arm.

Well . . . he said.

Giving in held sudden appeal. Wouldn't it be easier to relent? What harm could come from an hour outside of his established routine?

Oi, Mack, called a voice from behind. Get over here.

He grinned at the journalist again as though in apology and together they made their way towards the others. The men hyperactive in the wake of the meeting. Showing off. Cracking jokes. Play-fighting.

Didn't expect to see you, said Dai Eighteen Months, punching Mack's shoulder. Thought your lot ain't even going on strike?

We're striking, Mack said, glancing towards the journalist.

Scab bastards in security, aren't they? Coppers by another name.

How can anyone scab when they're closing the plant down? Curly asked. There won't be nothing to do in work even if they wanted to go in.

They'll find something for you, Bryn said. Whitewashing the walls if it comes to it. Anything so long as you're not sitting on your arse.

Security's different, though, Dai pointed out. They can just run their little patrols.

We're striking, Mack repeated.

Jackie said nothing. The chant got closer, a little out of time. It won't take long, the journalist said again, but the others were talking about a march of some kind. A procession to town. An early show of strength. Bryn reckoned they should make an afternoon of it. Grab something for dinner. Couple of pints. A chance for the apostles to bond before the opening night. Those boys had been close, hadn't they? Getting into character, that's what it was called.

The actor's show of solidarity had changed something. What had seemed like fun had become serious. The play was an intrinsic part of the strike now. Bryn was ready to commit to the performance.

Coming, son? he wanted to know.

Mack raised his palms as though it wasn't up to him.

I'm working later.

Join the fucking club, Peggy said.

You'll be all right, mun, Bryn insisted. Have a couple of shandies.

Mack laughed. A habit he'd picked up years ago on work experience. Teen Mack unable to tell when the men were yanking his chain so instead just laughing at everything.

Evenings you're on, aren't you? You'll have sobered up by then.

The men looked to the journalist as they spoke. Hoping to see her smile or else show disapproval.

I'm afraid I'm borrowing him for an hour, she said, taking Mack by the arm again. I'll return him in one piece, I promise.

Borrowing him for what?

Just a cup of coffee.

She held Mack tighter as though to protect her prize. He felt her weight against his flank. Smelled the shampoo on her hair as she pressed into his shoulder.

I don't know if I've got time, he said, stepping away from the woman. My shift starts in—

Another arm seized him from the opposite direction. Wrapped around his neck and gripped the top of his bicep. The smell of old smoke this time. Cigarillos. Royal Dutch. Dai's face lopsided with a grin. He was missing a tooth on the right side, halfway around at the top. The stubble on his cheek felt like pumice.

You can't have him, Dai laughed, clutching Mack close. He's one of us now.

Mack didn't deny it. He didn't say anything.

Aren't you, boy? Dai asked.

They swayed a little in search of balance. A three-legged creature lacking in symmetry. Mack ducked free of his captor and shoved him, only half playful, though Dai caught a hold of his sleeve. They locked eyes, Dai grinning wide enough to show his missing molars. Mack tugged, but Dai held on. Mack was about to shove him again but the man lunged forward with a hand.

Mack flinched. Dai ruffled his hair.

You had a petal, he said, motioning to the trees behind them. The cherries.

The actor was on the bullhorn now. Paused every so often in anticipation of applause. They couldn't hear what he was saying from the back, but they clapped along regardless. Mack saw his chance to slip away.

Hold up a second, the journalist called after him. Take this at least. Think about what I said.

She pressed a card into his palm. Her name and number printed in simple black lettering.

He left by the side gate and passed the junior school. Cut down the side of the hospital and followed Sandfields Road to meet the river by McDonald's. There was a weir there that provided water to the docks. They reckoned you could see salmon jumping when conditions were right. Today the water came over the crest as a trickle, stained green by thick blooms of algae. He looked over his shoulder to make sure the journalist wasn't tailing him.

The river led to St Joseph's church, the parish of his grandfather's childhood. One of the many families crammed into the terraced streets there. Irish families. Jamaicans. Italians. The Protestant St Mary's right next door. The grave-yard where Dic Penderyn was buried. He'd always been told there was once a castle around there, a proper castle with a moat and a keep, but now it was nothing but a bump in the road. He'd been told a lot of things he couldn't imagine. About the prehistoric settlers who built barrows and stone circles in the surrounding hills. The monks who mined coal from the mountains. Later the collieries and metal-works that scarred the land all the way back up the valleys. A railway line brought the coal out of Garw and Ogwr and Llynfi. Brought passengers too, the living and the dead, the train stopping at the bend in Goytre to unload the coffins to be buried.

Mack stopped before the church to catch his breath. The building was larger than his own parish, older, red brick with a campanile bell tower. His grandfather had once told him the bell weighed more than a ton and a half. It had a name, so the story went. Gabriel.

The entrance was open. He heard voices inside. Creeping through the vestibule, he cracked the door and peered in. The nave, he found, had been given over to rehearsals. Men and women dressed as Roman soldiers marched up and down the aisles.

When he got home, his mother asked if he wanted dinner. She'd already eaten but had laid him a place at the table. Since his return, she insisted on formality. They stood together as his plate rotated in the microwave then carried it through to the dining room. Mack added salt and then pepper. His mother sat and watched him eat.

The dining room had an armchair, an old television, a bricked-up fireplace and a sideboard along the back wall. Clara pushed the chair against the set when she pulled the table out. There was a mantelpiece above the fireplace. A carriage clock that no longer moved.

Any good books in the box? she asked casually. I noticed you'd gone up the attic?

Mack nodded slowly, chewing.

What sort of books are they?

He swallowed. Wiped at his mouth with his hand.

Well, they're not going to be *Playboy*s, are they?

His mother pursed her lips and looked off towards the window. The television talked in the other room. She left it on when she was home, as though afraid of what might emerge from a silent house.

The strike's going ahead, Mack said. Seemed pretty unanimous.

Clara nodded but offered no comment. Mack put down his fork.

To be honest, he said, I'm not sure the Steel Company care either way. We might even be falling into a trap. Rumour is they're not going to pay out redundancy to any striking worker. If that's even allowed?

His mother's lips remained pursed. Mack picked up his fork again but did not continue eating.

I don't know, he said. Sometimes it's like both sides are living in a fantasy. The men want to relive the past, the Steel Company are just thinking of money. For all the talk of the future, it seems no one's reckoning with—

His mother worried at the ring on her finger. Inhaled to speak but swallowed the thought and instead scratched at her shoulder through her top. Her hands reminded Mack of his grandmother, and a sudden sadness lapped at the edges of him. An evening feeling, the direction the mind turned in the hour between light and dark.

When he'd finished his food, he rinsed his plate and retreated upstairs. His room austere. A wardrobe, a desk with a lamp, a single bed pushed against the wall. A few belongings on the shelves but not enough to make it homely. Remnant patches of posters marked the paintwork. Little rings in the carpet where a TV cabinet had once stood. He made his bed every morning. A habit picked up in the seminary dorms. Not an instruction he'd been given but something that felt correct all the same.

He went to the closet in search of old clothes. A collection of vestments hung inside. He wasn't sure why he'd taken them from the seminary, but he liked the way they looked on the wire hangers. A stolen secret. A trinity of holy ghosts. A black cassock, a white alb, a chasuble of gold and white. They wore different-coloured chasubles for different times of year. White for Christmas and Easter, green for Ordinary Time. Red reserved for the Passion and Pentecost and the feast days of those saints who were martyrs. The most sacred of figures. Those stoned to death, beheaded, crucified.

He took the hooked pole from the landing again and climbed into the attic. Rocked the canon's box to the lip of the hatch and carried it down on his shoulder. He put the box against the wall in his room and went back up to see what else he might find. Signs of birds. Woodlice dried to husks. Long-roped cobwebs knotted with insect parts. In the corner was another box with his name on it. An assortment of old belongings. He decided to take that down too, but when he stood, he hit his head on the bulb and the light pitched sideways around him as though he stood in the bowels of a ship during a storm.

The water ran black in the sink when he washed his hands. In his room, he opened the second box and found the things his mother had cleared on his departure. Books, CDs, his favourite teddy bear. Familiar objects he hadn't seen in years. Near the bottom was a wind-up toy. A plastic duck on two legs that walked across the table when you wound it. Mack took it out and instinctively turned the key, only to remember the racket it made when released. So instead he just kept winding, until the strain of the spring had nowhere left to go.

He dropped the whirring duck into the box and buried it beneath his bed. He would go through the items another time, he decided. Put a few on display. Make the room a home again. But for now, he turned to the canon's books. When he opened *The Cloud of Unknowing*, a bookmark fell into his lap. A prayer card made for a monsignor's golden jubilee. The page it kept seemed charged by its presence. He took a seat at his desk. Could still hear the duck in the box.

His old notebook was in the top drawer. The cover creased now, the pages bloated. It felt surreal to have it before him again. A pen in his hand, the white of the page. An old compulsion calling.

God, he copied from the book, was beyond the intellect of man. Beyond even his imagination. When confronted by His face, the human mind seized. So on those occasions we might stand before him, we could only process an absence, a blankness, a nothing. For He was a knowledge we had no idea how to assimilate. In the end, we could only hope to be suspended within this space. To enter a cloud of unknowing.

V

At work, he reported to the office, clocked in, ensured the CCTV was operational, then prepared for their rounds. Denzil locked the door behind them and got the van going. Their shift operated according to a strict schedule. They drove with the headlights up at fifteen miles per hour. They stopped at every gate and door.

Bossman's offered double time, Denzil said, checking his teeth in the mirror. Thursday till Monday. Extra hours if we want them.

Mack said nothing. When Denzil braked for their first stop, he did so hard enough to raise a cloud of dust.

I'll tell him thanks but no thanks, issit? Hopefully this time he gets the message. Swear the cunt's deaf.

The teeth of a key clicked as they went into the cylinder. If you were careful, you could feel the delicate tension of the pins. Mack appreciated the order inside a lock. The elegance of parts in motion. A door was either open or fastened and there was nothing in between.

An unsecured access point was a source of danger, that's

what the induction video had said. An open door invited threat into the workplace. As though the entire world was full of malevolent forces waiting to test any vulnerability. Trouble slipped through the smallest of spaces. You had to hold the line.

They were on the haul road out by the coke ovens. So close to the beach you could hear the sea. Mack on foot, trying the padlocks on the gate in the fence there. Denzil crawling along in the van behind. He found himself wondering what would happen if he left a lock unfastened. If there would be consequences for such a curious, careless act. Did he dare do it between patrols one time as a kind of challenge? And if he could do one, why not three or four or five?

He tested the padlocks by pulling on them. Denzil drove with one arm out the window, an unlit cigarette between his lips. When the patrol was done, Mack returned the keys to Denzil and they went back to the office. An hour later, they would do it all over again.

The boss had rung in their absence. Requested a callback asap. Denzil paced as he figured out what he would tell him. We can't cross the picket line, he repeated under his breath. A mantra he was trying to remember. He shook his head as if to dissipate the gathering temptation, walking to one end of the room and back again, the keys on his belt rattling like a pocketful of coins.

We'll just have to tell him straight, Mack said.

Denzil nodded in agreement yet looked pained.

I'm going for a fag, he said, using his shoulder to open the door.

Mack took a seat behind the desk and loosened the laces of his boots. Quiet fell over him like something dropped from above. No sound but the straining computer tower and constant buzz of the screens. The telephone waited patiently at his elbow. Turned slightly, looking at him.

He took the receiver and put it to his ear. The flat tone entered his head again. An anchor to another space or time. He sensed Denzil might never return so long as he listened carefully. An entire shift filled with a single sound. He wished only that the window was bigger so he might watch the dusk descend outside. See the day turn purple then blue then black. His mind turned to the meeting then. The actor, the vote to strike. In his pocket was the card the journalist had given him, but when he raised a hand towards the phone, he punched a different number in.

She answered immediately on this occasion. He knew it was her from the intake of breath.

Hello?

She sounded small down the line. Mack clenched his teeth.

Hello? she said again. Who's speaking?

It's me.

He felt a shift on the other end. A slackening. He wondered if she'd been expecting someone else.

What do you want? she asked eventually.

He hadn't planned on getting so far. What did he want? He didn't want anything really. He wanted to talk to her.

They listened to the silence of the line together.

About the other night, he started.

But Siwan interrupted. She didn't want to talk about that.

I didn't mean to . . . He trailed off. He realised his hand was shaking. It's not that I . . .

The space between them felt like a hole. He wasn't sure who was at the bottom.

I didn't expect to see you, he said simply.

Her laugh was swift and stunted. A crackle of air.

I didn't expect to see you either.

I'm home now. I was going to say something. You know, when you visited at the—

She cut him off again. I thought you weren't allowed to talk about that?

About what?

The seal? Siwan said. The seal of silence?

Mack swallowed. Started to explain. He was never ordained, after all, so it hadn't been an official confession. There was nothing binding in his—

We never used to do this, she said. This small talk. Catching up.

The weary drag to her voice cut him. The sense of being indulged.

Then what do you want to talk about?

She hesitated. He envisaged her closing the door gently. Stretching the cord to sit at the table. Her body moving through the house. The phone was nailed to the wall in the kitchen, he imagined. Next to the cork board and the calendar. Adjacent to the sink.

We could meet, she suggested.

Her voice came different now. Right in his ear. Not louder, but closer to him.

Meet?

Isn't that what we used to do?

He pushed the phone harder against his head. A noise outside caused his body to tense. He found himself whispering.

I'm in work.

After work.

I don't finish until late.

That's okay, Siwan said. Late suits me fine.

He was about to explain that the Plaza wasn't open any more when she began to read out directions. He scrambled for a pen in the drawer and removed the lid with his teeth. With the phone in the crook of his neck, he scribbled on the palm of his left hand. The line began to break. Siwan's voice drifted away from him.

Hello? Mack said, taking the receiver into his hand again. Can you still hear me?

A short pause before the reply. Yes, she said, voice clean and clear. I can hear you.

Denzil gave him a lift when their shift ended. Dropped him off at the bottom of his street. Mack waited on the pavement to wave him off, watching the van disappear around the corner before pulling his coat tight around himself and setting off walking. The streets quiet at that hour. Security lights on motion sensors illuminated front gardens. Gnomes on ceramic mushrooms, lawns of bright green AstroTurf. A chained-up moped wrapped in waterproof sheeting like a body in a bag. The air smelled of sulphur, as it often did when the cloud was low. Part of the sintering process and the coke ovens. To make steel you needed iron ore and lime and coal. Temperatures over a thousand degrees. You removed the impurities, gases sometimes burned and sometimes cleaned and sometimes vented out into the atmosphere because where else could they possibly go?

Mack only noticed the smell when he stopped to think about it. A stitching to the air, a heavy sulphur thread. Not entirely unpleasant and with its own quaint history attached. The smell reminded him of his grandparents, and his grandparents were wholly good.

A car passed with its radio pumping. A deep bass beat, the pulse of the world.

He walked past the Plaza again. Thought of the posters that once lined the front wall. A near-unbearable variety. The films rated 18 the most alluring. Body horrors, chainsaw massacres, franchise slashers with dripping typography. The Japanese chillers. Italian freaks. He thought too of the food they never ordered. Buttered popcorn, pickled hot dogs, Thayer's ice cream. The slushies and the tip-tops and the Coke half flat with melted ice. The carpets with their isometric patterns and the trailers they played at the beginning of every picture. He had loved the trailers. Everyone did. The way the room went dark just before they started. How everything was Coming Soon.

It had always been Siwan who arranged their meetings in adolescence, when they were old enough to no longer be chaperoned. He was never certain when the call would come. She'd ring his house and hang up if he didn't reach the phone first. When he did, she spoke only to give a day and a time.

He crossed at the gates near the train station and headed away from town across the railway lines. The night cool but not cold, muggy with the cloud, the faint smudge of the moon like a bruise yet to show. He met the river and followed its line towards the docks. Heard the water but didn't see it. The lights from the works cast the clouds orange from below, as though the entire town were ablaze and he the only one to know it.

They couldn't go to the Plaza, but they were meeting regardless. He followed the directions on his palm.

The street lights changed from daylight LEDs to low-pressure sodium. A reversion fit for the surroundings. This rudimentary part of town bathed in a murky ochre glow. There were no homes this side of the line, just warehouses and outlets and corrugated sheds. A dismal space linked by roads of gravel and lined by high-security fence. Wide yards piled with discarded appliances and junked cars. Shipping containers and scrap metal and old railway trucks tagged with obscene words and signs.

Mack pulled his coat tighter and quickened his step. The gas monitor on his belt rattled a marching pace. Over his shoulder, the water pulled silently towards the sea. The river deeper there, its surface flat and silver, the blade of a knife. The road deteriorated. Just two tyre trails through rock and scrub. He dragged his feet so he didn't trip in the dark, until he thought to use the torch on his belt, the beam lighting his way among the litter and the brambles. Something congealed in his chest. Excitement, dread, any distinction lost in the night.

He bumped along slowly, a moth trapped in a jar. Up ahead something glowed. A light that caught the cloud like the works, only cleaner, without the rusted edge. A builders' merchant illuminated by towering floodlights. One in each corner like a prison complex, leaving no place in which to hide.

BRICKS, SAND, CEMENT, read the staked sign at the front of the lot. *GAS, FERTILISER, FUEL.*

Men moved in silence inside the fence. Smoking, breathing, loading things into cars. Every engine running, the air thick with exhaust. Mack hovered on the periphery, watched them lift and carry and communicate with their hands. Men gripping bags by the necks like throttled poultry. Men with wheeled trolleys, forklift trucks. Men shovelling grit into hessian sacks, casting four shadows, one in each direction, perfect compass points.

He heard the catch of an engine close by. A brief cough, then headlights. The car was on his side of the fence, its beams high and directed at him like spotlights on a stage. The glare was too bright for him to see through the windscreen, but then the driver's side opened and a figure emerged. Mack raised a hand to shield his eyes.

You found me, she said.

All he could see was the outline of her. A shadow with clouded breath.

Come on. Get in.

She reached inside the car and killed the engine. When he tried the passenger door, he found it locked. She had to reach over and pop it from inside.

The quiet was heavy in the enclosed space. He adjusted his belt, leather squeaking. The windows began to steam.

I've ordered something, Siwan said.

Mack crossed his arms, hands in his armpits against the chill of the night. She wore a knit cap and barely an expression. The low light caught the angles of her face. Harder than in his memory. Leaner. Taut with the weight of a private life.

I wondered, she continued, if you might go in and get it for me?

He couldn't help but look at her. Wished to remove the torch from his belt and really take her in. She appeared tired but used to it. At home in the dark. Her body and face moved but her eyes did not. A gaze he felt in his sternum. He tried to swallow but had no spit. Saw the builders' merchant through the misted windscreen as nothing but a blot of light.

I've got the slip here, she said, stretching her legs forward and arching out of the seat to get into her back pocket. Mack stole another glance sideways. Saw the pale strip of flesh between her top and her jeans. A pair of dimples at the base of her spine. A cotton label sticking up from the waistband of her underwear.

He looked away as she retrieved a sheet from her pocket. She smoothed the creases from the paper before handing it over to him.

Just go to the desk. Give them this.

Mack squinted, eyes adjusting to the dark. He didn't recognise the name at the top of the form. Male, generic.

Who's James? he asked.

Siwan was up to her wrist in her pocket again. When she moved, he smelled the detergent on her clothes.

I've got the cash here.

She counted out the money, passing the notes from one hand to the other, murmuring under her breath. He looked for rings on her fingers. The paper sounded like dead leaves and there was more of it than Mack expected. When she finished counting, she started over again.

A sudden despondence stirred within him. The sad alarm of expectations upended. The situation shifting in his head.

You're building a community garden, she told him, eyes on the money. An allotment for fruit and veg.

Fruit and veg, Mack repeated.

Your name is James and you're paying in cash.

He wanted to pause, ask exactly what was going on, but

things were in motion and Siwan didn't seem willing to stop. The night felt colder when he got out of the car. The lights in the yard unyielding and hostile. There was a van running somewhere, simmering, growling. The decisive sound of spade pitched into sand. It occurred to him he could walk away in that instant, never speak to her again. He could climb back into the car and demand she explain everything. In his hesitation, he looked over his shoulder, just about able to make out the shape of her in the driver's seat. A shadow of shoulders and head. She was watching, he realised with a prickle of disquiet.

He expected the staff to look up when he entered, but no one seemed interested in him. There was no shop floor inside. Just a thin room with a line of kiosk windows. A bell on the desk to let them know you were there. At the end of the row was a set of double doors where they brought out your order. *KEEP CLEAR* sprayed yellow in a box on the ground.

Mack rang a bell and waited. Leaned on the counter, acted casual. The window was Perspex and scarred with scratches. The warehouse floor was visible on the other side. A regimented world of steel racks and cardboard boxes. The sound of air conditioning. Rubber soles on concrete. Rotating orange lights.

He was debating whether to ring again when a woman emerged and took his slip without saying anything. She wore a flesh-coloured brace on her wrist, scaled like the belly of a crocodile. Carpal tunnel, she said, having caught him looking. Mack's own hands were shaking, so he hid them in his pockets. A television high on the wall played an old game show. The contestants were losing.

Something about the form seemed to bother the woman. Mack kept his eyes on the screen.

Have you bought this from us before?

He turned to face her. He said yes, no, well maybe not from here. He said his name was James and he was building a community garden. An allotment for fruit and veg.

The warble in his voice was audible even to him. The dip and break of a man on edge. The woman listened patiently before her eyes dropped to his utility belt. He could still hear the shovels outside.

Wait here a minute, she told him.

Mack removed his hands from his pockets and put them back in again. Looked to the TV on the wall and found adverts. You could cut the funeral now and go straight to cremation. The urn delivered to your door at prices starting under a grand.

He could leave, he told himself. Walk straight out the door.

When the woman returned, she appeared wary. Sorry, she said, what did you say your name was? He hesitated before he answered, a beat that seemed to last a day. He stepped closer to the desk and tried to smile, but she took a step back like he'd entered her personal space.

Could you please confirm your address?

My address, Mack said. I can confirm my address.

He grinned at the woman. She looked at him through the Perspex screen.

Is this correct? she asked, pushing the form through the little window. She spoke slowly as though across a language barrier. Like he was a witless child.

The form had been filled in by hand. Scratchy black ink, every letter capitalised.

Yes, he said, taking a moment to read it. That's my address all right.

She left him alone again. He tried to imagine how a relaxed man might hold himself. Leaned on the counter, then changed his mind. A small camera watched from near the ceiling across the room, its light a digital green, its glare like a needle. He pulled his collar higher on his neck and tried not to meet its eye.

The double doors opened and a man wheeled the order through on a trolley. Six white sacks, seamless polypropylene. A yellow diamond hazard symbol with a flaming circle at the top. James? the man called. Mack nodded. He asked if he needed a hand getting it to the van, but Mack told him it should be all right.

Just bring the trolley back, the woman said, a set of eyes back behind the window. He thanked her for her help but received no reply.

The bulk of the sacks made it difficult to push the trolley. He considered abandoning it where it was. Letting Siwan do her own work. Only another van was pulling up and he still felt the woman's gaze on his back. The closed-circuit camera. He imagined his face on a pixelated screen. He'd get the trolley to the car and no more, he told himself. Tell her exactly what he thought of being used in that way. He set his feet apart to brace himself and pushed.

He was all right until the paving ran out. Then the wheels dug into the dirt of the road and it felt like the brakes were on. But the ground between the warehouse and the car was open and he was determined not to linger. He hit a rock and the sacks threatened to topple. The wrappings were covered in a fine white silt.

She was out of the car already. The boot was open. She barely looked at him.

Get the other end, she said, wriggling her fingers under the first sack.

They had cameras in there, he said. CCTV.

They have cameras everywhere.

You could have warned me.

She stopped and looked at him, brow creased.

So what? she asked. You could have brought a mask?

She turned to the sacks again, but he didn't join her.

This isn't a game, he said. What if they—

An alarm interrupted. A car knocked in passing by someone else loading up. Hazard lights flashed amber in time with the siren and the sight sent a panic through him. He moved because that's what his body demanded. They lifted the sacks together, working on a count of three.

Only five of the sacks would fit in the boot so they put the other on the back seat. I need a bigger car, she joked as they lifted the last one together. Let me know if you see any going around town. When it was done, she got in and fastened her seat belt. Mack stood at the open door on the passenger side. She glanced up at him, one hand on the wheel, one on the gearstick, a little out of breath from their effort, then looked again as if confused by what she found.

The courtesy light by the rear-view mirror was their only illumination. Siwan's face pulled downwards in shadow.

Come on, she said. Get in.

He was awkward in his movement. Limbs suddenly unwieldy. His palms were tingling and it occurred to him they should have worn gloves. He got into the car and fastened his belt. When he slammed his door, the light snapped out. His palms were stinging now, but it might have been all in his head. Siwan turned the key and her face came alive in the iridescent glow of the dashboard.

She put the stick in reverse. Hooked an arm around his seat and turned to look out the back. He felt her hair on the side of his face. Thought back to that day at the seminary.

Bless me, Father, for I am about to sin. That's what she had told him.

I can't do this, he said to her now. She asked what he meant but he was already climbing out.

Mack, she called.

He set off walking. She crawled the car alongside and wound the window down.

You're being silly.

I'm being silly?

He could barely look at her. The car matched his stride. He wasn't sure what he'd expected from their meeting, only that it wasn't this. Perhaps he *was* being silly, he realised, to have brought himself there at all.

The men in the yard beyond moved stone and sand in barrows. The cold white light fell like a scythe. He felt suddenly queasy. The sense of having dropped a precious object from a cliff and peering after it over the edge. He wanted to lose the sensation but didn't know how. Could think only to put distance between them. He set off walking away from the warehouse and she followed alongside, window down and squinting. She called his name into the night.

He kept going. Her tyres inched over the road. Stones popped like ice in a glass. Mack, she called, voice almost a whisper now, but she soon realised he was not about to change his mind.

She rolled the window up and put the headlights on. The wheels spun when she accelerated, as though the car was weighed down by its cargo. He heard a screech of tyres, then something caught his temple. A stone that jumped up and bit him like a snake.

At first he thought he'd been blinded. A pain bright white then black, a vibration through his skull and teeth. He fell to one knee, fumbling in the weeds like a drowning man in search of the surface, a soldier under attack. His heart beating big, his limbs in spasm. When the initial shock passed and he opened his eyes, the world came streaming back.

With a hand to his face, he followed her brake lights for a way. Eyes in the distance, red and fleeting. A harbinger from ancient times. The pain in his head throbbed in rhythm with his heart. He suddenly felt like crying. If only she could see how she'd hurt him, he thought, she would surely come rushing back. But Siwan did not come back. Her lights kept moving. And when they finally disappeared and the night pressed in close, an immense self-pity came with it.

VI

Mass at the seminary was not as he imagined. They changed the translation in the months before he arrived. A new place full of unfamiliar people and even the service had turned against him. Those comforting old rhythms vanished when he needed them most. He lived in a grand old building of red brick and stone dressings. Six students to a dorm. Private bedrooms and a communal kitchen. A bathroom shared with the Filipino ex-soldier named Angelo next door. They took main meals on long tables in the dining room. Breakfast at eight, lunch at one, supper at seven fifteen. Lectures every day but Sunday. Morning meditation. Adoration of the Blessed Sacrament. Solemn prayer and chant practice and mass.

Mack did not believe in God completely, but he wanted to so strongly it came to feel meaningful. As though to will oneself to faith despite a lack of conviction carried a purity of its own. What better a man to serve the Lord than that? He bought black slacks, black shirts, black belts and shoes. Wool sweaters in dark grey and black. Washed with plain soap and didn't snack between meals. Got rid of his phone and took long walks in the evenings. Paid attention to birdsong and circling bats. He intended to become a contemplative man. Sculpted himself in that image. Someone serious, sensitive to the attendant sadness of the world around him. A man made white in the blood of the Lamb.

He did not visit home often. Came to see sentimentality as a function of nostalgia. Was done longing for what was past.

He got to know his fellow seminarians slowly. Coaxed by a gregarious third-year named Tom Murphy, a forty-something who insisted they call him Spud. Spud had had a wife and a kid once upon a time and he'd had them in the wrong order. Got married in Bantry Bay with his own little girl holding the flowers. The years that came later tested him, Spud said, but he liked to remember his family as they had looked on that day. He kept a photo of the three of them no bigger than a matchbox in his wallet. He'd show it to you if you asked.

They sat at a small table in the common room and played board games in the evenings. Risk, Scrabble, Monopoly. Catholic Monopoly, as Spud liked to joke. The winner the first person to give everything away.

Another of Mack's room-mates was into Marian apparitions. Saw himself as an investigator. Used the internet to edge closer to the truth. Garabandal, Medjugorje, Our Lady of Zeitoun. Anything the Church was yet to fully acknowledge. Cases with mystery still left intact. One knew the King James Bible by heart, another lifted weights. Not a penance, he was keen to stress, but a celebration. He felt God in every curl and rep.

They were taught by men from all over the world. Took classes on philosophy and Latin and the Acts of the Magisterium. The history of sacred music and the early centuries of the Church. The first year covered the basics, then they really got into it. Natural theology. Philosophical ethics. The philosophy of being and knowledge. Cosmology, psychology, ascetical theology. Apologetics, mysticism and metaphysics.

They played ping-pong in their spare time. Eight-ball pool, five-a-side. The men unfit but enthusiastic in their mismatched kit, shorts too baggy or tight. Balding men, beer-gut men, men unnaturally hairy or hairless. Legs milk-white and odd-looking, the sort never meant to be seen at all. They charged about and pushed one another and laughed. Mack wasn't sure which type of feller annoyed him more – the competitive ones or those for whom winning was a distant concern.

They didn't control your hours at the seminary, but they suggested a regimen. Lights out at nine p.m. You could stay up all night if you wanted, but no one ever did. What was a life of faith if not a submission to patterns beyond your control?

Advent, Easter, Ordinary Time. The feasts of saints and holy days of obligation. A wheel that turned. By the third year, the pattern grew tired. He went to mass, meditated, studied. He woke in the night and asked himself, was this really all there was?

He began to resent what the place asked of him beyond the liturgical rites. The communal meals, the camaraderie. He could barely walk ten yards down a corridor without a brother emerging from somewhere, eager to continue some previous debate. A life among enthusiastic men who only closed their mouths to sleep. He would try to go out alone. Take the bus to the supermarket, the hardware shop. They needed light bulbs and curtain hooks, he might say. Anti-fungal caulk to reseal the bathroom windows. But the others would invite themselves. Three, four, as many as would fit in a car. An outing of would-be priests in their slacks and their sweaters. Men with a certain aura. An energy that made people turn and look. He would go to the local cinema and watch a film on occasion. Obscure pictures playing for one night only. Lonely Swedish flicks in black and white. He sat alone, as near to the front as he could manage, and lost himself in the images. But more often than not, he found the solitude self-defeating. When you escaped to the desert, the silence shouted in your ear.

He sought other means of escape. Volunteered to help local nuns in the surrounding community. The sisters were impressive, nothing like the ideas in his head. They ran the convent as a de facto worker house where anyone could eat or sleep in exchange for good deeds. They picked him up at the seminary gates in a battered Nissan Micra. Cherry-red with three doors. Beaded seat covers and little cushions in the back. A woman named Sister Joan always driving. They grew vegetables and fed the homeless. Picked litter from woodland and riverbanks.

Sister Joan whistled as she drove. Wore jeans, a T-shirt, a baseball cap instead of a wimple. Played old folk cassettes with the volume turned down and talked about her ideas for the future. Ways to expand the operation. Make an impact in the world. The sisters were clued into the practicalities of helping people. Needle exchange programmes. Naloxone.

Clinics for sexual health. Such things could be transformational, that's what Sister Joan believed. It just required people who gave a damn.

Love, she liked to say, quoting Ignatius of Loyola, was shown more in deeds than words.

She'd been part of the Catholic Worker Movement in her youth. Moved from place to place, volunteering to help in the wake of disasters. Flash floods and fires. Oil spills that left mile after mile of coastline a glistening black. In her sixties now but no less enthusiastic. Sometimes Mack caught himself imagining she was Siwan's mother. Mrs Roderick allowed a future in spite of everything.

It was from the nuns that he learned names he'd never heard before. Althusser, Bonhoeffer, Merton and Boff. Gutiérrez and his liberation theology. He scoured the library and read everything he could find. If a particular author wasn't available, he wrote to Canon Sylvester.

The packages came wrapped in brown paper, samizdat with *Top Secret* scrawled in red pen along the top.

At night, Mack retreated to his room and read with a new-found hunger. His notes grew increasingly detailed. Through the nuns he discovered a context to unlock his faith, a thread between scripture and the real living world. The more he studied and the more he helped, the more he felt he belonged to something. Not the branch of the Church he was taught in the classroom, but a branch of the Church all the same.

Our Lady of Margam was not a church in the old tradition. There were no towers, no spires, no buttresses or parapets. No great columns or looming clerestory, no solemn figures carved from marble. Just a brick box, built in the seventies, social hall attached. Lemon-yellow walls and blonde-wood pews. None of the shadows of other parishes. None of the sorrowful murk. Even as a child, Mack had sensed something was lost in the arrangement. The old Catholic mystery sanitised in a surplus of light.

But if you could find faith there, without the seductive spectacle of shade and old stone, then you could find it anywhere.

The front doors were locked, so Mack went around the side. Entered the Blessed Sacrament chapel and found three stools lined along the wall nearest the confessional. Only one woman was waiting. Mack knew her face but couldn't remember her name. Knew she would know him and where he'd been. Knew she would be friendly with his mother. He considered leaving, but the woman had already turned to smile in his direction. He smiled too and closed the door, careful to minimise the noise.

He crossed himself and genuflected before the tabernacle, then took a stool to wait. They held mass in the chapel on weekday mornings. Essentially the church in miniature. Five rows of benches, bare plaster walls. A low ceiling with a shallow dome skylight set with stained glass. An abstract pattern, oranges and blues. The altar decorated with a pair of pillar candles in silver dishes and covered with white cloth. The tabernacle behind on a stand, a square box of hammered brass.

He'd gone to Siwan's before the church, compelled by a desire for confrontation. To demand she tell him everything or never again request his help. In the desperate early hours, he'd considered going to the authorities, explaining everything he knew or guessed at, getting out ahead of any trouble before it came to pass. Yes, that was him in the pictures at the builders' merchant, but he hadn't known what he was buying. He still didn't know and didn't want to. He'd tell them everything she had said.

Only he couldn't tell anyone so long as he believed in the seal of the sacrament. He'd decided to speak to her instead.

On Siwan's street, he'd found the car parked beside the house but the sacks missing. A thin pastel layer of dust coating the fenders and wheels. He'd made it across the road this time, right up to her front door, only to knock and receive no reply.

Have you been home long? the woman beside him whispered.

He could picture her family. A husband, three kids. A grandchild sometime later. He knew exactly where they'd sat in mass every week. The grandchild had been a girl. Mop of dark hair in thick ringlets. Liked to call out during the quiet periods of a service, would laugh at the sound of her own voice echoing from the walls. Mack wanted to ask the woman a question of his own but had no idea what might have happened in the interim. If her husband was dead, if she still spoke to her children. If you don't know a lot, talk even less, that was what they taught at the seminary. A parishioner will share what they want to share. There was a lot to be said for silence.

They waited. Light fell through stained glass. Mack's head throbbed where the stone had hit him, though the mark was modest. He'd approached the mirror that morning with trepidation and was almost disappointed by what he found. The woman beside him rooted through her bag then settled again. Whether there was someone in the confessional already wasn't entirely clear. The closed door kept its secret.

How's Mam? she asked eventually. She wore a silver brooch and a scarf. A long, pleated skirt to the ankle. If she noticed the bruise on his brow she did not betray the fact.

She's fine, thanks, Mack replied. Everyone okay with you?

Everyone's okay, the woman confirmed. I can't complain.

Mack nodded, pleased to hear it. He folded his arms, wondered the time.

Not that it would do me any good, the woman added. Complaining, I mean.

When the door to the confessional opened, the woman's husband emerged.

I always go first, he told Mack. She's got more to say than me.

They stood there smiling at one another.

The other feller come off worse? the husband asked, grimacing at Mack's face.

The woman swatted his arm and went into the booth. Her husband left to sit in the car. Mack considered what he might say when his turn came, but the throb filled his head with static. When he was younger, he would write a list of sins to take into confession. Canon Sylvester would demand he tear the sheet to pieces before he left the booth.

Every seminarian had been given a teaching parish to visit. A chance to shadow a priest on his daily rounds. They were not allowed to sit in on confession for obvious reasons, but occasionally parishioners approached them all the same. Like that woman one time who sat next to him in the pews.

Started talking before he could stop her. I hold negative thoughts, she had confided. I struggle to love my soon-to-be daughter-in-law. There were cultural differences. Clashes of habit and history. A certain disappointment, she'd admit it, that the girl did not match up to the image long held in her head. I told my son, the woman had continued, I said I don't care if she's got a bone through her nose so long as she's Catholic, but I can't even pronounce her family name.

Mack only had to wait a short while. When the woman re-emerged, she straightened her skirt, took a deep breath and told him it had been nice to see him. A person brighter than five minutes previous. Lighter in spirit or else plain relieved. Mack smiled and agreed, it had been nice to see her too. She genuflected before the altar and left. Then it was only him and the open door.

The confessional was more a cubicle. A small room bisected by a plasterboard wall. A window cut in the middle with a black curtain on a roller. A plastic chair to sit on, the kind they used in school.

Mack sat and listened to the quiet. Sensed a presence on the other side of the divide. He hadn't intended to go through with the sacrament, but now he was there he couldn't turn back. He wondered if the canon would know who he was by the sound of his voice.

Bless me, Father, for I have sinned. It has been some weeks since my last confession.

The squeak of a seat as Canon Sylvester rearranged himself.

Well, he said, tell me, son. What are your sins?

Mack wished he'd thought harder about what he wanted to confess. Had no idea how serious to be.

Someone recently lent me a collection of books, he found himself saying. I didn't have a bookmark, so I turned down the corner of the page.

He sensed movement behind the gauze. A bulge in the fabric. An eye pressed close.

Could it be? the canon asked. The prodigal son returned?

His voice sounded thin through the curtain. His old deadpan tone lacking its usual bite.

Mack said he wasn't sure about that. Hadn't the prodigal son run back to the father? He was running away.

The old rumour was that Canon Sylvester had once been an exorcist. Whispers swapped by schoolboys when he first arrived at the parish. A tall man, neither ancient nor boyish, in possession of tangible bulk. A man who dressed all in black, wore dark lenses in his glasses. Lent his vocation the gravity it deserved. He'd trained somewhere in Rome, the boys said, deep within the necropolis, but the canon wasn't an exorcist. He was a Jesuit. Had served all over the world. Even Latin America, he'd once told Mack, under the hot shadow of the Cold War. A man who might have confronted demons right enough, but not the kind to be banished so easily.

The chair creaked again. The old man exhaled through his nose. There was nothing to do in the box but stare at the blank wall ahead. No distractions from the sacrament. You might have been six feet underground.

And there was me, the canon said, thinking I had a ready-made replacement. I held on as long as I could.

He inhaled sharply between his sentences. A gasping effort, like he was sucking his air through a tube. When Mack imagined him on the other side of the gauze, he saw the figure he'd known in the past. A large man, shirt tucked tight over his belly, hands like the buckets of an industrial machine. A mark on his head, shapeless and rust-red. Like Jupiter's storm raging through the sparse hair of his scalp.

I've been meaning to visit, Mack said. I've just been—

Embarrassed?

A flash of heat came over him. He folded his arms and leaned closer to the gauze.

People get the wrong impression. Assume a scandal of some kind.

Oh, the canon said. You're going to disappoint me?

That or they think I wasn't cut out for it. That I'm not as serious or committed as I wished to believe.

The path of discernment is long and complicated. There's no superior outcome. Every man's experience is unique to—

You don't need to explain discernment, Mack said. I've heard it a hundred times.

Then you'll understand there are myriad ways to serve the Lord. I'm sure you will find a more fulfilling role outside of the priesthood. One without the friction that—

Who mentioned friction?

I sense friction, the canon said. Was there friction?

I didn't come here to explain why I left.

Then why did you come?

Mack fell quiet, a scolded pupil. Canon Sylvester seemed happy to sit with the silence. The pain in Mack's head made it difficult to remain still. It occurred to him he could walk out and never set foot in a church again. He wouldn't even have to look the old man in the eye.

Don't you ever get discouraged? he asked. Hold regrets?

I'm a priest, Cormac. Not a statue.

But, I mean, doesn't it frustrate you? The gap between what we say and what we practise?

The canon exhaled through his nose. Or was he laughing?

I always said you should have been a Jesuit.

I'm sure I'd find an argument with them as well.

Yes, the canon agreed, but a good Jesuit is always in some kind of conflict with the Church and the state. We get away with that sort of thing.

I don't intend to make conflict. I just feel—

The abandonment to divine providence has gone on long enough? The growing chasm between the rich and the poor is a stain on our souls? The desecration of the earth is contrary to the plan of the creator? We agree on these things Cormac. You know this. I suspect it's why you came to me. But there comes a time when we must stop waiting for them to meet us at this conclusion. Even the last Pope was sympathetic, yet their resistance remained. Better to get on with it. Commit to action. Remember St Joseph. Work with our bare hands.

That's what I looked to do, Mack said. I tried to explain.

What I've learned in my long years of service is that no one likes to be told things plainly. Be too direct in your words and they stop listening. Lose interest. Regard you as condescending. People prefer to think they figured something out for themselves or else receive a divine epiphany. Knowledge gained in the awe of some grand event. Which means we must be imaginative in our mission. Find the novel approaches that might get the point across.

Mack leaned forward, elbows on his knees. Between his feet, he could make out the swooping patterns on the floor where they polished the tiles. He wasn't sure if the canon was chastising him.

Is it wrong to attempt to do good? he asked. Because that's what they essentially told me. Yet even when I ignore them, focus on being devout and performing virtuous deeds, this sense of agitation remains. A restlessness that won't leave me be.

You've read Aquinas, yes? the canon countered. His ideas around the soul? Aquinas believed the soul a defective thing always yearning for perfection. A potential that wishes to realise itself. Every moral action is an attempt to reach towards this impossible height, but also the very thing that creates the urge to reach higher still. A better action. A superior expression of our love. You see, mere repetition is never enough when it comes to the habit of faith. The virtuous life demands an ever-growing intensity.

But intensity how? Mack asked, the morning's anger returning. What better action is there to take?

The pain in his head was worse now, intensified in line with his frustration. Canon Sylvester sighed quietly before continuing. His voice so quiet Mack was forced to press his ear to the gauze.

Opportunities present themselves, the old man told him. The question is whether we are ready to meet them. Willing to make ourselves available to the Lord.

There was a knock from somewhere off in the church. A single sound muffled through the closed door. Mack waited for the canon to continue but it seemed the old priest had finished.

Canon? he asked eventually, voice rising in inflection as though unsure he was still there. On the subject of the Jesuits? I've got a question about Ignatius and his principle of obedience. I understand that an individual's needs are not important. That a man of faith must put his own will beneath the needs of the Church and his society. But what about when those two needs appear to be in conflict? What is to be our priority then?

It's a question, the canon suggested, you might consider for your penance.

Penance? I haven't done anything?

The static of moving fabric. The wet crease of a smile.

Yes, the canon said. Precisely. And now I'm suggesting you reconsider.

His mother did a double-take when he came in. Reached to slow him down.

Have you banged your head?

My what? he asked, trying to play ignorant.

Your head, she said, peering closer. It looks bruised.

Oh, that. It's nothing.

Let me clean it.

She reached out, but he ducked away across the room. Some basic part of him felt it crucial she did not look any closer. As though the mark was a hole through which the previous night might come into view.

Honestly, he insisted. It's fine.

How many fingers am I holding—

Cormac, just the boy I was looking for.

His father bowled into the kitchen with a look of abashed hope. Like he knew he was about to be irritating but intended to do it all the same. Mack guessed what he wanted to ask before he opened his mouth. Jackie was already in his overalls.

Dad, he said, I'm—

The phone interrupted them. An unfamiliar tone, electronic. His mother made to answer, but Mack was closer to the table.

Hello? he said, taking the handset into the hall.

Hello? came her reply.

He moved further from the door. Lowered his voice and cupped the receiver with his hand.

Why are you ringing here?

Siwan hesitated before answering, halted by the question.

I've always rung you at home.

But what do you want?

Another pause. A small sigh or swallow. She sounded far away.

Are you free?

Free?

Free to help?

Mack laughed. A snort through his nose.

I wouldn't ask, she said, it's just I can't move these—

Don't ring here again.

Mack, wait. Please.

The desperation in her voice pulled at him and he hated himself for it. He closed his eyes and saw her brake lights moving into the distance. He wasn't going to indulge her any more.

You're right, he said. It always was you who rang. You who decided when we met, you who sent me scurrying to the phone. I was left to wait. Trust you hadn't forgotten me. The one always left in the dark.

Siwan made to speak again, but Mack cut her off. The tone of the dead line filled the space instead.

Wrong number, he said as he placed the phone back on

the cradle. His mother opened her mouth to probe further, but he didn't wait to hear it.

I'll be five minutes, Dad. Just let me get changed.

When he came back downstairs, his mother was rooting through the drawers of the freezer. She eyed him with something like disdain as she handed over a bag of peas.

Here, she said. Press this to your head.

On the drive, his father spoke of the Passion plays of yesteryear. *Behold the Man*, they'd called it. A summer tradition in Margam Park. They handed out blankets if the evening got chilly, lined their costumes with bin bags when it rained. People shared suncream and mosquito repellent, tins of lager and packets of salt 'n' shake crisps. Kids ran wild only to return as the gnats descended and darkness crept over the hill. No one missed the crucifixion.

Les Jones would experiment with crosses, Jackie said. Remember Les? He'd line his prototypes up in the yard in Central Junior's. Only the dullest sods would volunteer to test them out, but luckily there was no shortage of them. Les wanted the crucifixion to look as realistic as possible. It was important, he reckoned, that people understood how much it hurt.

Mack rearranged the peas every so often, in search of a deeper cold. The bag sweated thin condensation against his head.

What happened anyway? his father asked, as though only then noticing the injury.

Nothing, Mack said. Just caught it in work.

He could feel his father snatching glances towards him.

I only took the peas to make Mam feel better. You know what she's like.

There were more people on the streets than usual. Family

groups with backpacks and raincoats. Tourists from out of town. The length of Margam Road was lined with crowd-control barriers now. Lamp posts were emblazoned with signage to direct the expected flow. Mack watched a group pose for a photograph with the works behind them. Angled to include the blasts and the strip mills, the gas flares wrathful and baby-blue.

You should have gone for that cup of coffee.

His father didn't take his eyes off the road as he spoke.

What cup of coffee?

With that journalist. She seems nice.

Mack kept his gaze out the windscreen too.

But I don't drink coffee, he said.

Well you should think about starting, Jackie countered. It would be good for you.

When they arrived, Mack's father killed the engine but didn't get out. Bent low to the steering wheel to get a better look at the house looming before them. Distant all of a sudden. Somewhere off inside his head. He took the keys from the ignition and mumbled about bags in the boot. Handed the keys to Mack and said he'd follow him in.

The house still smelled like them. Plug-in air freshener, cold cream, old cigarettes. Grampa O'Brien had smoked all his life, though Gran hated it. It gave her a headache, she said. Did no one any good. When Mack was born, she forbade her husband from smoking anywhere but the bathroom. One per hour and no more. The top window cracked, his neck craned, face close to the frosted glass as he exhaled. Why don't you just go outside? Clara would ask, but Gran O'Brien wouldn't let him go outside. Let him smoke in the bathroom. His private, shameful thing.

Mack put the lights on. Opened the curtains and blinds. A house with a sheet thrown over it. Nothing had been touched. Not the ornaments or furniture, the pictures on the walls. The rugs, the clocks, the telephone. Framed photographs and stacks of books. Belongings he had grown to know intimately. The detail of his recognition caught him cold. The wear on the arms of the chairs, the teacup rings on the tabletop. He had brought his notebook, wishing to be proactive, ready to make a plan, but now he was there it seemed impossible to judge what to save and what to throw away. No such hierarchy existed. His grandparents were encoded in the very arrangement of the rooms.

How eerie to walk it. A family museum, a functioning shrine.

There was a *Western Mail* on the nest of tables, open to the crossword. Half the answers filled out in blue biro. Some scratched thick over a previous word as though Gran had changed her mind. They'd had a television each, Mack's grandparents. One in the front room and one in the back. At night they sat apart, watching different programmes in different rooms. Or sometimes watching the same programme, something they'd only find out later, stood shoulder to shoulder to spit toothpaste into the sink before they bade one another goodnight.

We'll just look around today, Jackie said, a sudden apparition in the doorway. Take stock of what needs doing.

The cutlery was still in the drawer in the front room. The best plates they only used at Christmas. Antique bottles of Jameson's, Babycham, Baileys Irish Cream. A packet of paper napkins, party poppers, cocktail sticks. Jackie examined every cupboard, crouched to his haunches. Looked but did not touch, as though to move the smallest object was an act of sacrilege.

Mack was beginning to understand his role in the arrangement. If Jackie was too close to all of this, it fell to him to grease the wheels. Coax his father into doing what they had to do. Ease the passage towards letting go. But now he was there, he realised he held many of the same emotions. The things that surrounded them meant the world to him too.

Upstairs, he found towels still on the rack. The medicine cabinet fully stocked. TCP, Aquafresh, a half-used bag of double-ply rolls. A blister pack of paracetamol sat on the bottom shelf, and Mack popped two into his palm. The pain in his head had deepened through the morning. An ache sinking into the teeth and skull. The cold tap spluttered when he ran it, and he waited for the flow to settle. The water tasted hard and stale but got the pills down his throat.

The curtains were drawn in the bedroom. There was a photograph on the shelf beside the bed. A team portrait, nineteen sixty-something. The Fighting Irish. The Green Stars. An invincible side, three whole seasons unbeaten. Men of hard faces and folded arms presented in three rows. Their ears taped down by bandages, thick wads of Vicks up their nose. Catholic men ready to bleed onto jerseys of green and white and gold.

Grampa O'Brien often told of their tours across Ireland. A welcome like a homecoming. Matches as eighty-minute fights. One time a car pulled up beside the bus and a load of fellers in balaclavas climbed out to salute a nearby monument. A strange time to be there. Tins passed under tables after matches, coins rattling like dice in a cup. Funds for the front, for the freedom fighters. Men blew on their change before they dropped it in.

There was a packet of photographs on the shelf too. Pictures from when Mack was a child. Summer holidays with Gran and Grampa. Days that felt like they'd never end. Near the back he found one with Siwan. A picture his mother must have taken inside the Plaza. The pair of them posing with a cardboard cut-out promotion. A dog-like humanoid wearing a quiver of arrows and an army commando with leather gloves.

Don't call it violence, call it action, read the tagline along the bottom of the display. *Kids love action.*

Mack held the picture closer. Their faces caught brilliant white in the flash. Mouths slightly open, expressions somewhat pained. As though the sudden light had surprised them. Like they hadn't wished to be caught there at all.

He put the picture in his pocket and went downstairs. Found his father in the living room, slumped on his knees on the carpet. He backed out of the door, ready to pretend he hadn't seen, but Jackie sensed his presence and scrambled to his feet.

Let's look in the garage, he said quickly, avoiding his son's eye as he pushed past in the hall.

Grampa O'Brien had kept the garage bolted like Fort Knox, but Mack knew where to find the keys. The junk drawer in the kitchen. The place they'd always lived. Grampa'd laugh if he could see us, he said, removing the drawer and setting it on the countertop. He wasn't sure what he meant but wanted to say something.

His father nodded slowly as Mack rummaged. A golf ball. A length of twine. A pack of cards with the jokers at the front. Several rolls of black insulation tape and a pair of needle-nose pliers. A flip compact mirror with no plate inside.

I can do this, mind, he said, not looking up from the drawer. Clear the house, I mean. Take care of everything.

He sensed his father behind him, swaying slightly.

I'll ask Denzil to give me a hand, Mack continued. We could borrow the van from work.

You could? Jackie asked.

Of course, Mack said. No problem.

He found the keys beneath a stack of instruction manuals and led the way into the garden. The space was not so kind in its preservation, full of dead-head flowers and untamed lawn, yet now his father's step seemed a little lighter. There were three padlocks on the garage door but only one was fastened. Mack assessed the ring of keys in his palm, trying to remember which it was.

I should be an expert on keys by now, he joked. It's all I do every shift.

A jackdaw watched from the adjacent fence. A snail traversed the wall. Mack tried a key but it didn't turn. The second wouldn't even go in.

I'm sorry the boys give you so much stick, his father said quietly.

That's all right, Mack said. He tried another key. Moved along the ring.

Just don't play up to it. Like dogs, they are. Ignore them and they get bored.

It's fine, Mack insisted. It's a laugh.

His father seemed pleased with the response.

Or do the opposite, he said. Give 'em both barrels back.

Bryn might take the piss, but he can take it too. He'd do anything for you really. Heart of gold. Salt of the earth.

He's great, Mack agreed. All the boys are. It's the same in work. Dai comes in all the time. Dai Eighteen Months?

Jackie grinned. Make sure they know who you are, mind. Don't take any shit.

That's the problem, Mack laughed, dropping a key, moving along the ring. They all know who I am. I'm a target.

His father thumped him on the back in sympathy. Said something about dogs having their day. A rite of passage. Part of the job. They'd tortured him when he first started, thought he'd be an apprentice forever. But there were always new apprentices.

Listen, he said, stepping closer. Your mother's going to ask you to go to church tomorrow. She's been stressing about it ever since you got back.

He spoke in a low voice, half whispered, inviting his son in on a secret he'd sworn not to divulge.

Don't worry about it, though. Tell her straight. She'll understand.

Mack selected another key. The works sighed at his back. He couldn't remember the last time his father had spoken in such confidence. How long it had been since the pair of them were a united front. He felt suddenly glad to be there. Eager to reinforce the bond. The same feeling he'd had on Sunday night at the club before Siwan's intrusion. The sense that his struggles could end should he only decide it. The realisation that a whole new path to his life could open up.

Why not work at the plant? Continue the family history? Banter with the men, fight for them too. Go for coffee should a woman happen to ask. Was there not nobility in performing the role expected of you? Wasn't the well-trodden road smoother, in the end?

What are you working tomorrow? his father asked tentatively.

I'm not working tomorrow. Our shift was due to start at eight, so we miss the cut-off point.

From the corner of his eye he could see his father nodding slowly.

I was thinking, fancy a pint before we meet the others? Just you and me? We'll raise a toast to Gran and Gramps.

The key clicked into the lock and twisted. A satisfying motion. The logic of moving parts. The sense of things working exactly as they should. The door swung outwards. It took a while for their eyes to adjust. There was no car in the garage. Just a gravel pit in the middle of the floor. Oil stains on the concrete like old shadows lingering. The dingy space neatly ordered and stacked full of tools. A drill and selection of bits. A-frame steps folded against the wall. A variety of bladed instruments. Saws, secateurs, hedge trimmers. A shovel, a spade, a rake, a hoe. There was a sledgehammer, a lump hammer, a claw hammer, a crowbar, and lined up neatly across the shelving tins of wood stain, white spirit, turpentine and creosote.

The air was cool inside. The order silent and pleasing. It occurred to Mack then that the pain in his head had passed.

A pint would be great, he said decisively. Let's do it.

VII

Denzil commentated as they patrolled. Knew the names of all the buildings and structures. Every urban myth and rumour. The scandals and the tragedies. An oral history passed down from his predecessor to be furthered and embellished. An ever-growing pool of knowledge authored by a chain of men stretching back through the years.

See that wall by there? he said, pulling over to the side of the road near the rolling mill. It's cursed, that is.

Mack knew the story but let him tell it again. A twenty-foot stone wall cordoned off by wooden fencing and buttressed with brick supports. The only remains of an old farmhouse that had once belonged to the Cistercians. Legend had it an angry monk placed a hex on the building when expelled during the dissolution of the monasteries.

If that wall collapses, Denzil said, the whole town's meant to come crashing down too.

A ghostly figure was said to stalk that end of the site. The old monk driven mad with fury, his habit the colour of blood. Denzil had an uncle who swore down he had seen him on one particularly long night shift. Not even joking now. On his mother's life.

He released the handbrake and checked his mirrors.

Imagine being so fucking raging you hung around here for five hundred years.

That's the Proddies for you, Mack said. Enough to drive anyone up the wall.

He was enjoying his shift this evening. Felt more relaxed than he had in months. Something to do with having been in the home of his grandparents, a mood strengthened by the knowledge of the imminent walkout. The job suddenly charged with meaning, every small action now possessing its own sentimental charm. As though only within the context of loss could the true nature of their work reveal itself. Him and his partner, shooting the shit, two fellers continuing something that had started long before they were born.

He could work ten thousand days like this one. Submit to the patterns and the history.

Denzil started the engine. Got onto the other bizarre things he'd seen at night. Glowing eyes in the reeds by the cooling reservoir. Balls of fog that rolled down the road like tumbleweed. There were foxes about, he said. The odd badger. Areas the workers had all but abandoned to the will of violent gulls. The trick was to run your torch along the railings before going into any enclosed areas. Clear out any unexpected life.

Denzil'd had a good look at the bruise on Mack's head when he first arrived but hadn't said anything. No big deal, was it? Every man came into work a little beat up from time to time.

Boys have died and all, he said as he let them back into the office. The contractor found slumped in a hot running channel. The feller who got turned around in a cloud of steam and fell into the molten slag. Eighty-five per cent burns, fifteen hundred degrees. The men followed his screams to pull him out.

Denzil hung his coat on the hook and retucked the hem of his shirt.

Not to mention, he said, the big bang.

A couple of months after 9/11. A massive explosion. Blast Furnace 5. Lifted thousands of tons a metre in the air. All hell came pouring through the gap at the bottom. Molten iron and sinter and God knows what else. Dust and gases rose skywards and ignited. They saw the fireball in Blaengwynfi.

Three dead, Denzil said. Remember it on the news?

Mack remembered. A few of the bereaved kids had gone to St Joseph's. Commanded an unnerving quiet in the corridors for months. There'd been little warning for the men on the casthouse floor. Some of the fellers reckoned the ground shook like an earthquake. The structure turned as it lifted and fell, rupturing the pipes from the cooling system and sending scalding hot water and steam over the men inside. They only found the third body some time the next day. A catastrophe triggered by nothing more than water meeting molten metal. The inside of the furnace let out.

You sort of forget it to look at them, Denzil said. So familiar now, aren't they, watching over us? The blasts might seem sturdy, but the forces inside are mental. If there's no outlet, pressure starts to build. All that heat has to go somewhere. Suppose it's inevitable really, they sometimes blow up.

They'd got a taste of the forces during work experience.

Two weeks where they hadn't so much worked as toured the site. Followed the steelmaking process from beginning to end. The blackened expanse of the coal yard with its bleating rubber belts, the steaming quenching tower and chambered coke ovens. The sandstone heft of the sinter plant. The men made a fuss at every stop. Wound the boys up, offered advice. Sent them on fool's errands and wild goose chases. The kind of jokes their fathers had repeated every day of their lives.

Nip to the store cupboard, will you? Need a new bubble for my spirit level.

Grab the skirting-board ladder while you're there.

One man had cornered Mack in a quiet moment. Warned against getting stuck in such a place. Go travelling, he said. Chase skirt, enjoy yourself. A ginger bloke with yellow teeth and a tranquilised manner of speaking. Tattoo of Roy Keane on his arm wearing a Celtic top. The induction video said the workers put a small piece of soul into every ton of steel, but the plant put out five million tons a year. Wasn't long before a feller didn't have much soul left to give.

But it was the blasts that left the lasting impression. Twin beasts blind and atavistic. They had watched the hoppers ascend with coke and iron ore. Climbed the riveted steps and entered the casthouse. The heat struck you first. The heat then the smell, the sulphur, the sense of standing deep within the earth. A shadowed cavern of ferric winds and livid flame attended by men in visors. The floors sloped and stonelike. A tangle of pipes above and below and chutes and gates and tuyeres. The men had explained the tapping drill and the molten rivers of iron, and deafened by the sound around them, the boys edged as close as they dared to peer over the edge.

Mack had sensed something wrong in the scald of the luminous pit. Something to be respected and feared. A malign reptilian life. Hot metal flowed and slag hardened on top like a skin. Pig iron passed in runners beneath their feet. Looking down had made him feel dizzy.

Makes you wonder why we ever thought it was a good idea, Denzil said.

Mack looked at him.

What was a good idea?

The blasts, like. I mean, mess around with stuff like that and someone's gonna get burned.

Thousands of men have passed through, though, Mack pointed out. Only a fraction have gotten hurt.

Well I wouldn't fucking work in there, Denzil said. Would you?

Mack laughed and sort of shrugged. Denzil widened his eyes.

You'd wanna work in the blast furnace?

My dad did, Mack said, shrugging again. Both my grandfathers. Why shouldn't I?

Well it's too fucking hot for starters.

Oi, came a voice across the room. This is a hold-up.

Dai Eighteen Months at the door, fingers mimicking pistols. Mack felt his spirits sag at the sight of him but raised a hand in greeting, determined to maintain his mood.

We don't have to worry about it much longer anyway, Denzil said, ignoring their visitor. Blasts will be gone.

Will they bollocks, Dai interjected. Pessimists, you pair. I can see it on your chops. Glass-half-empty sort of twats. It's your first ever strike tomorrow. Should be buzzing, mun. Full of gumption.

The tone of Dai's voice went through him, but Mack thought of his father's wisdom. The rite of passage. Giving both barrels back.

We were full of gumption till you came in, he joked. Sucked the air out the room.

Dai seemed stung for a second, but soon a grin dawned on his face. He walked right up to Mack and dug an elbow in his ribs.

Baby's coming round then? he said to Denzil with a wink. Been training him, have you?

We train all the new recruits on how to deal with knob-heads. It's in the manual.

Dai's grin grew wider. The same smell of smoke came off his clothes. When he looked at Mack again, he did a double-take.

What do you want anyway? Denzil asked. Hanging around like a bad smell, mun.

I was wondering if you fancied a break, Dai said, chin gesturing towards the door. You know I don't like smoking on my own.

He's got time to smoke a pack every shift but reckons he's too busy to be in the play, Mack said to Denzil. Doesn't seem all that busy to me.

Oi, that's different. Got stuff on this weekend. I couldn't do it.

We've all got stuff on, Mack said. But we—

I'm fucking serious, Dai snapped. Anyway, stop complaining. Better off having supper with Jesus than standing on a picket line. If it wasn't for this play, you'd be holding placards all night, freezing your bollocks off.

Come on, Dai, what happened to that gumption?

I'll fucking gumption you now, he said, raising a fist.

The men looked at one another, smirking in new-found respect or uneasy truce. Mack couldn't tell if he'd won him round or pissed him off. Wasn't sure there was any meaningful distinction.

You really think it's going to make a difference? Denzil wondered aloud. The strike, I mean? Walking out on a company that wants us gone in the first place?

Posturing, that is, mun, Dai said. Tryna make themselves look big. Shitting it, they are. I'm telling you. Got 'em on the ropes.

Swagger already rebounded, Dai wandered the office like he owned the place, hands linked behind his back.

We'll have our way yet, boys. Just need to buy some time. These things work in cycles, see? And the mood's about to turn. All these new politicians aren't convinced by this net-zero crap. We'll be building another blast at this rate. Making so much steel they'll have to reopen the pits.

Mack felt a sudden pain in his head and blinked against it. The paracetamol must have been wearing off.

There you go, Cormac butt, Denzil laughed. You'll have your dream job after all.

His dream job is down the mine?

In the blast, Denzil said. He was telling me earlier.

Mack smiled, trying to stay connected to the conversation as the pain flashed again. A lightning strike, trailing thunder. He blinked and shut his eyes. When he opened them, the faintest smudge had appeared at the edge of his vision. A misty frame, translucent white.

He can do double shifts once the new era starts, Dai continued. Once we give the control-freak socialists the boot.

Mack placed his hands on the desk to steady himself. He felt tired all of a sudden. Had a taste on his tongue like tin. He'd heard the symptoms of a concussion could sometimes be delayed but didn't want to make a fuss in front of the others. In search of distraction, he looked off across the room to the bank of monitors. The pain in his head dilated. There was something on one of the feeds.

Up on the right, two screens from the top. A figure just standing there. Hood up, coat like a robe. Shot white in the monochrome.

I'd have a three-step plan, I would, Dai was saying, counting on his fingers. Deal with the scroungers, the nonces, the immig—

Who's that? Mack asked, pointing.

Who's what?

There, look, on the screen.

By the time Denzil got to his feet, the feed had cycled to a different frame.

Which screen?

It's gone, Mack said. It was . . . a person?

Denzil narrowed his eyes.

You having me on?

I'm serious, Mack said. There was someone there.

Denzil scooted his chair to the screens and Dai followed, keen to be involved. The three of them watched as the monitors moved through their sequence. Agitation built in Mack's chest. A desire to be right, trepidation about what that might mean. There'd been something unnatural in the figure's gait but he couldn't have described it. He'd seen the outline of them, seen them reach up to remove their hood, but couldn't have said if it was a man or a woman or how tall they might have been. His mind was jumping to conclusions. He regretted having said anything.

By the time the right shot came back, the figure had vanished.

They were in that one, Mack pointed out. Near the level crossing behind the knuckle yard.

Oh fuck. Not a jumper?

The screens flashed scenes silent and peculiar, greyscale in the dusk.

Now you mention it, I saw someone down there yesterday, Dai said. By the side of the road like.

Wasn't a woman? Mack asked quickly.

Not that desperate, are you?

Denzil swivelled his chair around. We checked all the gates down there, didn't we?

Yeah, Mack said.

And everything was locked?

Mack considered the question. He thought so.

Smackhead, I reckon, Dai said. Tons of 'em up town last week. Like fuckin' *Dawn of the Dead* it was. I said to my Trish like, I said forget about any actor. That's where the cameras wanna go. Half an hour on Station Road with a fixer and translator. Bet they'd find a couple of new species.

What did the prick look like? Denzil wanted to know.

I didn't get a good look, Mack said, growing warm under interrogation. Just happened to glance over.

Dai was still talking about the smackheads. Asking for change they was, but Trisha says you shouldn't give a beggar change unless you want him to be a beggar tomorrow—

They might have had longish hair? Mack offered. A long coat or cloak or something?

Beard? Nail holes in his palms? He's probably from the play, isn't he? What did they call it, immersive?

The play doesn't start until tomorrow.

I know that, aye, but the programme says to expect signs around town all week. Could be practising or something?

Mack nodded, unconvinced. The pain in his head brought to mind the builders' merchant. Tyres over gravel. Tail lights. Siwan.

Well you're the one fucking in it, Denzil said. Have you been practising or what?

Mack swallowed. Looked at Dai.

You're better off asking him.

We did some practising, Dai said, rubbing his neck. But not in costume or nothing. And not in the middle of fucking nowhere either. We met in the YMCA.

Denzil frowned and pushed closer to the screen, as though an answer lay within the pixels themselves. The picture disturbed by choppy static and rolling distortion. An electronic ebb and flow that belied the stillness of the scenes.

All right, fuck it, we haven't got a choice.

He was on his feet and moving now. Frisking himself for his gear. A checklist in his head.

Might mean stumbling into the dress rehearsal, he said, but we can't know it's not some bastard about to top himself.

He moved to the peg for his jacket and put it on. Retrieved the second and threw it at Mack.

Come on, Father O'Brien, he said. If this is a jumper, d'you think I'm gonna talk to him?

The sun had set when they went outside. A damp came down with the dark. The van's lights blinked when Denzil unlocked the doors. Dai was still with them, still yapping, continuing his previous thread as though they were hanging on his every word.

The thing about smackheads, he said, is they've got no consideration for anyone. Nothing matters to 'em except getting that next fix.

The mood was stilted when they got in the van. Mack put on his seat belt, eyes set forward, his vision clear but confidence dented, the nagging fear of some internal injury like a thorn stuck in his mind. The radio started when Denzil turned the key in the ignition and he quickly silenced it. He gripped the head of Mack's seat as he turned to look out the rear window. The truck shuddered when in reverse.

He's harmless, mind, Denzil offered as Dai waved them off. Bit of a cock, but harmless.

Mack wasn't sure anyone was harmless, but he didn't say anything.

Denzil shifted gear and they pulled forward. The grit under the tyres sounded like fire moving through dry brush. Cans of something rolled in the footwell, sugar-free and caffeinated, pick-me-ups for the graveyard shift.

I meant to say, Mack said. I need to borrow the van.

They hit a bump in the road and jounced around. Denzil changed gear again before he answered.

You telling me, or asking?

It's just my grandparents passed away recently. We're clearing the house. My old man wanted to do it in the car, but there's hardly any room in the back even with the seat down.

Denzil raised a hand to interrupt. There was no need to explain himself.

I was thinking this weekend? Mack suggested. Seeing as we're not in work. If you could drop it off, say, Friday morning?

Denzil nodded, eyes set dead ahead. The route nothing but twin tyre tracks, a path cut by the men who'd driven that way for years.

The boss got in touch again earlier, he said eventually. His final offer. Triple time and the days back as leave.

And what did you tell him?

The seats shifted slightly as Denzil turned.

I thought you said we shouldn't cross the picket line?

I did say that.

Right, Denzil said, eyes on the road again. Exactly. That's what I told the boss.

Mack waited for his colleague to elaborate on the exchange, but nothing was forthcoming. He glanced at him, looked away. Denzil sniffed and wiped at his nose. The track deteriorated further and their heads swayed in tandem. The weave of their jackets whispered with every bump in the road.

Do people try it often here? Mack asked, just to fill the space. Killing themselves, I mean?

Denzil clucked his tongue. It's the easiest place to get on the line. I've only seen one, but he was spread from Tollgate to Pyle so that was enough for me.

He changed gears. A jerking action. The van the kind you had to fight.

You'll have a word with him, though, won't you?

Mack straightened the belt at his neck, took the grab handle to steady himself.

You know I'm not actually a priest?

Denzil said nothing. The high beams caught the spectral dust of the road.

I'm just saying, Mack warned.

But you've done this before?

Done what before?

Dealt with desperate fuckers. Talked a man down.

Mack's turn to say nothing. Denzil swore to himself.

Hell they go, innit? Just tell him that first as last.

Hell they go. A mortal sin. A remote attack against God's work. Not as true as it used to be. The Church's position was changing. One drastic act did not a sinner make.

But Mack only swallowed. Looked out the window. Saw his thin reflection in the glass.

Dunno what I'd prefer, Denzil said. A jumper or an actor.

He laughed at his own comment, though his face was flat and sombre. Mack couldn't shake a third option from his head. Siwan and her confession. Loose change slid down the dashboard as they took a bend. The windows kept steaming up. He put the blower on cold and directed it at the windscreen. Night bugs darted through the beams of the headlights. Their heads bobbed with the pothole jolt of the road.

Every bump met Mack in the bones of his skull. The ache in his head stirred.

When they reached the spot, Denzil cut the engine but left the headlights up. Mack took his torch from his belt, popped his door. You go and look, Denzil said, not moving from his seat. I'll do a loop around the site. We'll keep in touch on the radio.

Mack shivered as he got out. The beam of the torch made him feel vulnerable. Too conspicuous in the gloom. He didn't know what he would say to a suicidal man. Had no idea how to deal with actors. Let alone Siwan or someone working with her. Another man, a stranger.

A bird screeched in the dark. The gravel beneath his feet crunched like snow. The equipment on his belt clacked in time with his footfall and the works thrummed like a vacuum cleaner left running, a contraption powered by the night itself.

The moon hung yellowed overhead, some pickled thing suspended in a jar.

He turned in time to see Denzil's brake lights disappear. Felt the pain in his head again. A flash across the brainpan. The sense he'd done himself some dire injury. Knocked something out of place. With it came the taste in his mouth and shimmer in his perception. A sound, too, or was that something different?

A plea, perhaps? A prayer? A voice coming from the railway line.

He straddled the fence like a cowboy, a leg over each side, and shone the torch to find a figure on the tracks. Back hunched, head between his knees. When Mack called out, he hardly recognised his own voice.

Are you all right?

I've had a drink, came the reply, as though that explained everything.

Come and tell me about it. You must be cold.

He swung his other leg over the fence and edged towards the tracks. Swore under his breath as the scene came into focus. There really was a man crouched over a rail, smack bang in the path of danger. Mack looked both ways down the line as the reality of the situation dawned. He'd have to act, he realised. Save the man. Drag him if it came to that. He'd see the lights of any engine, he told himself. Hesitation would only make things worse.

He dashed as though before an audience, awkward under their scrutiny. He grabbed the man by the back of his coat and pulled, but immediately felt resistance.

Ahh, the man said, voice stretched animal-like. The smell of beer came off him like gas from a bog.

Mack let go and put the torch on him. The man's wrists were fastened to the rail with a zip-tie.

I'm protesting, he said, eyes squinting into the beam. It's my public right.

His face was half familiar. A stranger from a place Mack knew. Work perhaps, church, school. Not a feller he knew by name, but someone he might have nodded to in passing.

Do I know you? he asked, though he received no reply. The dark had a weight to it. He heard his own breath ragged and quick. He considered running and not looking back, but his fear curdled into something different. A sudden urge to kick the man. Claw at his face. Punish him.

You're going to get us killed, he said. Who else is with you?

He turned to scan the surrounding bracken. When he shone his torch on the ground, it felt the ground was looking back.

The man sat with his shoulders hunched like a sulking toddler.

I'm protesting, he slurred.

Do you know Siwan? Siwan Roderick?

The lack of response only riled Mack further. He snatched the hood from the man's head, hard enough that his shoulders rocked. The man's legs jumped in surprise. The stones between the sleepers clinked like billiard balls. Mack knelt before the man and tried pulling at the tie, only the cable was cinched too tight.

The man yelped as Mack struggled. He might have been anchored to the centre of the earth.

The nylon strip was secured fast at the top of the wrist, impeded by the protrusion of the thumb. Mack tried digging his nails in to break it. Bent in an attempt to sever the cable with his teeth. Frustration kept him busy before he suddenly remembered where he was. His body tensed in on itself, sensing impact was imminent. His head no longer hurt as such, but something didn't feel right.

Then a voice emerged through his radio, startling them both.

Mack? Denzil called. Mack?

He jammed his finger against the talk button and asked for scissors. Asked for pliers, bolt-cutters, a knife. He cradled the radio in both hands, something precious, alive.

Hold on, came Denzil's reply. I'll be there as soon as I—

The transmission faded into garbled static. Stop the trains, Mack shouted, hands shaking as he squeezed the button. He's tied himself to the tracks.

The sound of his voice rose into the dark and a panic sprang within him. As though speaking aloud granted fear its permission. He felt his body clench again, lurched away from the rails as if burned.

Where are you going? the man asked. Don't leave me.

Mack ran blind through the weeds, stiff-limbed and gasping. A bug unearthed from beneath a rock. A man made of tin. When he reached the fence, he threw himself over and rested in the safety of the other side. The ground was damp, his head spun, his heart pounded. The voice called out again.

Please, the man said. Please, please, over and over. The pitiful whine of a dog locked out at night.

Frisking himself for the radio, Mack tried to call for help again. Denzil, he yelled into the night. Denzil? His own voice thin and desperate. The dark pressed close to his face as the same self-pity from the previous evening roused itself. A feeling of victimhood grown too familiar in recent times. Floodwater rising around his neck.

The childish notion of a tantrum occurred to him. The idea that someone more capable would intervene should he only burst into tears and kick his feet in protest. But the man was already whimpering somewhere off over his shoulder, and no help had materialised. Mack knew he had to get to his feet.

Forcing himself to his knees, he used the fence post to stand. Climbed over again and told himself to breathe. In through the nose, out through the mouth. He returned to the man slowly. When he spoke, he tried to calm his voice.

We could try to break it?

It's too tight, the man said. We need a knife.

I don't mean the cord.

The man's face changed.

If your thumb wasn't in the way, Mack continued, the hand would slip right out.

Even in the dark he saw the man blanch.

I don't think so. Thumbs don't work like that.

The man spoke clearer now, sobered by the threat. Mack squatted and examined the binding again. Ran his fingers over the man's hand. Felt him flinch and attempt to pull away.

What about your butty? the man stammered. He said he's coming.

Mack got his fingers under the tie and pulled with all his

strength. He was cold now, beginning to shake. Night dew leached through the thin fabric at his knees.

Refusing to admit defeat, he focused on the problem before him so his gaze did not wander down the line. The train would arrive as a light, he decided. Something vast and all-bright that would engulf them in an instant. To imagine it was in some way to hope for the conclusion. How better to end than completely and all at once?

Do you know what the worst thing is? the man asked eventually, voice mild and shy. I can't get at my pockets. I'm dying for a fag.

He arched his back as though to demonstrate the fact. Grew agitated with the movement, the depth of his predicament occurring to him again. The momentum pitched him sideways so his shoulder hit the ground. Mack watched his feet kick in an effort to right himself. A terrapin stuck on its back.

He shone his torch at the man. Saw his wrists blood-raw against the cord.

Don't, he said, placing a hand on his back. I can help you.

The man continued to struggle as Mack leaned over him. Took some time to fall still at his touch, reluctant as a beaten animal. Mack felt the man's pockets, smelling beer again as he frisked for his cigarettes. Found a lighter in the front. A wallet. Tobacco and papers at his arse.

Sit up, he told him. Relax.

He blew on his hands to warm them. Took a paper from the sheaf and flattened it best he could.

You're going to have to instruct me, he said. I've never rolled a cigarette in my life.

The man found that funny. Conviction returned to his voice as he outlined the simple steps.

Some of the tobacco strands caught on the breeze when Mack opened the pouch. He had trouble rolling the strip even. The man told him he was pressing too hard. He opened the paper and started again, hunched over his work to protect it from the wind.

Don't worry, the man said, leaning close to watch. I'm not picky. That'll do.

Mack licked the gum strip and twisted the paper to seal it. Reached over and put the cigarette between the man's lips.

You're not having one? the man asked from one side of his mouth.

There was a sound behind them. Mack spun around but the night gave nothing up. How far could Denzil have gotten in the time since he'd left him? How close would an engine have to be before they felt its energy coursing through the rails?

He struck the lighter three times before drawing a flame. Cupped his palm around it and leaned closer to the man. New details of his face revealed themselves in the glow. The spark came back double in his eyes.

The man puffed and Mack removed the cigarette from his mouth. He breathed a moment, then Mack put it back in.

So what's this protest all about then? he asked.

The man appeared embarrassed by the question.

I'm just pissed off, he said.

About what?

He attempted a shrug and spat at the ground between his knees. You know, he said. Fuckin' everything.

Mack smiled, forcing himself to keep eye contact for the benefit of them both.

Fair enough, he said. But if we're waiting here, you might as well be more specific.

The man smiled in spite of everything. The reluctant reflex of a person finally listened to.

Well, he started, I'm going to lose my job for one. My dad worked the cranes most of his life. My uncle was a machinist. In the control room, I am. Thought I was moving up in the world. Shifts with coffee and computers. Now everything's gone to shit.

No one's lost their job yet, Mack said, and the man laughed. A bitter sound devoid of humour. A single, shunted syllable.

To be honest with you, I've felt this way for ages anyway. Long before redundancies were threatened. Just this help-lessness hanging over me. A mood I couldn't shift. I'll give you an example, right. Take my boss. He's younger than me by a decade or something but still orders me around. I'm pretty sure he's cheating on his wife. Every lunchtime he goes out in one shirt and comes back in another. He's got a picture of his family on his desk. She's a nice woman, his missus.

The man's voice gathered momentum as he spoke, as though some gate had lifted and everything had poured through. Mack edged forward, loose gravel slipping beneath his feet. That this man could sit and talk with catastrophe looming was a marvel to him. That his earthly concerns lost none of their weight.

I considered telling her, he was saying. My boss's wife, I mean. Or confronting him at least. Just to do something, you know? To make things right. I try to be good like that. A solid citizen. Someone who cares. I scrub graffiti from the walls in my street. Pick up dog shit. Write letters to my MP about those foreign wars. But you can only do those things for so long before the penny drops. Before you realise it's impossible to change anything after all.

I think change is possible, Mack said, but the man just shook his head.

Not in this day and age. Not for the likes of me and you.

Now that the man had started to talk, it seemed he couldn't stop, as if on some level believing quiet was death and sound his only defiance.

Do you know how long we've been discussing this strike? How many years we've fought against the company? Go on, have a guess. Right back to the day it was privatised, that's how long. Probably longer than that. And all that effort for what? There's strength in numbers, the union boys reckon, but I'm afraid it's total bollocks. None of that romantic shit makes any difference nowadays. The power's shifted. Believe otherwise if it helps you sleep at night.

Mack was close enough to touch the man. Smell the yeast of drink on him. The sour sweat of his skin. He was still waiting for the rails to hum through the soles of his boots. Placed a hand on the man's shoulder in an effort to calm him.

So what? he asked, fighting to keep desperation from his voice. We just chuck ourselves in front of a train? What's that going to solve?

I'm not chucking myself anywhere, the man protested, suddenly indignant. I'm *waiting*. That's all that's left to us now. The hope that something better is coming. A great flood would do it. A cleansing water to wash the world clean.

He stared at Mack as though daring him to disprove the notion. Mack forced himself to sit.

But what if waiting isn't the answer? he asked, feeling the cold metal of the rail through the seat of his trousers. What if we've got it backwards? Someone once told me we shouldn't sit still in the hope that God might act on our behalf, but instead consider what He would want us to do.

But the man shook his head. All God asks of me is to prepare for His imminent arrival. The one true Messiah will walk the earth with us.

Messiah? Mack asked.

We must repent, for the kingdom of heaven is at hand.

What Messiah? Mack asked again. Are you a part of the performance?

Performance?

The Easter performance. The Passion play. The famous actor arriving as the town's salvation.

I don't know anything about a play. I only know who comes after. They are better than you or me.

Stop it, Mack said, a familiar fury rising. If you're part of the performance, you need to tell me. This isn't a game we're playing. I risked my life to roll you a cigarette.

The man studied him calmly. Not everything is a performance, he said. It's important you remember. Don't let the pretenders obscure your judgement. Seek out those who are true.

Mack felt a sudden pull of dizziness. His head rang like a struck bell. The shimmer in his vision had returned, worse than before. So thick he might have been peering through a veil.

Who are you? he demanded.

I am the voice of one crying out in the wilderness, the man said. Make straight the way of the Lord.

The announcement seemed to tip the world at an angle. The vertigo worse than ever, Mack shut his eyes. In the silence that followed, he became aware of a faint sound nearby. Or not a sound, a vibration. A hum beneath his feet. Terror arrived as quickly as the force that was doubtless haring towards them. The bright light, the singing lines, the screaming fury of the impending train.

He stood, knowing they'd dallied too long already. Ignored the man's protests as he seized his arm. Pushed his opposite shoulder down so the man fell sideways again, disabled on his back. It would hurt, but the man would thank him in the end. The trick would be getting the correct angle. The wrist on its side, thumb pointing up. A large rock would do the job, but he had no time to look for one. He settled for the weight of his boot.

Clench your teeth, he told the man. So you don't bite through your tongue.

He took a depth breath, nose filled with the smell of industry around them, a shadow-stink born in the guts of machines. He heard the pulse of the furnaces, the rush of wind in the weeds, and on glancing up saw a shape high in the sky above the works. A cloud, white and hanging, glowing as though lit from within. He blinked to clear his eyes, a metallic taste filling his mouth, then he inhaled once more to brace himself and stamped down with all his might.

PART TWO

High Mass

VIII

He set his alarm early Thursday morning. Rose before dawn and brushed his teeth, unable to stomach breakfast. He dressed, sat with the quiet a moment, then took more painkillers and left the house. He walked the long loop around town, down past the Plaza and along the front of the works. Stood before the furnaces and felt the vibrations in his head. The previous evening was like a dream he saw in flashes. The split second as he brought his boot down, the cold of the air, the snap of the bone, the singular pleasure of submitting to his own convictions. That knife-edge moment when there was no going back, a terrified wonder shining in the man's eyes.

Sleep had proved difficult. Better to be out on the street. Let the sounds of the morning push away the night. The groan of washing lines raised on rusty pulleys. Wood pigeons calling ghost-like from the trees. The droll robotic voice of a vehicle reversing. Alarms in the works, a frenzied tremolo, two-tone anxiety.

The man had fled before Denzil returned. Paused only to

peer at Mack in accusation, his mangled hand tucked close to his chest, face gaunt and ashen white. Denzil brought the police with him, but there was nothing to see by then. They couldn't even find the loop of cable on the rail. The police searched a while but their hearts weren't in it. Asked questions as though not quite believing the events described. Mack stood in the cold, blue lights rotating over him, and tried to convey what he had been through. The officers nodded politely and shook his hand and thanked him for his time.

He'd left work shaken and unsatisfied. A feeling that persisted even as the sun lifted itself again and made the previous night unreal. He longed for someone to confide in, a sympathetic ear to listen and understand. He put one foot in front of the other and walked the streets, tiredness a dense liquid in his sinuses.

The alarm in the works ceased. Mack glanced at his watch. In a matter of hours, the men would down tools and everything would grind to a halt. Signs along the roadside foretold of closures that evening. Decorations had replaced the adverts on billboards and bus stops. The preparations were finished, the morning hush misleading. One last intake of breath before they took the plunge together.

It seemed too much all of a sudden. The strike, the play, the emergent sense of history. Mack was overcome by a fear that the day would prove too large for him to match. He was exhausted, sore, shivering as though fevered. Wished for nothing more than to retreat to a dark place in which he might wait it out.

As he neared the centre of town, he found activity ongoing. Crews of strangers in yellow vests and hard hats, supervisors authoritative with their clipboards and their stares. People working with the busy quiet of a plan long set in motion. The invisible hand that would bring the play to life. He crossed the road to avoid the action, pulled his collar high and looked away, though on passing the entrance of the shopping centre, a familiar figure caught his eye.

The journalist stood in the square with her assorted team, all of them looking up as a man on a cherry picker fixed a printed backdrop to the top of the civic centre. A woman in a lanyard explained something to them. The journalist followed the point of her finger, nodded enthusiastically. Mack lingered in the door of the mall, allowing himself to watch her for a moment. The way she clasped her hands in front of her chest, eyes wide with curiosity. Her golden ponytail bobbed as she nodded along with whatever the woman was saying. She wore her jeans tight and high-waisted. Kept her phone in her back pocket.

They could get coffee, she had told him. Some place more relaxed. She'd said she wanted to hear what he had to say. She said it was important.

Not wishing to approach her in front of the others, Mack cut up Forge Road instead and headed for the payphone near the barber's. He'd call ahead, he decided. Arrange to meet, act casual. He couldn't remember the last time he'd used a phone on the street but he had change in his pocket. For a second he feared the box had been decommissioned, but then he picked up the receiver and met an unending tone.

Her card was somewhere in his jacket. He frisked himself in search of its crisp edge. Only he came across something larger than he was expecting. The photo of him and Siwan at the Plaza, the pair of them side by side. Placing the receiver back in its cradle, he smoothed the crease from the middle of the picture and studied the image more closely. Young Mack leaning to put an arm around the cardboard display. Siwan stood straight, hands almost painfully at her sides. Their eyes cast red in the glare of the flash and their expressions nakedly troubled. He'd knock her door, he decided in that instant. Forget the previous days. Start again.

Excuse me? called a voice. Excuse me, mate?

A car had pulled in at the kerb, hazards blinking. The man wore a black baseball cap and aviator shades. Leaned one arm from the window. Wanted directions to a place Mack had never heard of in his life.

I'm sorry, he said.

Are you sure? the man demanded. There's nothing you can tell me?

When the man left, Mack walked the short distance to Siwan's. The blinds were still shut in the windows. No sign of life inside. He crossed to where her car stood out front and placed a hand upon the bonnet. The engine felt warm to the touch. He felt he was being watched.

Her confession came to mind again. The way she'd sat before him. Vulnerable and serious. Late repentance brought desperation, Matthew had written in his gospel. So what exactly did early repentance bring?

Losing the nerve to knock, Mack instead took the photo from his pocket. If he'd had a pen, he'd have written a message on the back. A debrief of his encounter on the railway line. A set of questions. A list of demands. The sky looked like rain, but it wasn't raining. The man in the car had unsettled him.

He took great care when lifting the flap of the letter box. Only had second thoughts once he'd threaded the photo through the bristles of the brush seal and let go. *Get the picture back*, his better sense demanded, a twitch through the whole of his body. His hand grasped in reflex but nothing was there. The time for reconsideration had lapsed.

On the way home, he walked the underpass that cut beneath the motorway. A long concrete tunnel with a ninety-degree turn at the bottom. Goalposts spray-painted on the far wall, three wickets in the middle. The names of bands and declarations of everlasting love. Mack spoke to himself just to hear the words echo back from every surface. Hello, hello, hello. Cars thundered overhead. The walls were solid concrete. The ceiling, the floor. When he shouted, his voice became the whole world.

His mother was watching her tapes when he got home. Watching and praying, lips moving in silence. The screen showed a funeral cortège descend into chaos. Nineteen eighty-something. A reversing hatchback, a Volkswagen Passat. Mack had seen the footage before, or something like it. Knew which side he was on but couldn't tell who was who without narration. Everything a blur in the mayhem. A swarm of bodies over the bonnet and roof.

Clara would pray for anyone and everyone. The only thing she had to offer. Small pennies thrown in the hope of shifting salvation's mysterious economy. She'd pray for bank robbers and serial killers. Pray for Judas Iscariot when she remembered him.

Mack sat on the sofa, hands in his lap. His eyes burned whenever he blinked. The screen showed men in mourning dress, men in tracksuit tops and tennis shoes. The flash of a gun, a hasty retreat. A plain-clothes corporal hanging halfway from the door. The crowd returned and fell upon the man. Dragged him from the car, beat him, stripped him of his coat and clothes. When they dragged a second man from the car, a priest tried to intervene. An army helicopter buzzed overhead, propellers disturbing the air like angel wings. The crowd bundled the two men into the back of a van and drove out to a stretch of waste ground. They removed the men and shot them there in nothing but their socks and briefs. The priest arrived again and knelt beside the one still breathing. Waited with the man as he shivered and moaned, face as bloodied as Christ Himself. He crossed the man's lips and administered the last rites. Final words for a soldier before his soul raised itself sluggish from the chill ground and considered its next direction.

When adverts started, Clara crossed herself.

Let me clean that for you.

He felt her gaze across the room.

It's fine, he said. There's barely a mark.

But his mother was already out of her chair and after the first-aid kit in the cupboard. She put the big light on to see better. Got her glasses from the top of her head. The injury wasn't severe enough to warrant cleaning, but he did not begrudge the attention. He felt an urge to squirm when she touched him, but fought the reflex. If it had to hurt, let it hurt, he told himself. Let her do whatever she thought best.

Is it sore? she asked.

It's fine, he repeated. Feels more like a headache now.

I've got a headache this morning too, his mother said, her fingers gentle at his brow. Hope it's not a migraine coming on.

What's the difference? Mack asked, eyes on the screen.

Migraines are a different animal altogether, his mother

chuckled wearily. Feels like someone's driving a nail through your skull. I can't bear the light. I get feverish, a bit loopy. I see these weird halo sort of things in the corners of my eyes.

Mack fought to keep his voice even, his attention on the TV.

What brought them on?

Anything, really. Hunger. Dehydration. Tiredness. The weather. You know when it's muggy and—

I mean in the first place, though. Did you hit your head or something?

No, his mother said, confused. It doesn't work like that, does it?

I don't know, Mack shrugged. Just wondering.

Your father might make me want to bang my head against the wall on occasion, but I've never followed through. He's not worth it.

Mack grinned, eyes still on the screen. A two-storey mural. A bombed-out shop. The tricolour, the balaclava, the Kalashnikov. He could hear his father's voice somewhere in the house but not what he was saying. Just bass notes as they rumbled through the wall.

He's all wound up today, his mother said, dabbing now with a piece of cotton wool. Who knew a strike could be so exciting?

Her voice was thick with disapproval. A chemical smell stung the air.

The canon's moved mass an hour early in the hope people will still attend, she continued. I hope a fair crowd come out, it being his last week and everything.

She let the sentiment hang between them.

The whole play thing feels wrong, she said, talking so

softly now it might have been to herself. I mean, most people involved aren't even Catholic. It's no wonder Canon Sylvester has—

I went to see him, Mack said suddenly.

He felt his mother's hands pause, resting on the crown of his head.

See who?

See who? his father echoed, entering with his morning porridge.

Denzil, Mack said quickly. That boy in work. We can have the van, no problem. We'll sort it, me and him.

Oh, right, Jackie said. Great!

His voice was bright and spry and paper-thin, distracted in tone as though he wished to change the subject. It occurred to Mack that his father had told his mother nothing of their prior agreement. He watched as he blew on his porridge. He hadn't intended to embarrass him.

The television showed new images now. The same tape, a different programme, a row of children blinking in the aftermath of some calamity. The picture riddled with static as though rewound one time too often. Mack was so tired he could barely support his head.

You were home late last night? his mother started as though reading his mind, only his father happened to speak at the exact same moment. They both ceded way to the other. Insisted their point was of little consequence. Mack listened to them squabble, unsure who he wanted to come out on top. Go on, his father insisted, gesturing with his spoon, but his mother fell silent and rested her face in her hands.

What's wrong now? Jackie asked, rolling his eyes in bewilderment.

Mack's mother remained silent for a long moment, then revealed her face again.

It's nothing, she said, blinking. I think I've got a migraine coming on.

Mack excused himself and went to his room. The two boxes were still under his bed. He retrieved the one with his belongings inside and slowly sorted through the contents. Came across an old poster at the bottom, rolled up in a tube, and carefully flattened it on the carpet. A film poster, double crown, thirty inches by twenty. The woman at the Plaza would give them to you if you asked nicely enough. He could see it now. Walking through the foyer and into the screens. The dark inside, the peace. The knowledge of someone beside you even though you couldn't see them. A sense in the air, a smell perhaps, small movements passed through the back of your seat.

He was examining the image when he heard the front gate. Peered out to see Siwan closing the latch carefully behind her. He left the poster where it lay and bolted for the stairs, stopping only to grab his shoes and coat before beating her to the door.

Oh, hi, she said, tucking her hair behind her ear.

Mack stepped out and closed the door behind himself.

C'mon, he said. Let's walk.

They headed away from town, down the side of the rugby field and across the river to the chapel. The path at the end of the road there led up through a smallholding with ragged ponies and muddied tarpaulin and out onto the face of the hill that overlooked everything. He'd climbed that way often as a child, his grandfather leading the way in his pac-a-mac and off-brand trainers, clearing brambles with his walking staff. He had a collection of such sticks lined against the wall of his shed, let Mack choose his weapon at the beginning of each excursion. No trees on the mountain by then, lost to intermittent wildfires and a steady wash of fumes from the works, but still the closest thing to wilderness they had. For the paths to be accessible, they had to declare war on the fast growers. The brambles and nettles, the ever-unfurling ferns. Keeping the path clear was a civic good, Grampa O'Brien told him. He came to take pride in his work.

You know I have to ask, Siwan called over her shoulder, panting a little with the climb.

Have to ask what?

What happened to your head?

He was too heartened by her sudden appearance to return to the incident now. Tried to think of a clever answer but came up blank.

Oh, he said quickly. That's nothing.

The footpath was narrower than he remembered, muddy underfoot and hemmed in on both sides by gorse. Siwan went first, pulling down the sleeves of her coat to protect her hands against the needles, pollen shaking free across her shoulders, the air sweet as coconut. Small critters moved amid the bracken. What sounded like a river was just traffic on the motorway below. Soon the mud became a bog, but Siwan waded through it. She'd come prepared in her boots.

You need better shoes, she said, voice thick with playful judgement. Didn't you go walking in priest school?

Mack eased his way slowly, moving duck-footed to spread his weight. Some part of him refused to register the moment as real. Him, her, together in daylight. The product of a stubborn dream. He kept his elbows in, hands covered, afraid a prick from the gorse might wake him.

Siwan grinned over her shoulder, hair sent back in the breeze, and he kept his head down and followed behind, cheeks warm with her attention.

I called by yesterday, she said. After I rang? No one came to the door.

I was busy yesterday.

Right, she said. But if I came across a certain way on the phone, I'm sorry. I didn't mean to upset you.

You didn't upset me.

His voice came out a little too high, a little too quick, unconvincing even to himself.

We're clearing the house, he added. My dad and me.

Siwan stopped on the path. Waited for him to catch up. The house? she said. Which house?

My grandparents'. We haven't touched it since they died.

She rubbed at her shoulder with her opposing hand, studying him. A scar lined her first knuckle, one he didn't recognise.

They passed away, he said. Back before Christmas.

I didn't know.

Why would you know?

She nodded and looked off down the path.

Did I ever tell you I went there once? To your grandparents' house, I mean? When I was little? Dad was away and Mammy couldn't get out of bed. There was no food in the fridge. I didn't know what to do. But I knew your mother's number was written on the calendar. I rang and she came immediately. She was going to see your grandparents anyway, she said, and they only lived around the corner. I didn't believe her even then, but what did it matter? I remember she went up to see Mammy. I remember the way she smiled at me when she came back down the stairs. Your gran gave me hot chocolate and shortbread fingers and afterwards the three of us walked to the shops in Groes Wen.

Mack examined his shoes as he listened. Tried to scrape the mud off one sole with the other. He had never heard the story before. Felt his picture of the world rearranging itself in his head.

Well anyway, she said, I'm sorry for your loss.

She turned as though to hug him then, but instead just rested a hand halfway up his arm. She left it there a moment, then took it back and carried on walking.

You didn't upset me, Mack called after her. He had to skip to keep up.

They followed the path as it cut back on itself and lifted to a grassy knoll where the bushes cleared and old stumps lay upended like driftwood brought in by the sea. Siwan removed her coat and placed it on a log to sit. Clouds moved over the sun but the day was not cold so long as you were out of the wind.

He'd imagined her apology countless times since she'd left him in the dark at the builders' merchant, only now he had it, he felt a strange deficit. The guilty sense of having let his own small feelings cloud the wider context.

Listen, he said, studying the ground between his feet. I'm sorry if I was short when you rang. I wasn't expecting it to be you.

You don't need to be sorry.

I just don't want you to get the wrong impression. It's not that I—

You don't need to be sorry, Siwan repeated.

Mack let it go and considered the view. They could see the entire town from up there. A thin, constricted strip regimented by the things that surrounded it. The docks in the distance, the waste ground and industrial wharves. The works themselves, mindless and sprawling like a geological thing present long before men happened to stumble upon it. And below them the vast sweep of the motorway bypass.

They'd erected the road years before Mack had been born. Four lanes raised on great stone pillars, built straight through people's gardens, their homes if it came to that. Both part of the town and not. Something you heard and felt and saw only from underneath. A long shadow-lane through town you could follow if you were so inclined. To sit above it felt like a small victory. To look down at the commuters. See rather than be seen. Kids had been known to throw stones from the hillside. Indiscriminate and ruthless. Suddenly higher in the world and convinced the owners of vehicles deserved everything that came their way.

Siwan hadn't mentioned the photograph he'd put through her door, so neither had he.

How's your mother? she asked eventually.

The blandness of the question caught him out.

She's fine, I think?

You think?

The vehicles whistled as they passed below, the wet road fizzing in their wake like foam left on the shoreline. Siwan brushed her hair from her face and the wind brought it back.

She's fine, Mack repeated. She's got a migraine today, that's all.

Hasn't she always suffered with migraines?

That she knew such a thing brought blood to his cheeks.

They don't last long. My forty-eight-hour affliction, that's what she calls them. Wouldn't be surprised if she was right as rain by tomorrow.

A bird soared above them. A raptor mute and vigilant. Siwan ran her hand over the bark of the dead tree on which they sat and watched the buzzard hover.

Chris swears by chiropractors for his migraines.

Chris?

My boyfriend.

Your boyfriend.

What? she asked.

I didn't say anything.

Yeah, that's what I mean.

The bird drifted in lazy circles, an orant in the sky above.

Isn't jealousy a sin?

I'm not jealous, Mack said. I'm just surprised.

Surprised about what?

That you spend time with someone into that sort of thing.

She laughed. What sort of thing?

Aren't chiropractors quacks? I thought you were scientific.

Well, Siwan said, rising to her feet. I've been known to spend time with all sorts of superstitious folk.

She brushed the back of her trousers with her hands and struggled into her coat. They kept walking, down the grassy bank and along the path south-east towards Margam. Soon they came upon the culvert where Mack had played as a child, damming the stream with rocks and sticks, ducking to go under the bridge and out the other side. He'd scratch his name into the concrete with stones there, not as permanent as the graffiti left before him but a memorial all the same.

Each branching path brought back a memory. Grampa O'Brien had known all the landmarks on those hills. The Iron Age fort, the baths where ancient monks had washed. Entrances to abandoned pit shafts, open-cast quarries, the reservoir and the place where witches were said to convene. Mack wished he had paid closer attention. Learned the routes by heart so he might impress her with his knowledge.

Siwan, he called ahead. She was walking too quickly for him.

The works were before them now. The blast furnaces and the slab yard and the long parallel stretch of the hot and cold mills. The casting plant and coke ovens. The coal yards and the silos. He'd seen it as a fairground when he was young. A carnival. A place of wicked alchemy. The various belts and structures like rollercoasters, the furnaces helter-skelter slides. The site had barely changed in the thirty years he'd known it. A land of tangled pipes and licking flames and heat and steam and sound. The mystery of the place remained intact even if he knew better now. It still felt like a primeval thing stumbled upon, not so much built as tamed towards the benefit of the town.

I've been meaning to ask, she said when he caught up. Which apostle are you?

He looked at her warily. Apostle?

In the play, she said. I've been trying to guess. What was that one called? Thaddeus? The patron saint of lost causes?

He narrowed his eyes. Who told you I was an apostle?

Or maybe . . . she continued, studying his face, Doubting Thomas?

Why does everyone assume I'm doubting?

Well, the last time I saw you, you had a collar on. And then you're in the club, half cut with your father's friends.

I wasn't drunk—

And besides, would a truly pious man get himself into fights?

He felt the pull of her gaze. Brought his fingers to his head reflexively.

That, he said, was a so-called friend getting me in trouble.

She nodded slowly, not quite understanding, then suddenly her face changed.

Wait, she said. *Me?*

A stone, when you drove away.

She reached out and put a finger lightly on the bruise. He winced and realised she was laughing.

You should have ducked.

I didn't see it coming.

Her fingers were still at his face. Part of him longed for her teasing to continue, but he didn't want her to see him blushing.

My office is just down there, he said, turning towards the town. The little brick bunker, see it?

She stood with her hands on her hips. Followed his finger. Said she saw it, or pretended she did.

What was it you said you did again? Security?

Mack feigned confusion. I'm the site chaplain. I hear the men's confessions. Administer the viaticum if there's ever an accident.

Security, you said. Signing people in and out.

Isn't that more or less the job of a priest?

Her punch surprised him. A jab in the meat of his arm. He told her it hurt, enough to leave another bruise, but

Siwan's attention was back on the plant before them.

I can't believe they trust you with the keys to the place. You could let anyone in.

They don't trust me with the keys. They trust Denzil.

Denzil *McCarthy*?

You remember him then?

I could hardly forget.

Mack grinned and studied the works too. The structures always appeared agitated, boiling with steam, run through with electric.

Do you ever get any trouble?

Smoke rose from a stack as he considered the question. If he'd craned his neck he'd have seen the knuckle yard and the thin incision of the main line. He recalled the man's face then. The look in his eye when he realised Mack was serious. The way the dark had seemed to close around them. The terror of the imminent light.

But Siwan had already moved on.

What about animals? Do you see anything like that?

Animals?

You know, she said, hand raised against the sun. Birds nesting on site? Mice? That sort of thing?

Mack thought about it. We get some birds, he said. The odd fox. Denzil reckons he's seen badgers. He always makes a racket before going into any enclosed space on patrol. Runs his torch along the railings. Says it flushes out any unexpected guests.

Siwan examined the works with a faraway look.

That's smart.

Smart wasn't the word Mack would have used, but he didn't argue.

What about you? he asked.

What about me?

Do you enjoy what you do? I'd swap the works for a garden any day of the week.

A garden?

You're building a garden, no?

He sensed her turn towards him. Felt the dagger of her glare.

Mack, she said, don't do that.

What? I'm making conversation.

No. You're prying. That's not how this used to work.

He didn't disagree, but things were different now. They were older, more mature, not hidden in the murk of a late-night Plaza screening.

You're the one who asked about my mother.

I like your mother.

Okay, I like Chris. What does he do for work?

She considered him, that line in her forehead again.

Are you sure you're not jealous?

He tried to grin, but the blood was seeping back to his cheeks.

I'm just curious. I—

What exactly did you want me to do, Mack? Wait a decade or so on the off chance your faith lapsed? Just hang about around town in case you wanted to see another film after all?

I was just making conversation.

Okay, she said briskly.

Okay, he agreed.

They stood in silence. Traffic on the bypass. Wind in the ferns. He felt he'd put distance between them but wasn't sure how to close it. The wind lifted and brought his arms out in goosebumps.

You could have waited, he tried slyly. Wouldn't have killed you.

She turned to him, hand still raised to her face against the sun.

Impatient, he continued, that's your problem. Always been the same.

She laughed. A proper laugh. A reflex of surprise.

Impatient?

Mack shrugged, maintaining a straight face. I'm just saying.

What do you think patience looks like? Do you understand what would happen if I wasn't patient?

She raised her arm to punch him again. This time he managed to catch her fist.

They looked at one another. Now he had her hand, he didn't know what to do with it.

I'm patient, she insisted. I am.

They struggled. She stepped closer, tried to poke his ribs, but a clank off behind made them stop and turn. A terracotta cloud rose above the works. Small, but growing. Swelling outwards. A dirty ghost in ascension.

I got your photo, she said, voice suddenly soft as she watched the smog rise.

Mack watched too, unsure if he was embarrassed at the gesture now or glad he'd followed through with it.

How old would we have been then, do you think?

He wasn't sure, couldn't have guessed. Old enough to know one another, not so grown his mother had stopped accompanying them.

I loved it in there, she said.

Mack nodded in agreement, gladdened by the fact it had meant as much to her.

We should go back, she continued. Tonight.

To the Plaza? I'm not sure what'll be showing. It's been shut for years.

All the better. We'll have it to ourselves.

He laughed and turned, expecting her to be laughing too. But instead found something like hurt in her eyes.

You don't have to if you don't want to, she said quietly. It dawned on him she was serious.

Siwan, the place is falling down.

Like I said, you don't have to.

She angled her body away from him, watching the cloud climb before them. He tried to put a hand on her arm, but she pulled away.

It's not that I don't want to, Mack tried. But it's the start of the play tonight. The Last Supper. I've got to—

Her laugh interrupted him. A sound stripped of amusement. A rush of air through her nose.

Oh right, she said. Of course.

I think it's as silly as you, he started, speaking quickly with the urge to make his feelings plain. If I had a choice, I wouldn't go within ten miles of something like that, but I've told the others I'll be there.

Well, if your friends are expecting you.

They aren't my friends, Mack said.

Who are they then?

It means a lot to my father. I've given my word.

Okay, she said. You do what you think is most important.

The meekness of her voice made him want to shake her. He felt an anger rise again.

It would be easier to judge what was important if you actually spoke to me. If I knew what exactly it is you want. You can't expect me to drop everything when you won't tell me what's going on, Siwan. Not when you act as if you think I'm stupid.

The cloud ahead had drifted. A high mass dissipating to the point of translucence. Not disappearing so much as embedding itself in the world.

All I'm asking is to meet at the Plaza, she said simply. And we both know you're not stupid, so you might as well stop acting like it.

IX

The poster was still furled up on the carpet when he returned to his room, though he no longer wished to see it. What satisfaction he'd felt in Siwan's company had slowly evaporated during their walk home. He'd left with the sense of having been scolded without quite knowing what it was he had done. The feeling came with an odd combination of guilt and injustice. The needling suspicion that he was lying to himself. A rising desire to repent. Slotting the poster back into its cardboard tube, he placed it in the box with the rest of his belongings and turned to the canon's books instead.

He reached in without looking and removed a slender volume by John Ruskin. *The Storm-Cloud of the Nineteenth Century*. A transcript of lectures on a blight of bad weather. Eighteen eighty-four. A wind blowing cold from every compass point.

A new affliction ever returning, that's how Ruskin had described it. A cloud appearing again and again.

Mack heard his mother climb the stairs and move down

the landing. She went into the bathroom. The bolt on the door fired like a gun. He looked at his watch as the shower started and saw that evening was approaching. In three hours, the furnaces would stop, the workers would walk out, and everything else would begin. Only his mother, he knew, was preparing for a different event. She was getting herself ready for mass.

A dry black veil. A wind of darkness. A plague-wind peculiar to the times. The cloud of the nineteenth century looked like a storm but wasn't. It looked like the lost souls of the dead.

He turned the page. Ruskin didn't know what caused the blanched sun and blighted grass, but he had an inkling. The explanation, he reckoned, would have been obvious had the year been a little earlier. If Man had not moved on so swiftly. For England and countries like her had taken to blaspheming. Allowed their men to mistreat one another however they saw fit. There would be consequences for such actions, not just in the next world but here and now as well.

Mack went to his desk and put on the lamp. Retrieved his notebook and pen. He took up the book again and transcribed the series of diary entries Ruskin had provided as evidence. Catalogues of the weather as seen from the window of his room. A deep, high filthiness. A dense manufacturing mist. Terrific double streams of reddish-violet fire with grand artillery peals close behind. A thunder that ceased then returned, the air collapsing into black fog. A double-forked flash rippling in a frightful ladder of light.

He made notes through to the end of the chapter. Wrote as though the words were his own. What is best to be done? Ruskin asked on the final page. For him, the answer was obvious. Because regardless of whether a man could affect the signs of the sky, he could affect the signs of the times. And if he could not bring the sun to shine again, he could assuredly return a cheerfulness to himself. Bring back his own honesty.

The path of rectitude was still there before him. The promise of those old times might hold yet.

Mack closed his notebook and rose from his desk. Got to his knees on the carpet. He crossed himself, bowed his head. Had no prayer to offer, no demands or requests. Instead, he drifted into the silence, mind as flat and blank as a pool of oil. Only it wasn't silence. For beyond the shower and the creak of the walls, a constant drone still plagued the distance. An idling engine, a jet plane roar. Alarms and pressured gases, intense fires, molten flow. A sound with smell and light, its own clouds in the sky. A tone that had been in his head for as long as he could remember. The unending hour of the furnaces, refusing to give up quite yet.

The lock on the bathroom door jolted him back into his body. He looked at his watch again. Half an hour until mass. Getting to his feet, he opened the wardrobe. Pushed past the vestments to retrieve a shirt, a pair of trousers and a black sweater. His old daily uniform. He dressed quickly then went to the bathroom to brush his teeth and wash his face. When he descended the stairs, he sat on the bottom step and put on his shoes. He waited for his mother in the hall.

She spoke of family histories on their way to the church. Nanna Caitríona's stories of Easter in another time. Women attending Good Friday mass barefooted with their hair down over their faces, bending low to kiss the five wounds of Christ. She spoke of the black fast and other superstitions. The swallow, the heron, the robin. The bad luck on drawing blood. She spoke as though to wrap him in the heritage of their faith. To enchant him in the dark allure of that which had become lost.

Traffic was building on the main road, all headed in the same direction. The curtain-raising shutdown was still a couple of hours away, but the audience raced for the best spots. On reaching the church, they found it half empty despite the canon's efforts. Only the most devout were not seduced. Mack trailed behind his mother to their usual seats, head down to avoid any familiar faces. Fearing not so much their questions as the answers he might give. The look in their eyes as they nodded along without a shred of comprehension. Even the prospect of seeing Canon Sylvester on the altar made him suddenly uncomfortable. Better as a voice in a curtained booth.

They sat and crossed themselves, then lowered the kneeler to pray. He closed his eyes, listened to the ambient quiet. Felt the hard wood through the cushion at his knees. There'd been no cushion at the seminary, but he had gotten used to it. Some of the others had insisted on kneeling on nothing but the cold tile.

When he finished, he leaned close to his mother.

How are you feeling? he asked. Has the headache gone?

Clara remained facing the altar, only batted his concern away.

Mam? he probed, voice a whisper. You know we were talking about migraines. Do you ever get, like . . . a taste?

But his mother was too distracted to answer the question. Suddenly nudging at his shoulder, gesturing with her chin. She didn't open her mouth, but her face said enough. Mack knew who it was without even looking.

A few rows ahead. The very front pew. That hair, that ear, that curve of neck. A view he'd had in church for years. He felt the push of his heart in his chest as his mother peered at him, seeming to want a response or confirmation. But there was no mistaking who it was. Siwan's family had always sat in the same place at mass too.

Come on, Clara said, already rising to her feet. We can't let her sit on her own.

He stayed where he was as his mother stepped forward. Watched her tap Siwan on the back and bend to whisper into her ear. He knew Siwan would decline the offer, insist she was fine on her own, but he knew too how stubborn his mother could be. Siwan tucked her hair behind her ear as if to hear Clara better. His mother had both hands on her arm now, willing her agreement.

He stood to greet her into their row. The pair of them awkward, feigning surprise. She looked brighter than their previous encounters. Wore a red sweater and a chain around her neck. Her hair brushed and loose. Dark mascara on her eyes. When he hugged her, he felt her shoulders and spine hard through the back of her jumper. Was struck by the same surprise he'd felt on first stroking a cat to find there were bones inside.

Hello, stranger, she said into his ear. Long time no see.

A frisson followed her voice. He suddenly felt too warm. How much was coded in the interaction? Would a casual observer see it on his face? He sat on the end of the pew, Siwan's leg pressed against his own. He wanted to say something but couldn't. Shy before her all of a sudden. Troubled by a nagging unease. Unable to shake the sense that her presence had betrayed something between them. Broken rules they had never spoken aloud.

The dream world and real life colliding. A shadow scheme drawn out into the light.

He picked up the Roman missal. He'd brought his own. The cover worn, pages gold-edged and translucently thin. A present from his grandparents when he'd first moved away. He'd wanted his mother to see him using it, but felt foolish now before their unexpected guest.

Clara whispered questions. Clasped Siwan's hand as though afraid she might slip away. How've you been? How's your father? Dear Lord, do you know how much you look like your mam?

The missal had three ribbons to hold his place, frayed velvet strips in green and white and amber. A message inside the front cover. Black ink, handwritten, dated to the day. *With love from Gran and Grampa.*

A bell sounded from the sacristy and the people rose to their feet. A stranger played the organ. Mack held the hymn book open but didn't sing, didn't even pretend. The song hesitant with their low number. A murmur from a humble congregation. The server with the processional cross came first, then a pair of candle bearers. Siwan sang but barely, her words a soft vibration.

Canon Sylvester followed his acolytes. Gave no sign he had noticed Mack. At the altar, a server prepared the thurible and handed it over. There were rules to the instrument, a proper technique. Three double swings for the book of the Gospels and the Paschal candle, three double swings for the people themselves. A series of swings around the altar before being handed back to the server so he might offer three double swings to the priest.

Incense clouded the air. Mack felt an urge to explain the process. Impress them with Latin and Greek. The thurible, the tabernacle, the humeral veil and aspergillum. The monstrance and lunette.

The incense ceremony had finished by the time the hymn ended. The canon raised his hand and crossed the air.

In the name of the Father, and of the Son, and of the Holy Spirit.

Amen.

Brothers and sisters, he said, let us prepare ourselves to celebrate these sacred mysteries.

They spoke as one. I confess to almighty God, and to you my brothers and sisters, that I have greatly sinned. In my thoughts and in my words, in what I have done and what I have failed to do.

Mack succumbed to the rhythm. Took heart in the metre and verse. Siwan's shoulder against his, his mother beside her, the same words in their mouths, stood in the very pew from which his grandparents had spoken them too. If he could not convey his thoughts directly, then let his voice in the chorus say it instead. For what else was love but an unthinking action? A beat persisting in spite of everything?

The altar servers rang bells during the Gloria in excelsis. Then the bells fell silent and would remain so until the Vigil Mass.

The first reading was from the book of Exodus. The response to the psalm was: The blessing-cup that we bless is a communion with the blood of Christ. His mother rose to give the second reading. The first time St Paul bothered the Corinthians, a little story he'd heard, too good to keep to himself. For on the night he was betrayed, Jesus took bread and thanked God for it and broke it, and said: This is my body, which is for you, do this in memorial of me.

Some part of Mack was moved to hear his mother read. They stood in the aisle when she returned so she might retake her seat. Siwan caught her arm as she stumbled over the kneeler. I'm fine, Clara said, pinching the bridge of her nose. Just a bit of a headache.

The gospel was according to John. Jesus knew his hour had come. For it was written that the devil had already gotten into the mind of Judas Iscariot. He kissed his master in the garden.

Simon Peter drew his sword and struck the high priest's servant, cutting off his right ear. The servant's name was Malchus.

Siwan fussed over Mack's mother in a series of silent gestures. She had Aspro Clear in her purse. She'd get a glass of water.

It had long been assumed the disciples could not fathom what was happening, Canon Sylvester said in his homily. That the big picture was beyond their reach. The path to glory led through the garden, but all they could see was the dark of the night. In reaching for his sword, Simon Peter struck out in dumb anger instead of submitting to the higher plan. He let his pride get the better of him. Grew foolish enough to think he might take God's will into his own hands.

The canon sucked breath between his words. Gripped the lectern as an overboard sailor might a buoy on the open sea. He paused to fish a handkerchief from deep within his vestments. Wiped at his nose and mouth before continuing.

Biblical scholars have long puzzled over why Jesus was crucified. Was our Lord not a pacifist? What did he do to deserve such a violent end? A new line of thinking blames the disciples for arming themselves. For being more militant than they let on. The Romans would not have tolerated such a band roaming the streets of Jerusalem during the Passover. Had Peter not drawn his sword in the gloom of the garden, Christ might never have been killed at all.

The canon started to cough then. Brought the handkerchief to his mouth as if to muffle the sound. He coughed slightly longer than was comfortable, for both him and the congregation. For a moment he seemed ready to admit defeat, only to hesitate as he made to turn away. He leaned to the microphone instead.

But of course, he said, breath short, our salvation depended upon it. If the crucifixion was the whole point of the story, then Peter's outburst might have saved the world.

They skipped the washing of the feet, unable to summon the required number of men. After communion, the canon put more incense inside the thurible, blessed it and took it, then knelt before the Blessed Sacrament and incensed it three times. He rose, wrapped a white humeral veil around his shoulders, took the ciborium within the veil and led a procession of the servers back to the place of repose.

After a moment of silent adoration, the priest and ministers genuflected and returned to the sacristy. A few of the congregation took the opportunity to leave. The sound of kneelers raised, books gathered. People sneaking through the mist of incense with thoughts of some better place to be.

We can go too, Mack whispered, leaning across Siwan to speak to his mother. If you're not feeling well?

But she shook her head, adamant. Mack made to protest, looking at his watch. Remembering his father and the pint he'd promised. But when he faced back towards the altar, a metallic tang crossed his tongue. The strangest sight before him. The smoke had coalesced into a ball of fog up near the ceiling. Or not a ball. A cloud.

A hand seized his wrist. His mother reaching across Siwan, her grip so tight it shook. Her face blanched as though in shock at the sight before them, though before she could speak, the service resumed.

The canon wore a violet stole upon his return from the sacristy. Together with the servers, he stripped the altar of its dressings, its books and flowers and cloths. What could not be removed was covered with black veiling. Every candle was extinguished. The room left as empty as a tomb. All the while the cloud hung above. Left of centre, just in view. A lingering apparition that strobed translucent. A metallic click, a censer's ticking, the taste thick in Mack's mouth.

When the canon and the servers returned to the sacristy, the congregation made their exit. But when Mack put on his coat and stepped from the pew, he headed not for the doors but the altar. A spare veil had been left there. He bowed before he took it in his hands. Then, without acknowledging the cloud, he covered it with one graceful motion so that it hung cloaked above them, a dark phantom in the centre of the room.

Stewards protected the entrance to the plant. A line of red and white warning tape strung across a series of cones. Only the workers were allowed through. The hastily arranged prologue written for them alone. Without ID, there was no way to witness the walkout from such a clear vantage. Those of the scant few who had hoped to bend the rules settled on lining the roadside.

When Mack showed his badge, the stewards lifted the tape so he could duck beneath it. The action made him light-headed, though he told himself it was just hunger or nerves. After getting his mother home to bed and changing into his work clothes, he'd only had time enough to take another dose of painkillers with a slug of milk straight from the bottle. He would eat later, he told himself in consolation. He would see a doctor if it got any worse.

He found his father huddled with a handful of the apostles, waiting for the strike to start and the rest of their number to emerge.

I'm sorry I'm late, Mack said, halfway breathless, but was interrupted before he could explain.

Not sneaking in for a shift, are you?

Bryn squinted through hooded eyes.

I told you about them boys from security. Can't trust 'em as far as you could throw 'em.

Mam isn't well, Mack told his father, ignoring the jibe. She's got a migraine. I've never seen her so bad.

Jackie only grunted, eyes set on the ground. A hand caught Mack by the arm.

Oi, Bryn said, spinning him to face them. We're talking to you.

Mack squared his shoulders. The apostles looked back. Jackie, Curly, Peggy and Bryn. Crazy Horse O'Leary and one of the Bowen brothers. Each man with a pin badge on his breast. *Save Our Steel. SOS.*

He eyed the men before him. He felt tired again now.

Sensed a rush of blood to the bruise on his head. Considered turning on his heel and not looking back, but then the stewards parted and took the cones with them. A car pulled into the entrance, tinted windows, all black, and the back door opened and a man climbed out. Hair wild, face thick with beard. Their Messiah before them in sackcloth tied at the waist with tasselled rope.

Are you ready? the actor asked the gathered men, rubbing his palms in anticipation. The time is almost here.

A call went out. A countdown. Only sixty seconds left. The plant hissed like the static of a dead television. Its lights cast the sky above them brass. The gathered men called out each passing second. Fifty, forty, thirty, hardly any time at all. The works responded in anger, its noise escalating as though rising through a narrow column, needle-thin and accelerating, a dropped bomb in reverse. Behind this noise came another, like something hooked on the first and dragged from deep within the earth. The second sound grew louder, engulfing that from which it was born, then the bleeder valve opened and effluvia burst forth, and with it a desperate thunder, a gas scream, a cloud.

The men stood motionless. Lights began to snuff out one by one. The furnaces, the ovens, the sinter plant. Every part of the site slowing to a rest as it gradually fell into dark. Then the doors opened and its workers emerged. A few at first, then more. Mack looked for familiar faces among them, but too many bodies spilled out of the plant. A vast cumulus climbed white above. And when the comrades met on the forecourt and the last lights extinguished, a great stillness finally fell, and silence sealed their ears like the skin of a drum.

The Saviour led the way to the supper. A procession in eerie hush. Not even the audience that lined their path said a word. A quiet striking enough to raise the hairs on their bodies. Hinting at the holy and the sacrosanct. Even Mack was awed by the strangeness of it. A man more than familiar with the power of repose. Something in the dusk light and sense of common purpose. The total commitment to spectacle.

The silence held until they reached the bottom of Dalton Road. The entire town seemed to have gathered outside the club. Or more than the town. Outsiders too. Tourists. A swelling audience wishing to see history unfold. Revellers drank, people yelled, money changed hands. Gaunt men in paper aprons handed greasy burgers through stall windows. An ice cream van chugged its exhaust. At the entrance, a row of men wearing pin badges and works uniforms were there to greet the pilgrims. A picket line, already translocated. A welcome like coming home.

A screen had been set up on a scaffold in the corner of the car park. An image from inside blown huge. Backs of heads, silhouettes. A long table lit from above.

The club had never been so busy. There was no stage, just the table slightly raised under the snooker lights. Thirteen places set with napkins and paper plates. Pints already filled to the brim. Chairs had been arranged around it in concentric circles, like an amateur boxing event. Cameras, kino lights, loudspeakers and microphones. A system of rigging to adjust the scenery. The crowd hushed as the disciples entered and the actor took the seat in the middle. The apostles fanned out around him. Bryn to his right, Jackie on the other side. Mack took the last seat on the left.

Peggy couldn't keep still in the neighbouring chair. Mack hitched an inch further leftwards, but Peggy put an arm around him. How about this, butt? he asked, his breath sour on Mack's cheek, though Mack had no answer. He imagined the people watching outside. Himself as blurred pixels on a hanging screen.

The actor, on his feet again, raised a pint in the air. The men returned the gesture and a cheer went up in the crowd. Soon the audience followed, a sea of hands and sloshing liquid, light playing magic through the glass. When the toast was over, the actor took a long pull from his beer. He sighed with satisfaction and wiped at his mouth with his sleeve.

Applause broke out. People called and whooped. The actor waited for the sound to fade before he started. When he finally spoke, he did so with great flourish, his voice projected theatrically.

Would you believe it, he asked, if I told you one of these men is about to betray me?

Easter week had been the toughest of the year at the seminary. The days harder and longer. Alarm clock shrieking at four fifteen. Time only to piss and wash his face and fall into his clothes. The end of Lent. The beginning of a journey towards deep shadow. The days when they followed Jesus into his last hours. Endured with him the cruelties and ridicule.

Total quiet in the courtyard those mornings. Hands under armpits. Hoar frost on the ground. No hats, no coats, a growing cloud of breath. Then the sound of something shifting. A key in a lock. An open door. A tight bustle as they pushed towards the pews. No warmer inside, but no wind at least. Every man gathered in the still-dark morning to chant the matins and the lauds.

A candle hearse stood on the altar. A wooden triangle on a long, narrow stand. Prickets like the teeth of a harrow. Fifteen candles, their wax unbleached save for the white candle at the summit. Their flames the only light in the room.

For every psalm, they extinguished a candle. Shadows danced freakish up the walls. Nine in the matins, five in the lauds, until only the white candle remained. At the conclusion, this candle was taken and hidden behind the altar, the room cast as dark as the hollow eyes of a skull. They sat within this moment, sat as if darkness was all there was, and then from somewhere in the room the strepitus sounded like thunder. A racket meant to convey the loss of the Lord. The sound frightened them at first, but soon the men responded. They stomped their feet in the total dark, beat their hymnals against the pews. Faced down their blindness with noise as though that was all that was left to them. Made chaos like something risen from the ground.

The night was black after the glare of the club. The absence of the works hit like cold water. Like some key layer had been stripped from the town itself. Its ambient depth, its texture. The loss threatened to reveal something dreadful. The pure silence beneath everything. Once the supper concluded, a band had taken to the stage as though in defiance. A singer wailed like a manic street preacher, cymbals crashed, bass pounded. The audience had pushed forward and subsumed the apostles. Their Saviour not too proud to bop along with the rest.

The scene had been too much for Mack. The paracetamol worn off by then, the noise thumping a sinister feeling into his head. He slipped out the door without a word, what his grandfather had called an Irish goodbye. And though he now groped his way through the empty streets, he understood where he was going. It was not too late, he told himself. He had made up his mind.

He knew the light was her the moment he saw it. A sanctuary lamp burning at the end of the road. She did not greet him when he appeared or say how long she'd waited. Siwan with her coat over her church clothes, face still made up. She'd brought a torch for each of them.

They stood shoulder to shoulder before the old cinema. Facade still proud in its ruin. Most of the leadwork scallops had fallen from the parapet. The billboard and poster frames were blank. The Pepsi sign still clung beneath the canopy, but every door and window was barricaded. She put her torch down and began to prise the boards loose. Grunting with effort, breath misted in the dark. Mack joined in and together they worked under the feeble light of the moon.

Everything was damp and rotting. The building smelled like mulch. It felt good to be near her, to work in tandem, to feel her effort and her force. If she knew the purpose of the trip, she did not speak it. When Mack pictured the inside of the cinema, it looked just like it always had.

If he pulled with all his strength, he could open a gap large enough for her to squeeze through. They'd go on the count of three. Only they were interrupted before the count could start. A headlight shock, an engine. An angry horn. A voice.

Oi, called a man through the driver's-side window. What the fuck do you think you're doing?

The door flung open and the figure came climbing out. A feller in full works uniform, still in his steel-toed boots. The engine was running, a Mondeo the colour of red wine. Mack raised his torch upon the man and recognised him immediately. Only half an ear. Dai.

Hand raised against the light, Dai staggered forward, only to stop as recognition hit him too.

What the fuck? he asked. Voice softer now, inward. Face contorted as the cogs turned in his head. His overalls were splattered in what looked like white paint. His cheeks too, his arms and hands. His hair was damp with sweat at the back of his neck. A man, it occurred to Mack, on his way home after an evening shift.

Dai seemed to sense the penny had dropped. He got back in the car and slammed the door. It took him a second to roll up the window before he could speed away. His brake lights smeared red on the wet of the road. When Mack returned to the boards, Siwan tugged at his sleeve.

We should go, she said, voice hurried and spooked.

He ignored her. Braced himself and pulled. Only she kept a hold of his coat, trying to wrench him towards her, so that it felt he was fighting in two directions simultaneously.

We can't linger, she said, hanging off his back. Not if we've been seen.

I know that man, Mack said, turning to face her. He wouldn't dare tell anyone.

She evaluated his face with a frown. He didn't look away, not once.

Siwan, he said. Trust me.

She held his eye a beat longer. Swallowed whatever reluctance she felt and wiped her hands on the seat of her trousers.

They counted down from three. Pulled with force enough to make a gap Siwan could crawl inside. Once within, she braced her back against the door frame and kicked the rest of the boards right out. There was no glass in the front doors. Room enough to duck through. A small set of steps led into the lobby. The same brass handrails and concrete floors. The smell of leaves as plucked from guttering. Bird shit everywhere. The inside doors were more difficult. Full of water, swollen shut. She tested the frame with her shoulder. They stood together and pushed.

The tiles from the lobby floor had been ripped up, but the ticket desk remained. The ice-cream chest and wire racks for chocolate bars. Everything ominous in the beams of their torches. Surfaces discoloured by mildew bloom and saltpetre, the once cream walls now cadaver-yellow and blistered with the damp. Paint fell in long, hanging tatters from the ceiling. A skin in the process of shedding.

He understood the rules instinctively. She would lead the way. He would follow.

Adverts were still everywhere. Nestlé and Lyons Maid. Thayer's Real Dairy. Hot dogs and burgers, buttered popcorn, salted popcorn, small, medium and large. Posters heralded films new no longer. Limp cardboard standees of cartoon characters grinning through rot as though crazed by the state that had befallen them. Siwan kept raising her beam towards the ceiling. A winding stairway led out of the foyer towards a green door. The path had been roped off in their memories, but no one could stop them now.

Upstairs they found the projectionist's room ransacked. Chairs upended, cabinets pushed to the floor. Metal tins and cardboard boxes. Film unspooled and piled into a corner. A bonfire never to be lit. Even the old logbooks had been left behind, their paper brittle but legible. Handwritten notes on each screening – the trailers to play, the title cards, the silence.

The walls had corroded back to the concrete. The rust on their hands smelled like blood.

Siwan pushed past the reels and the xenon lamp to peer through the small window into the theatre. Mack scanned his torch around. It felt like a bunker with the vents and lockers. A place to see out the end of the world. *No Smoking*, read the sign on the wall. *Nitrate Film Is Flammable*. The quiet took on a new depth without her moving around and he didn't like it. He stepped forward to be nearer her, and when he raised his torch behind her head, he imagined her face blown giant and projected to the screen.

Thank you for coming, she told him. Her words echoed from the walls.

They backed out into the corridor. Dust fell through the beams of their torches. Soot lined the floor, thick enough that they left footprints. He paused at the top of the foyer stairs. Saw the room different from that vantage. The full ruined scene.

I didn't expect to see you at mass, he said.

I didn't expect you either. I thought you were busy with your new friends.

He turned towards her on the steps. Raised his torch to see her face, but she brought her hands to her eyes.

Mack, she said. You're blinding me.

Downstairs, they pushed through to the main theatre. The door had a porthole window. It felt warmer in there. Old air sealed in. The ceiling was caved, the carpet pulled up.

Boards had come loose from the bottom of the stage, but the velvet curtain remained. The seats looked like someone had died in them. An entire audience turned to ash.

Well? she said. Are we going to stand here all day?

They chose their usual spot, halfway up on the left. The fabric was greener on the cushions than the backs. It smelled like an attic, a dungeon, a grotto hollowed out from the ground. He looked to Siwan but found her face barely visible in the reflected light. An eye-shine gleam, a gilded nose in silhouette.

They killed their torches and sat for a long while, time distorting around them. The dilapidation was easy to forget in the dark. They were in the same old seats, facing the same direction. They half expected the screen to slowly come to life. The alluring trailers to begin. The future condensed into promises.

They had always arrived early in their youth. Stayed seated long after the credits rolled. Sat until the lights came up and the cleaner kicked them out. Stretched the moment as far as it would go.

Why did you leave the seminary?

Hearing the question he'd long anticipated was not the trial he'd imagined. He felt something more like relief.

They queried my motivations, he said. Claimed I didn't feel a true calling. Doubted the path was what God intended for me. Not the easiest thing to hear after years of training and preparation. Your attempts to be good are a personal failing. You do not know God after all.

He felt a movement on the armrest. Her fingers searching for his in the gloom. He extended his hand so that she might find it, and she did.

There's a refusal to confront reality, he said. I see it every day. Those who wish to believe things can continue the same way forever. Who place their faith in a future that cannot hold.

He felt the warmth of her, the pulse of blood beneath her skin.

What I mean, he said, is that I think I'm ready to stop acting like I'm stupid.

Siwan didn't respond. He sensed the smallest twitch in her hand.

I can get access to a van. I have two hands and two feet and a willingness to work. There's space in my grandparents' garage should you need it. There are supplies in there you might find useful.

He looked dead ahead as he spoke, though it was so dark he might have closed his eyes. Siwan sat with the thought before speaking. Absorbing the offer, recalibrating the picture in her head.

You don't have to do this, she said slowly, careful to ensure her words were comprehended. You understand that?

He felt the springs through the cushion of the seat. Was aware of his own beating heart.

I understand, he said.

And you're going to have to trust me, she continued. Appreciate I can't answer every question. Listen to what I tell you.

I'll listen, he said. I trust you.

She gripped his hand tighter. Shifted her body closer to his. Something warm in the dark. An animal with hair and skin. He didn't move, but he didn't need to. Hair brushed his face. A weight leaned into him.

Then her chair snapped upright. A puff of dust, a fungal smell. She put her torch back on and walked away from him. He watched the light pass along the row and down the aisle. An errant beam, a will-o'-the-wisp. Down the stairs and up onto the stage via the small steps at the side. His pulse grew quick to see it. He could still feel the phantom weight where she had pressed her body against his.

Meet me tomorrow, she called, stood in front of the velvet drapes. At your grandparents' house. In the evening.

X

His room at the seminary had been cold, but he learned to ignore it. He came to know the marks on the ceiling, the cracks in the wall. The previous occupant had smoked, and the smell had never quite departed. There was a railway line somewhere in the distance. He heard the trains when the wind was right.

There were days, kneeling alone in the chapel, when he prayed someone might walk through the door. A person to talk to, anyone on earth. There were days amid the closeness of the men in the cloisters when he would hide in the toilet just to hear his own thoughts. Sometimes he wished he'd pushed himself further. Joined an ascetic order, the Carthusians in their alpine retreat. Some days he wished he'd never set foot inside a church at all.

His reprieve came from the nuns. They had a garden nearby and accepted volunteers. He felt better in their presence, better in the soil. Attuned to the cycles of the earth. They grew potatoes and carrots and turnips. Sweet peas, beetroots, courgettes. They took the veg and cooked it and fed those who were hungry. They did their best to offer shelter, clothes and medical care. Sister Joan was always thinking of ways in which to expand their endeavours. Just hearing her talk of them was to edge closer to God Himself.

His free time was devoted to reading. He read the work of Hélder Câmara and Des Wilson. The Berrigan brothers and Dorothy Day. Came to believe Christianity could be rehabilitated, the religions united. Conceived a world changed by sufficient compassion and rage.

I have come to set the world on fire, Jesus Himself had said. I only wish it were already burning.

His mindset won few friends among his fellow seminarians, but he wasn't looking for any. They teased him at first. Approached during supper, eager to debate. Hanging out with the hippies? they'd joke, seeing the mud on the knees of his trousers. The dirt beneath his nails. One last commie slipped through Pope John Paul II's net. The Holy Father spinning in his grave. But Wojtyła, God bless his soul, wasn't the Pope any more, as Mack liked to remind them. Theirs was a church on the cusp of something different. Better to adapt, he said. Embrace the new age.

With his fervour came a sense of action. The line between hope and delusion was thin. The seminary was built on an old monastic site, grand buildings surrounded by manicured grounds and rolling fields. They didn't use half as many of the rooms as they had in its heyday and much of the land was neglected. He saw no reason why such space should not be put to use.

He spoke with the vice rector. A large man with a bald head and one leg longer than the other. They sat together on a wooden bench outside the rectory. There were flowers in the beds there. A freshly mown lawn. A small rockery with a plastic Holy Mother in the centre. Birds called in the trees.

God was present everywhere, the Jesuit way of thinking.

The nuns did good work, Mack explained. They had so many plans to put into motion. If they could spare them an office, he said, a base from which they might operate. A couple of acres for vegetables and flowers. Five rooms, ten rooms, accommodation for the needy.

The vice rector sat through the sermon with a wry smile on his face. As though he had seen fools before but didn't mind suffering them on occasion. He waited for Mack to finish before he commenced speaking.

Cormac, he said. Do you think all this pays for itself?

He gestured to their surroundings. The bowling-green lawns, the carefully maintained masonry.

We're lucky to get a handful of seminarians each year. Our projections continue to trend downwards.

Then space is not an issue. Why have whole wings of the building gather dust?

But can't you see, Cormac? We're against the wall ourselves. Forced to become imaginative with our income streams. We could convert those empty rooms into a hotel. Offer the lay person novelty holidays. It's a growing market, is it not? To someone other than ourselves? We've got idyllic surroundings. We have peace.

You want to rent out the rooms?

What I want doesn't enter the equation. We're broke and the planet spins on money. The Church cannot be above adapting to the world in which it finds itself. Either we change or we are buried.

We could have a gift shop, Mack said. Go all the way and become Calvinist.

The vice rector said his name like the bark of a dog. He was always saying his name. Mack didn't like it.

Cormac, the vice rector said, surely you're old enough by now to understand idealism is not a virtue?

He set his alarm early yet woke before it. Felt his body clench like a fist. He made his bed and got to his knees on the carpet. He held his breath and prayed. In the bathroom, he drank from the tap until he could drink no more, then showered in cold water. He stood before the mirror and considered his head.

The bruise had receded now, yet the longer he studied his face, the stranger it became.

He walked, his route extended. Past the Plaza, the shopping centre, St Mary's and St Joseph's. Around the school and back again. He wanted to see everything. The new-found quiet of the morning cast familiar things different. The very air changed without the factory thrum. Absence as a kind of clarity. If he'd had the time, he'd have gone to the beach, walked the seafront in the early morning, felt the sting of the sand on the wind. But instead he followed the river back the way he'd come, stalking waters clogged with discarded shopping trolleys and plastic bags shredded and drifting like the hair of the recently drowned. From there, he passed the works, still standing despite its silence. He made his way towards Margam. He went to the underpass and screamed just to remind himself of his own voice.

The hardware shop opened at nine. He was waiting outside when the owner arrived to raise the shutters. A system of pulleys and gears, a chain to be yanked hand over hand. The shutter ascended slower than the man's effort seemed to deserve. Inside, Mack chose two pairs of work gloves and took them to the counter. The man asked if there was anything else he needed and Mack said yes, in fact, there was.

He took a key from his pocket, the one for his grandfather's garage.

If possible, he said, I'd like to make a copy.

The key-cutting machine was behind the counter. A motor with a belt, a carbide steel blade, two vices side by side. The man placed the original key in the first vice, teeth facing upwards, then selected a blank from a series of hooks on the wall and placed that in the second. He put on a pair of ear protectors but offered Mack no warning. The belt whirred like a film projector. When the blade met metal, it wailed.

The man worked with the agile disinterest of an expert. Soon a perfect duplicate emerged.

Her street was quiet when he arrived. Her car out front, still in need of cleaning. He checked his watch. Walked down the road and back again. Biding time. Waiting for something. When he finally stood before the door, he saw a shadow for his reflection. He paused a moment to compose himself. Felt the key in his pocket.

His early arrival would impress her, he thought. Prove he was ready and willing. He imagined pressing the key into the warmth of her palm. Pictured her taking him by the hand again.

It took a while for her to appear after he knocked. She did not take him by the hand. Only appraised him on the front step, squinting with one eye closed, distrusting the sight before her, arms folded tight across her chest.

What are you doing? she asked.

Her body was angled to fill the doorway. She wore an oversized jumper and pyjama bottoms. Her hair a mess, her feet bare.

I thought, he said. I—

But he was no longer sure what he thought. He'd made a mistake, he realised. Wished to take it back. But a car started in the street behind them and the sound appeared to cause her panic. She leaned against the wall and beckoned him inside.

The house was not as he'd imagined. The air thick, the hallway narrow and cluttered. Pictures adorned the walls, but he dared not stop to look. Behind Siwan was the door to the front room, but she pressed herself tight against it and waited for him to pass. He worried the key in his pocket as he walked. Siwan was right behind him.

She spoke only to ask if he wanted tea. He said he was all right, but in the kitchen she filled the kettle anyway and set it to boil. He helped gather mugs from the rack, dried them on a towel hung from the oven door. She got two tea bags from the tin and set them on the counter.

He folded the towel neatly. Ran his hand along the countertop. A row of ceramic pots lined the windowsill. Rainforest flora, rubber-like and reaching. Unlikely plants grown wild. He couldn't help but look for something in the room. A clue, a glimpse of her life.

Siwan kept her back to him. Unable to bring herself to look him in the eye.

When the kettle boiled, she poured a thumb of water in each mug to warm the bottom through, then cast the water into the sink. Mack handed her the towel and she took it without thanks. He got the milk from the fridge and set it beside her. She got a spoon from the drawer and worked the tea bags.

He tried to listen to the house, judge whether they were alone. Thin radio music, a lurching combi boiler, the slow click of the kettle as it cooled.

The arrangement of every object seemed charged with cryptic meaning. The lack of obvious sign its own foreboding weight. He felt foolish in his coat, a man overdressed. It was warm in the kitchen. A humidity in the air. The succulent plants breathing.

She gestured for him to sit. A fruit bowl on the table but no fruit. Takeaway menus. Kebabs, Indian, Chinese. Pamphlets selling chinos for old people, teddy bears and commemorative coins. The scam junk born in the middle of magazines. She cleared a space and set his tea down before him. Asked if he wanted toast, but he shook his head no. Asked if he wanted a biscuit and went to the cupboard before he could decline. She presented a selection on a saucer. A couple of digestives, a KitKat, custard creams.

Their silence seemed almost remorseful. Or were they still two kids playing a game?

Couldn't sleep, she said when she finally met his eye.

He wasn't sure if it was a statement or a question. Over his shoulder, the tap dripped. There were plates in the sink. Pans. Forks and spoons. A wad of papers pinned to a cork board on the wall. The radio played the pips before the news.

He blew on his tea, felt the steam fog against his nose. Took the KitKat and snapped it. He pushed the remaining finger across the table. Siwan looked at it but didn't move.

How's your dad? Mack tried. I haven't asked about him.

She brought her mug to her face, eyes not moving from his.

The tap was still dripping. He got up to tighten it. If he was moving, he thought, his presence would not weigh so heavy. He could feel the gloves in the pocket of his coat. A nebulous grease was suspended through the bowl in the sink.

This probably needs a new washer, he said, examining the tap from various angles. Pretending he knew what he meant.

He crouched to look in a cupboard. Could feel her watching him.

My dad's probably got a spare, he said, turning around.

She studied him, mug still close to her face. A crinkle around her eyes that might have been confusion. It was clear to him now that he should not have been in her house. They had rules to follow. What on earth was he doing?

He leaned against the counter. Smelled the loam of the plants at his back. The fridge was opposite, a wheezing contraption decorated with magnets. Souvenirs arranged north to south. Welcome to Vancouver. Seattle. Portland. Salem, Oregon. Eugene. A Polaroid photograph was pinned between them. A young woman posing beneath a canopy of trees.

He couldn't help but step closer. Was struck again by just how much Siwan looked like her mother.

He glanced back to the table, remembering she was watching.

Denzil's dropping the van off this morning, he said, trying to sound calm. I was just killing time, thought I'd call in.

She ignored him as though he hadn't spoken. Her eyes unmoving, observing him.

The radio was on the traffic now. A head-on collision. Jams on A roads.

I'm sorry, he said, turning towards the window. I shouldn't have come.

Yeah, she agreed. You shouldn't have.

He fingered the key in his pocket, its fresh-cut notches and grooves. He watched the gulls outside and the gulls looked back, eyes like painted coins.

I just wanted to . . . I don't know. I thought you might . . .

He turned to see her tuck her hair behind her ears and place her feet up on the chair. Her eyes were still pinned on him. She hugged her knees to her chest.

Mack, she said. Stop.

But what if we need to talk? he asked, returning to the table. What if—

We need to be careful, she said. Calm, deliberate, organised. You need to do exactly what I say, when I say it, or else do nothing at all.

She spoke with an even tone. A dismayed parent determined to hold her nerve before a stubborn child. Her manner embarrassed him, and with embarrassment came a sense of injustice. He did not like to be made to feel unserious. Couldn't help but raise his voice.

It was you who came to me at the seminary, he reminded her. If you don't want my help, I'll go.

They eyed one another. Mack made to speak again, but something stirred above their heads. A pitch, a crick, the slow track of what might have been footfall. He glanced towards the ceiling. She glowered at him, then stared down at the tabletop as though chastised. The sound lasted thirty seconds or thirty minutes. Then a different sound. A sluggish shuffle approaching down the hall.

He rapped on the door with a knuckle as he came in.

A guest? asked a voice with genuine affection.

Siwan's father shambled closer to see Mack better. He looked older than Mack expected. A man grey and dried out. Something washed up on the shoreline. He had also worked in the steelworks once upon a time. Something research-based. Science. Chemistry. Doc, the men had called him, on account of the title before his name. Mack knew him only as the smartest man in church, a husband older than his wife. A tall man and awkward with it. Always slightly hunched as if regretting the space he occupied.

Doc had rarely drunk with the other men, and when he did, he stayed only for a pint.

This is Cormac, Siwan said, neck reddening as she rose from her seat. Clara O'Brien's son. You remember Clara?

Mack looked into his mug. I was in the area, he said. Just passing by.

Siwan's father made to sit, waving his daughter off as she tried to help him move the chair.

I get there eventually, he said, smiling towards Mack. Just don't expect me to rush.

The trio sat at the table. Red crept higher towards Siwan's cheeks. She kept tucking her hair behind her ears. They picked up their mugs again, quiet but for the radio. The weather. The local news.

Your mother makes a fine casserole, if I remember right?

He looked at Mack like he expected an answer. Mack didn't deny the claim, but had no idea why this man would make it.

She was one of the only people who visited, Siwan's father

continued. After everything that happened. We didn't forget it.

He ran his palm over the table. A slow gesture, absentminded, like he was reminding himself of where he was.

A good Samaritan, your mother. Always thinking of others. My wife, she might have rubbed people up the wrong way, but Clara didn't let that—

Dad, Siwan interrupted. You've got your jumper on back to front.

He looked down at himself. Chin to his chest, knowing where to look but not what he was expected to find there.

Put your hands in the sky, Siwan ordered, rising from her seat. Her father did as he was told.

She pulled on one sleeve then the other, holding his shirt by the belly so it didn't untuck from his joggers. Once both arms were free, she told him to lower them and rotated the sweatshirt around by the shoulders. Not the gentlest action but not intended as such. The practical efficiency of a hand learning the necessity of things.

Mack felt he had trespassed on something. The shame was overwhelming.

Don't let us keep you, Cormac, Siwan said as though reading his mood. I know you have places to be.

Mack rose to his feet, but her father dismissed the idea.

So soon? He'll have another biscuit at least?

Mack grinned as he sat back down and examined the plate before him. Siwan wouldn't meet his eye. He selected a custard cream only to find it had gone soft. If he asked about her mother now, he thought, he'd find out everything he'd ever wondered. But instead he put the biscuit in his mouth and forced himself to chew.

Oh, Siwan said. He listens to you.

Both men looked at each other and exchanged half-smiles. She sat back down and hugged her legs again. When Mack took up his mug, he found it empty. He brought the cup to his mouth and pretended to drink anyway.

Could I use the bathroom? he asked carefully.

Siwan looked at him, but her father intervened.

Upstairs, he said. Last door at the end of the corridor. You can't miss it.

He felt he was on a timer and hurried to maintain his innocence. A heightened attention on his movements. The glare of her eyes through the wall. The door to the front room had a latch but no handle, just a square hole in the backplate where a handle might go. He pushed the panel with a fist and found it steadfast. He tested it with his shoulder, though the door resisted as stubborn and blank as that of a confessional. When he looked down, he noticed marks on the carpet. A parallel track of grooves dug into the weave. A thin, spotted trail of white dust.

He did not linger. Ascending the stairs, he crossed the landing and found Siwan's bedroom door open. The air musty. Mammalian. The bed unmade. A framed picture of her mother on the table beside it. A woman younger than Siwan was now, again in an old-growth forest. Hair braided, teeth showing, her T-shirt sleeveless and reading: *What Would Jesus Do?*

In the bathroom, he found a large shower cubicle, three glass walls housing various pulleys and handles and a squat seat in the centre, sturdy on four legs. He lifted the lid of the toilet and unzipped himself. Tried to piss but couldn't. His coat was weighed down by the gloves on one side. The key was in the other pocket. With both hands on the edge of the sink, he studied his face in the mirror. He was pale, he thought. Exhausted. He flushed the cistern. He waited. He soaped his hands, ran the tap, and washed them until the water became almost too hot to bear.

She was waiting for him in the hall when he descended the stairs, back pressed tight against the door of the front room. Take care, she said, showing him out and standing aside so he might exit. The uncanny quiet of the morning struck him again. He put his hand in his pocket.

Siwan, he said, I only came to give you . . .

He hesitated as his fingers found the key. The cold cut of its teeth sharp against his skin.

You know what, never mind. I really should be going.

XI

Mack had arranged to meet Denzil in the back lane so they could put the van straight into the garage. It would be more secure that way, he told him. Less likely to have its windows put in. There was a sticker on the back doors declaring that no tools were left inside overnight, but such things depended on the mood of the perpetrator. How brazen they might be. How desperate.

Denzil beeped the horn when he saw him. They shook hands through the open window. I'll reverse it in, he said. Make it easier to get out. He knew Mack didn't drive but didn't say anything about that. Lights came on when he started going backwards. Mack used his arms to guide him in.

He locked the door behind them and led the way through the garden. Denzil had asked a mate to follow behind and pick him up.

How long do you reckon you'll need it? he asked, bending on the patio to remove his boots before entering the house.

Not long, Mack said. I can't imagine it taking more than a few days.

Denzil nodded slowly, picking at his laces.

Why's that? Mack asked.

Ah, no real reason. It's just if you were done by this evening, I'd come back and pick it up.

I thought we agreed the whole weekend?

Yeah, I know that, but—

If you need the van, just say.

Nah, don't worry, forget about it.

Denzil seemed overly occupied with his boots. Mack felt a lick of alarm.

What's the matter, Denz?

Nothing's the matter. It's just . . .

Just what?

Denzil finally removed his boots and straightened.

Mack, he said, I've got a confession to make.

They made eye contact then. Mack felt his heart flip in his chest. The last twitch of a landed fish on the wet deck of a boat. He thought of the previous evening. Dai in his dirty works clothes.

I don't want to do it, believe me.

Denzil's guilt registered as a lame smile.

They're offering triple time.

You can't.

I can. *We* can even, if you—

No, Mack asserted. You don't understand. It doesn't matter how much money they're offering. You can't go in over the weekend. The works have to be empty.

But that's where you're wrong see? Denzil argued. It *does* matter how much money they're offering. I'm fucking broke, mun, and nothing's getting any cheaper. I've got to think about my old man too. Since his pension went up in smoke he's hardly bringing anything in. He'd be on the street if it wasn't for me.

Mack didn't know what to say. Needed time to think. Turned to let them into the house but could hardly get the key in the door.

There's no picket line as such, Denzil reassured him. You won't see anyone. When you stop and think about it, we're not doing anything wrong, are we? Just making sure everything's sound during the walkout. Looking after the place while they're gone.

The key went in but jammed a little. It had always been a sticky lock. The trick was to lift and twist. Inside, they stood in the hall, unwilling to disturb the empty rooms, awkward in close proximity. Mack had intended to make them a cuppa but suddenly felt unwilling to offer anything.

If you need the van, he asked, why even come today?

Denzil's eyes dropped to the floor, acting as though mesmerised by the carpet.

Well, he said, the thing is . . . I've come up with a bit of a plan.

The men would never forgive him if they found out. And some of them lads were busy. The sort who slept with one eye open in the hope of catching a mate fall short. Mack knew the ones he was on about. The men with two-up, two-downs in Margam village, two cars on the drive, drank up the golf club no matter how often they spoke of solidarity. The sort of men you couldn't trust.

It occurred to me in the middle of the night, Denzil said. I get one of the boys to come and fetch me now. We make a big deal about you having the van as we're not going to need it. Everyone's happy then. They're convinced we're both on board, you get the van in the day to do whatever you need. I'll just swing by before the shift to pick it up, drop it off again when I'm done.

He looked up at Mack suddenly, boots in hands, shame-faced and appealing.

It would only be you who'd ever know, he said. I thought I'd be able to trust you with a secret?

The hall seemed claustrophobic, so they waited on the doorstep. Denzil stooped to put his boots back on by the gate. He made two loops with his laces before tying them. The old bunny-ears method. He flinched at every passing car. Mack was filled with a desire to help but knew he couldn't. He kept opening his mouth to dissuade his friend, but didn't know what words might do it.

Ah, here he comes, Denzil said, standing as a car pulled into the street. They watched it approach together. A wine-red Mondeo. The window slowly wound down.

There he is, look, Dai said, squinting with one elbow out. Our holy monk.

Our *priest*, Denzil corrected.

I'm not a priest, Mack said.

They stood there looking at one another. The exhaust was almost blue. Denzil went around to the passenger's side but hesitated before opening the door. He looked at Mack over the top of the car.

You getting in or what? Dai asked, eyes still on Mack. Up town, we're going. All the boys are there. Was just talking to your old man.

Mack hesitated, but didn't see he had a choice. All right,

he said eventually, coming down the path and opening the car door.

The interior smelled like wet shoes. A box of fishing tackle on the back seat. A book about calming the mind. The driver's headrest had a chunk missing from the foam as though someone had taken a bite out of it. Dai's seat was pushed back tight against Mack's knees. When Dai put the hand-brake down, he accelerated away from the kerb then braked hard like he was trying to shake something from the roof.

Got your belt on, butt? he called into the mirror. Not an instruction but an observation. An expression of surprise. Dai never put his belt on in the car. Didn't like the way it felt around his neck.

The main road was even busier than the previous evening. The pavements full of people too. A flock headed towards the centre of town, eager to see the next part of the Passion. Word was spreading. They spoke of it on the news. Mack imagined their Messiah sat somewhere nearby, locked in character, deep in contemplation for what came next. There'd be a trial, the people would be consulted, but the familiar arc of the narrative would remain. A crowd would gather, their Saviour's fate decided. Everyone knew how the story had to end.

What's the matter with you? Dai asked suddenly.

With me? Denzil answered.

With Niblo by here. Swear we was driving to his trial.

Both men turned to look at Mack in the back seat. He dug his hands into his pockets.

His gran and grampa fucking passed away, mun, Denzil said. I told you that. That's what we're doing here. He's bor-rowing the work van to clear the house.

Dai's eyes in the mirror again. Mack met his gaze and held it.

You know, Denzil added. 'Cos I won't be needing it, will I?

They left the car by the old police station and walked the rest of the way. Joined the crowds already heading down Station Road. An entire populace slouching towards Bethany Square. A scaffold stage had been erected in front of the civic centre. A sound system and two LED screens. It wasn't clear if the riot police were uniformed officers or actors in costume. At least half of the audience were strangers. Tourists descended from elsewhere. Various pedlars moved among them, hawking slapdash souvenirs priced like relics of the saintly dead. The union men had formed another satellite picket line near the entrance to the shopping centre. A long banner strung up on the wall there. *Save Our Steel*. *SOS*.

They arrived in time to hear the Saviour suffer under Pontius Pilate. The latter in an unconvincing Roman uniform. A red curtain wrapped around his shoulders as a cloak. Chest plate made metallic with rolls of tin foil. Behind them hung the printed backdrop of an old stone temple. When the sheet rippled in the breeze, the corners lifted to show its blank reverse.

Are you the king of this town? Pilate wanted to know. The question whistled through the sound system. An accusation the Saviour neither denied nor confirmed. He'd come only to reveal the truth, he explained. If he was a king, it was them who said it.

The microphone thudded with feedback. The backdrop snapped in the wind. When the trial ended, Pilate washed his hands and said he could find no fault with the man, but his fate was up to them.

The crowd cheered and called out in unison.

Crucify him, they demanded. Crucify him.

They met the others in the pub after the performance. Station Road was rammed, so the men settled on the Tavern in Forge Road. Maggie Mays they used to call it. More of a members-only place now but happy to make the exception. Net curtains in the windows, plastic flowers on the sills. A barometer on the wall behind the bar with an erratic needle. No food was served in the Tavern no matter what the sign outside suggested. A chalkboard listed the specials of the day: car bomb, snakebite, diesel.

They usually only let you in here if you show your giro card on the door, Dai said out the side of his mouth. They had to stoop to enter. It was busy inside. The room long and narrow but wider at each end. A pub in the shape of a femur.

Then again, he said, suppose we are out of work now.

The apostles hollered when they saw Mack. Shook his hand and demanded to know where he'd been hiding. He'd missed the best part of the previous night. Hadn't followed the actor to the sunken gardens on the beachfront, waited there before an audience of hundreds as the dark found its depth and the dew came down like frost. Hadn't heard the footfall of gathering soldiers or seen the wink of their lanterns in the night. The crowd had objected when the guards seized their Saviour. Protested angrily from behind a rope line as soldiers bound his feet and hands. Because it wasn't easy to watch such a thing, the men said, pretend or otherwise. They'd all felt an urge to fight.

Call yourself a disciple, Bryn said, finger poking at Mack's chest. Missing something like that.

I had things to do.

Things more important than this?

Grinning, Bryn poked his chest again. Mack slapped his hand away.

Would you give me a break for a second? Jesus fucking Christ.

The group fell quiet with the outburst. He hadn't intended to shout. Bryn peered back, wounded. Denzil filled the space.

His gran and grampa passed away, he said. He's borrowing the work van to clear the house. Barely been on strike twenty-four hours and he's already grafting. He's a fucking good egg, Cormac. Leave him alone.

Denzil put his arm around Mack's shoulders. A gesture surprisingly touching in spite of everything. The men, softening at the news, shot embarrassed glances at Jackie. Bryn put his palms in the air in defence.

We're only pulling his leg, son, don't worry. We all know the boy's a little saint.

There were buckets on the door for the strike fund. Every man got a pint on the house. The woman behind the bar pulled them without much attention. Filled oversized trays to be passed through the crowd. Mack was handed a drink. The last thing he felt like, but what choice did he have?

A toast, Bryn shouted, raising a cheer from the men. To the death of the Saviour. To rising again.

To living forever, someone added.

They drank. Mack took a long pull and found the beer yeasty on his tongue, like the barrel needed changing.

Someone behind him was saying net zero would soon be a thing of the past. Technology was the future, they said. Carbon capture. Leave it to the nerds. Mack nodded at Denzil in thanks and Denzil clinked his glass against his before taking another mouthful. When he came up for air, he looked like he was about to say something, but drank again instead. He was two thirds through his pint already.

The men left them after the toast to push deeper into the room, though Mack's father lingered.

Moving, weren't it? he said, gesturing towards the door with his chin.

What was? Mack asked.

The performance this morning. The trial.

He thought back to Pontius Pilate and his curtain. The background printed in two dimensions.

Yeah, he said. It was good.

Jackie studied the pair of them with a smile on his face. It occurred to Mack that his father was well beyond his first drink. Jackie put an arm around their shoulders, quiet of voice, eyes as wet and straining as the wall of a dam. I can't tell you, he said, how much I appreciate it. He spoke as though they'd already cleared the house. As though Denzil had carried half the load. He said the works were lucky to have boys like them. Fuck, the luck was the entire town's. Because that's what it came down to in the end. Mates looking after one another. Helping each other out. There was a lot of shit in the world, but stuff like this warmed his heart. It was the whole point of the strike, wasn't it, when you really stopped to think? The next generation. Honest grafters. Good men needed a proper place to work.

All drinks are on me, Mack's father declared, clapping

them on the back as he set off towards his pals. Chuck it on the tab. Order anything you want.

When Mack looked at Denzil, it seemed he was about to cry. He leaned close to Mack and told him to forget everything he'd said earlier. His head had been a mess. He hadn't been thinking. He was no scab and never fucking would be. He was proud of where he came from. Took pride in what he did.

He nodded slowly along with his own words, hoping to shake the sentiment further into his head. He thanked Mack, apologised, then dug deep into his pocket and retrieved the keys for the van. Remember the back doors can stick, he said as he squeezed them tight in Mack's hand. Don't be afraid to give it some welly.

He thanked Mack again, then was back in his pocket, frisking for his fags. Gonna get some air, he said quietly.

Mack watched his friend fight towards the exit. Everyone seemed to be shouting in the Tavern. Laughing. Braying. He considered following Denzil and slipping away, but on looking up he saw a familiar face coming in. The journalist removing her coat at the door.

He averted his eyes, but it was already too late.

Cormac? she said. It's Cormac, isn't it?

I'm sorry, I haven't got time for this. I was just leaving.

But we haven't had a chance to talk properly yet.

The woman looked flushed in the face, like she had rushed from some place else. She reached out and touched his shoulder gently.

I know I've been pestering you, she said. But it doesn't have to be like that. Why don't we just grab that coffee when all this is over? I'm sticking around for a few days into next week, if you happen to have any time off?

There was a new shyness to her face. A sense of hopeful vulnerability.

But he hasn't got time, a voice echoed. Dai suddenly behind Mack. Rank breath in his ear. Fingers at the back of his neck like a pincer. We was just going to the toilet, wasn't we, son? Dai grinned towards the woman. And I'm sorry to say, we're desperate.

He kept his hold of Mack as he steered him towards to the bathroom.

You do need a piss, don't you, boy? he asked, though it wasn't much of a question. Come on in here with me.

The bathroom was small but empty. A single cubicle and a metal trough on the wall. Dai gestured to the urinal. Go on then, he said, reaching to unzip himself. Mack didn't need to go, but thought it easier to play along. He stood at one end, maximising the distance between them. There was chewing gum in the trough. A tangle of hair in the trap of the plug. Dai hawked and spat, then proceeded to piss like a racehorse. Mack tried to clear his mind as the frothy tide ran down the gutter towards him.

There was a radiator at his hip, paint bubbled and rusting from the splashback. He could feel heat against his leg. The radiator was on.

You didn't see anyone last night, did you?

Last night? Mack asked.

No fellers on their way home from work, anything like that?

Mack concentrated on the wall ahead of him. Breeze block painted white. A bristle from the brush caught in the emulsion.

What are you asking? If I saw any scabs?

Dai finished and shook himself. Arched his back to zip his fly.

Well? he asked eventually. Did you?

They washed their hands together, side by side at the pair of sinks. There was a soap dispenser on the wall but nothing inside it. A bar of Imperial Leather rubbed yellow and tough as unbleached wax. Dai rolled his sleeves up his forearms like a doctor and began to scrub. Four fingers, a thumb, a practised method. There were still flecks of white paint on his arms.

I can walk out right this minute and tell your old man about the girl you're seeing, he said. I can tell him where you go to fuck her. And I can say her name, which is where things might get interesting.

Mack held the man's eye in the mirror. The water ran cold on his hands.

Not that I want to, Dai continued. Never like to embarrass anyone, me. But loose lips sink ships, or however the fucking saying goes.

He flicked his hands and tore himself a paper towel. Patted them dry carefully, eyes back in the mirror again.

One thing I did wonder, he said, is what you talk about on your little rendezvous? What secrets does she share?

Mack took a paper towel too. Dai was stood between him and the door.

You can tell me, butt. Pals we are. Colleagues.

David, Mack said, voice quiet and even. Just don't go in over the weekend, all right? Or else don't say I didn't warn you.

Dai grinned, lips as tight as the skin of a balloon.

And that's a threat, issit?

He took a step closer, eyes still in the mirror. Mack

continued to dry his hands. He scrunched up the paper and aimed for the bin, but Dai got in the way.

At least tell me if she's a decent screw, he said, squaring his shoulders. She any good or what? All things aside, I'd have liked a go on her mother.

Mack tried to push past, but Dai lunged. His face big all of a sudden, forehead against Mack's, hands grasping at the breast of his jacket. They grappled, a strange dance across the lino, no sound but for the soles of their shoes. One led, the other followed. Momentum shifted, they pushed and pulled. Mack felt the edge of the sink against the bone in his hip, felt the wall at his back, the radiator's heat. Dai breathed flat with the exertion. They twisted one way, the other. Dai seemed to want to hit Mack's head against something. Anything hard. The mirror, the wall. Wanted to take his skull in his hands and squeeze. Crack him in two like an egg.

Mack had no plan or idea of how to end it. Knew only he had to stay on his feet.

Dai's fingers groped higher. Mack's Adam's apple, the hollow beneath his chin. Mack strained his neck to get away, rolled his eyes up in his head as though not to see was to escape.

They twisted again. Dai grunted. Suddenly a thumb hooked in Mack's mouth. Large and hard and salted, an unexpected thing still moving, probing blind. The surprise of it closed his throat and he bit down without thinking. Dai retracted his hand but didn't scream. He didn't make a sound.

The tension slackened. Panic hit Mack like lightning. He saw himself as though from above. With the shock came a surge in his limbs as if a sluice had been opened. The light had a flicker to it. It seemed suddenly bright.

Dai instinctively cradled his thumb. Mack did not miss his chance. Gripping Dai beneath the arms, he drove him into the wall of the cubicle. The bones in his elbows vibrated with the force of it. He drew Dai's body close and slammed him again. The third blow took the wind from his lungs. The wall of the cubicle rattled hollow like the plywood floor at a wrestling event.

Dai fell forward. Mack struggled to hold him up. Was about to hit him again when the door banged open and a stranger came in. A man unaware, whistling a tune he only half remembered, already at the zip of his slacks. Mack let go and Dai staggered forward. A serpent hiss filled the room as the urinal purged itself.

Back in the bar, the journalist was waiting expectantly, but he shoved towards the exit. The scratches at his neck burned as though aflame. People complained in his wake but he did not stop to apologise. When he reached the pavement, he spat on the ground and saw blood.

XII

In his room, he retrieved the box of his belongings from beneath his bed and put it up the attic. He stripped the linen from the mattress and stood on a chair to unhook the curtains from the pole. He took the shade from the lamp, the plugs from the wall. Worked his fingers beneath the edge of the carpet. He gripped the fabric. Pulled.

He changed into his trousers and sweater then put on his coat again. The work gloves were still in the pocket. The duplicate key and its newly cut blade. He removed the gloves and put them in the drawer of his desk then made his way across the landing. He found his mother's room dim, a shape beneath the blankets. A tepid light canted through the blinds.

I'll explain to the canon, he called from the door. He'll understand why you have to miss the service.

Oh, his mother said, propping herself up on her pillow. I won't miss it. I'll watch it on the screen.

She spoke so softly, Mack had to step closer.

The what?

The screen, his mother repeated, finger extended towards the empty wall at the foot of the bed.

He followed her hand but saw nothing. Felt unease tighten like a fist at his throat. Mam, he started, leaning closer, do you see strange things when you have a migraine? Did you see it yesterday, at—

He stopped, unable to bring himself to finish the question. He wasn't sure if he wanted an answer, or if it would only make things worse. Instead, he brought a hand to his mother's brow and found her fevered to the touch. Announced he was ringing the doctor only for her to cut him off.

I'm fine, she said. Everything's fine. You go and do what you need to do.

He hesitated before submitting to her will. Bent to kiss her head, demanded she drink more water. He pulled the door shut quietly behind him and descended the stairs to put on his shoes in the hall. There was a chill on the air, he fancied, or was he fevered himself? He pulled his coat tighter around his shoulders, then headed out onto the street.

Traffic queued to get closer to the town centre. A race to beat the afternoon's road closures. Those who had decided to walk to the next scene lined the pavements on each side. Babies pushed in prams, kids carried on shoulders. Entire families following the directions set out in the programme. Spectators in such number they became a spectacle themselves.

Mack fought against the tide towards the church. Found the car park empty. The doors unlocked but mass books still stacked in the vestibule. No one waited in the pews. Hesitating at the back of the nave, he removed his coat and folded it over his arm. The altar was still bare from the previous evening. Scoured down to its angles and lines. A votive stand was set against the back wall and he considered lighting a candle, but just who to pray for he couldn't quite decide.

He checked his watch. Felt exposed in the empty church. The sole focus of God's eye. He took his missal from his pocket. Stopped to dip his hand in the font and crossed himself before walking down the centre aisle. At the altar, he bowed his head and genuflected, then took a seat in the fifth row.

The place the O'Briens had always sat. He put the kneeler down.

With his elbows resting on the back of the bench in front, he crossed himself again and closed his eyes. Beyond the stillness of the room blared impatient traffic, the gathering crowd, a whine of distant sirens. He might have been suspended within a glass box. A place away from the world.

Dear Lord, he started in his head, though the prayer refused to take.

Quiet like the eye of a storm. The beginning of an end. He felt a twitch in his eyelid and blinked against it. An errant trigger, a bug trapped beneath skin. He knelt with his hands clasped before his face and tried to focus on his breathing. The taste of blood still in his mouth. He wanted to pray but the words kept sliding from his head.

The sirens outside grew numerous. Expanding and contracting as they passed.

Mack became aware of another sound. An animated whisper from another room. The murmured hum of a lowered voice in reply. A conversation, it seemed, was taking place within the sacristy.

Rising to his feet, he stumbled over the kneeler and into the aisle, pausing only at the altar to bow. He stood before the vestry and put his ear to the door, sensing movement within.

Two distinct voices. Agitation in their tone.

Canon? he called softly as he pushed open the door.

They were deep in conversation, though stopped abruptly at the sight of him. The canon in a simple cassock. Siwan in her coat and jeans. The pair of them looking back, dumbfounded by his sudden appearance. He felt like an intruder. Wished he'd never left his seat.

Is there no service today? he asked awkwardly, wishing only to turn and leave. Not a soul has shown up.

He expected the old man to push past and confirm the sorry truth for himself, but Canon Sylvester merely frowned.

But they have, he said, ushering Siwan out of the sacristy. I count two souls before me now.

Siwan followed when Mack returned to his seat. She knelt and closed her eyes. Canon Sylvester emerged a few minutes later. Fully dressed now, his chasuble a ruby red. Mack watched as he stepped into the adjoining chapel, genuflected before the tabernacle there, then let himself outside through the side door. He followed the red smudge through the stained glass. Around the flank of the church and in through the main entrance. Mack and Siwan stood as he re-entered, a small cushion in his grasp, his procession lonely and jaded and silent save for his heavy breathing. At the altar, he got to his knees and laid the cushion before himself. He placed his head upon it and lay prostrate upon the ground.

His trouser legs rode up a little. Showed skin between sock and hem. When he got to his feet, he stood before them with his hands extended, palms raised, and said:

Let us pray.

They conducted mass in the usual order. First reading, second reading, the Passion of our Lord according to John. The solemn intercessions with their kneeling silent prayer. Prayers for the Pope, for catechumens, for the Jewish people and those who did not believe. The scant attendance charged the service with a peculiar energy. A clandestine secret shared in quiet. The altar just a slab of stone before them. A priest and his two recusants.

Later, the canon disappeared into the sacristy and returned with a large wooden crucifix. The one that usually hung from chains behind the altar.

Cormac, he asked, a hand?

Together they stood at the foot of the altar and held the cross for adoration. The voices outside grew louder, the rumble of a gathering tempest. Siwan approached, genuflected, then bent towards the feet of Christ, reaching with her hand to steady herself. She kissed the carving upon His feet and straightened again. The canon took a handkerchief from within his vestments and wiped the kiss away.

Mack swapped places with Siwan so he might perform the action too. He crept towards the cross and bent to kiss the figure. He felt the nail through Christ's feet knock against his teeth.

She wiped her feet on the mat before going into the house. Followed him into the rooms one by one, an impromptu tour of what had once been. His grandmother's kitchen. His grandfather's favourite chair. The framed papal blessing on the wall, congratulations for a milestone wedding anniversary. She did not ask what he was doing and he did not explain it. He showed her the bathroom, the bedrooms, the cupboard beneath the stairs. He knew only that he wanted her to see.

The stillness was dizzying against the motion of the day. The sense of stepping from a boat to the harbour wall. The only quiet he could compare it to was the year a sickness descended on the seminary. A flu of some kind that struck the men in quick succession. You could almost watch it go down the corridor. A sore throat, a growing sense of heat, an ache in the marrow of the bones. Fever enough to spin the heads on their shoulders, have them seeing the faces of angels and saints on the walls. An eeriness came over the place. A quiet held so fast it seemed like a queer competition. Who could remain silent through the worst of it? Who might still every splutter and cough? By the end of the first week, Mack could imagine the place no different. As though an empty room was the proper state of things. Silence the first and the last.

Here, he said, reaching into his pocket. He'd put the keys to the garage and the van on the same ring.

Outside, he removed the padlock from the garage door and let Siwan go in first. She squeezed around the side of the van to examine the contents therein. Aerosols and acetone. Paint thinner. Gasoline. She could only open the door of the van a crack. Had to flatten herself and shimmy in. Her in the driving seat, him the passenger. All sorts of junk littering the dashboard. Gum wrappers, rolls of tape, the accumulated detritus of men at work. She placed her hands on the steering wheel. Wiggled the gearstick. Felt the handbrake. Flipped down the visor and met her own face. When she took hold of the handbrake again, she released it. Mack gripped his seat, caught unaware. He felt that he was falling, and then she pulled it back up.

The air was heavy in the garage, so dark it might have been night. There was a calendar on the wall but he couldn't read the year of it. Tins of shoe polish, Brasso, wood treatment, white grease. She sat with her hands on the wheel, pretended she was driving. Moved her feet over the pedals, her hair out of her face. There was a cassette player in the console between them. When he opened the glovebox, he saw the ring of Denzil's work keys.

What were you discussing with the canon? he asked.

A private matter.

I didn't know you were close.

Siwan didn't answer. She gripped the wheel so tight it took the blood from her knuckles.

So, she asked eventually, the men don't go back until after the resurrection?

He still had the padlock from the door in his hand, the shackle wet with lubricant. Her voice made him jump a little. He heard the sigh of his seat.

Tell me, Mack, she demanded. At daybreak on Sunday morning, will the works still be empty?

On the way back, they found the road closed and full of people heading to the crucifixion. Had little choice but to join the crowd. The spectators and hecklers, the singers and revellers, the bewailers and denigrators and ridiculers and slanderers. The giddy and the righteous. The lamenting and the damned. The people who sang and swore and danced around. Carried banners in the Saviour's name and against his name, carried family trinkets and treasured heirlooms and framed photographs of relatives long deceased. People who bore these most precious objects close to their chests so they might prove who they were or what they'd once been. Characters in an old story slanting deathwards. The Saviour's Golgotha would be the roundabout before the blast furnaces. The drummers called them in.

Another scaffold had been erected. Giant screens stood blank. The police had long since abandoned any hope of control and the crowd pressed tight around the scene. People expectant, excited, stamping their feet. A population turned outward, awaiting their Saviour. The mood was jubilant.

The union men had brought their banner and fixed it to the stage. A mural had been designed, a blue-sky vision of the works expanded. The future they believed they deserved. The real blasts stood motionless behind, blind to the un-folding event. Two colossal figures primitive and looming yet sorrowful in the moment. Lost without their usual hiss and smoke and winking orange heat.

Together Mack and Siwan climbed down the verge and over the crash barrier. The wind was damp and cool. A woman in front fell and Siwan stopped to help her up, only to stumble herself as the crowd spilled down the bank. Mack lost her for a second in the turmoil. Someone walked into the back of him. The drum felt like a second heart in his chest.

The crowd gasped when the Saviour stepped onto the verge, flanked by Roman soldiers. Thorns upon his head and cross upon his back. His face bloodied and his robes bloodied too but still shining white before them. The crowd parted for the procession to pass. People reached to touch the hem of his sleeves.

Night was beginning to fall. The beat of the drum was unerring. Mack couldn't take a step, so tight was the crowd. He felt the breath of them, the smell, the energy. He could see Siwan but not reach her. He used his arms to hold himself upright.

The Saviour made his way towards the scaffold, bent nearly in half. Now that he was closer, Mack saw the blood was not quite convincing. A little too luminous. Lacking the shadow and rust. Near the front, he saw his father and the rest of the apostles clearing the path to the gibbet. Hand-to-hand combat to prepare the way of their Lord. All of a sudden, Mack dropped his elbows and ceased struggling against the people around him. The whole thing abruptly ridiculous. The crowd contracted and convulsed.

The screens flashed and came to life. The Messiah's face in close-up. A head cast colossal, blinking in delirium. A low moan as the scene descended into farce.

Mack felt a hand in his. A warmth. He grasped at it. Squeezed tight.

The hammer started then, a steady rhythm. The actor wailed and the mallet kept going. The audience clapped along in time. Someone in the crowd mimicked the screaming to shushes and titters of laugher. The actor fell quiet and the silence of the works asserted itself. All the while, the blasts stood behind like penitent thieves awaiting their partner in execution. The rest of the plant still enough to be dead already, splayed beneath a looming sky.

Once it was done, the men gathered with ropes and pulleys. A voice over a Tannoy announced a countdown from ten.

Nine.

Eight.

Let's go, Siwan said, back already turned on the spectacle. I think we've seen enough.

They were at the verge again when the cheer went up. Could not help but turn to look. The cross erect and the actor upon it, half-naked and smeared with blood. The crowd fell dumb before the sight. The ribs, the thighs, the cries of agony. And when the Saviour called out to his father, not even the works could muster a response. A mimed last breath and it was finished. He let his head hang low.

XIII

The liturgical ordo spun much like the earth itself. Advent, Christmas, Ordinary Time. Lent, Easter, Pentecost, Ordinary Time again. The lectionary on a recurrent pattern. Two cycles of readings for weekdays, three for Sundays. Cycle I and Cycle II. Years A, B and C.

Little could disrupt this repetition. Not the strangest shock or freak event. When a seminarian named Nigel attempted to hang himself with a belt in his dormitory, barely a service was missed. They got him down before his last breath, one brother lifting his legs as the other ran for a knife. Nigel said it felt like his eyes would pop out of his head, but his vision persisted long enough to see it.

Please believe me when I tell you, he said. I saw the awesome light.

They practised the liturgy and sacraments like a band in rehearsal. Echoed the prayer of absolution back and forth across the hall. A handbook was given out. A text they were to study. Their script to follow. The updated Roman Rite.

They learned the proper actions of the torchbearer. The

thurifer. The master of ceremonies. The deacon, the sub-deacon, the assistant priest in surplice only.

They visited schools. They visited hospital wards. The burns unit. High dependency. They visited prisons where men sat in regulation clothing, chairs arranged in a half-moon. Men unrepentant and men converted, bright-eyed and born again. Men who might have been capable of great violence. You had no idea what they had done.

Only on going out into the world did his isolation reveal itself. He found he pined for the safety of the seminary even while begrudging the slow crush of its walls. One time a nurse in the burns unit stopped to ask him how he could bear devoting his life to one conviction. Then she wiped her glasses on her sleeve and took a gulp of coffee and started her rounds again.

Only things did begin to change. He barely noticed at first. A quickening step away from him in the corridor. A distracted glance beyond his shoulder in the middle of conversation. Nothing said directly. No confrontation, no criticism. Just a widening distance between him and his fellow seminarians, as though he was a temperamental mutt who might at any moment jump up and bite.

Excuses were made. Rotas altered. Whispers echoed in his wake. An ideologue, the rumours said. An activist. A man willing to place politics above dogma. He did his best to stay away, started to feel infectious. Was it really so bad, he asked himself, to put Christ's teaching first? But once an image was established, there was little hope of changing it. Unsure how to deal with his deepening isolation, he sank further into the solemn routine.

He turned to the Roman Rite. Studied the church and

its furniture, the vessels and the instruments, the common actions of the ceremonies.

On changing from sitting to kneeling, you stood then knelt, never slid directly to your knees. On genuflection, the hands were joined before the breast, the right knee touched the ground in the exact place the right foot would have been. On prostration, the action was followed by the left knee and a bow of the head.

A genuflection was made to a relic of the True Cross, should it be exposed. To the cross on Good Friday. To a bishop in his own diocese, a metropolitan in his province, a papal legate in the place of his legacy, a cardinal out of Rome.

The general rules for bowing were to keep the hands before the breast unless they were holding something. A medium bow to persons of higher rank. A low bow at the beginning and end of mass. The celebrant bowed lower to the cross than the congregation. The head alone was bowed to greet persons of equal or less dignity.

He learned the high mass and low mass. Sung mass of the simpler form and the more solemn form. Mass before a bishop, mass before a bishop not in his own parish. He learned the extreme unctions, the five absolutions, the vespers for the dead and the funeral of an infant.

He went to the chapel at night to practise. The early hours when everyone was asleep. Moved from the vestry down the aisle to the altar. Performed the rituals he'd learned in the dark. He was not afraid of getting caught, felt not the slightest bit sacrilegious, yet he lacked the nerve to speak aloud so mouthed the words instead.

When the rector's summons eventually came, he stopped to finish the tea he was drinking before going up. He knocked lightly on the office door and stood in the echoing corridor, waiting to be called.

The rector wore a short-sleeved shirt and a collar. A cross on a cord around his neck. Small bottles of holy water lined the front of his desk. Plastic representations of Mary the Mother, translucent white with a blue crown stopper. Trinkets collected from holy places. Retreats to Fatima and Lourdes. Mack could make out the waterline inside the figures. One appeared to have less than the others. The blessed evaporated into thin air.

He seemed to cut an isolated figure, that's what the rector said. They couldn't help but notice. His brothers were concerned.

The man spoke in a kindly voice. His smile was not without sympathy.

Don't take this the wrong way, he said, but I get the impression you chose to pursue the priesthood out of a desire to do good, rather than feeling a true calling.

Mack looked back at the man, dumbfounded. Listened as his fate was spelled out with euphemistic grace. When it was finished, he returned to his dorm and began to gather his belongings. Clothes, books, barely enough to fill a bag. There was nothing behind him and before him only a black wall. They were taking not only his vocation but his time, his structure and routine. And if not God Himself, then at least the formality of their bond. If doing good was not what was being asked of him, then what exactly did the Father want?

With his things packed, his room looked so empty he got them out again. He dropped to his knees, crossed himself and prayed.

He felt like an abandoned child. The black wall had never been so close to his face.

Lord, he asked, direct in his desperation. What am I to do?

The knock at the door came later, dragging him from a shallow sleep. He lay there in the wake of it, unsure he had the will to move.

Cormac, came the voice beyond the door. Spud and his unflagging wonderment. You've a visitor outside. She's waiting for you.

She asked if he was ready and he told her he was, then she asked again as though looking for a stronger reaction. The pair of them shoulder to shoulder, walking slowly on the side of the road. Heading back into town, away from the crucifixion. The streets empty, the traffic lights changing colour in aid of no one. Red, amber, green. A short pause, then red again. With the crowds behind them, the true quiet of the night revealed itself. When the lights changed, there was a second where there was no light at all.

Go home, she told him. I'll pick you up in an hour or two. She told him to wear something dark, but he was wearing black already.

There was no lamp shining in the house when he returned home. He lingered in the hall, listening for signs of life. His father must have remained out there with the other apostles, gazing up at their dead Messiah. His mother likely still sick and delirious, confined to the stale sheets of her bed. He crept up the stairs and across the landing. The bareness of his room surprised him. He switched the light on but turned it off again. Put Denzil's work keys in the drawer of his desk and changed his clothes in the dark. For a while he stood at the window, waiting for her lights to pull onto the street, but waiting so blatantly made him nervous so he descended the stairs instead. The house creaked, contracting in the night. The seconds passed sluggish on his watch. When Siwan came to the door, she did not knock. He saw the shape of her, a shadow pressed close to the glass.

Putting on his coat, he made to follow her to the van but remembered the gloves he'd bought. Siwan, he called, I've got something for you. Come in a minute.

She glared at him in the hall but said nothing. He took the stairs quicker this time, eager to retrieve her gift. The gloves seemed silly the moment he picked them up, but it was too late to backtrack. When he handed them to Siwan, she looked at him with something like pity.

Was it good?

A voice from the other side of the wall. They looked at one another, eyes wide. Siwan seemed to shrink.

Cormac? called the voice.

He stepped into the living room. His mother alone, a woman of solitude.

Cormac, is that you?

You scared me, Mam. I thought you were upstairs.

I've been sleeping all day, she said. I'm feeling better now.

He could see the shape of her but not the details. A dark mass on the settee.

That's good, he offered. You were out of it earlier.

She scoffed, never willing to endure the concern of her own child.

Did you go to the crucifixion? she asked. What was it like?

It was silly, Mack said quickly. Melodramatic.

His mother nodded as though in vindication. Shifted herself on the sofa in attempt to sit.

Have you been drinking? she asked. Where's your father?

Mack shrugged. I suppose he's still there, Mam. He won't be long, I'm sure.

His mother nodded again and swung her legs over the side of the settee. Waited a second for the blood to return to her head then reached a hand for the lamp. Only she hesitated at the switch, thinking better of it. Her eyes had long adjusted to the conditions. She saw far better than they understood.

Siwan, love, she said. You don't have to hide in the hallway. I just wish you'd said you were coming. I'd have run a brush through my hair at least.

Siwan stepped into the room with a glance at Mack. He could almost feel her ears burning.

I'm glad you're feeling better, she said gently.

Mack's mother, reaching for the lamp again, waved away the concern like she did not deserve it.

Well, Siwan said, we missed you at mass.

The light came on. Mack's mother appeared bemused.

You went to mass?

I told you that, Mack said. I came into your room.

His mother nodded as though the memory had returned, though the gesture lacked conviction.

I didn't know you'd started back to mass.

I came with you last night.

Yes, his mother said, but that was for my sake.

The room got lighter as the bulb warmed. Mack suddenly self-conscious in Siwan's company, familiar surroundings cast back to him anew. The pattern on the cushions and the curtains. The telephone table and widescreen TV. The fireplace with its faux-marble grate and black-and-white portraits framed along the mantel. Long-dead faces with half-remembered names.

They stood on the carpet, unsure how to extract themselves. The light strengthened. Clara cleared her throat.

Was there a tidy crowd? she asked. At mass, I mean.

Mack looked to Siwan.

Modest, she said. I think that's the word?

Mack's mother did not look surprised. The more the conversation dwindled, the worse Mack felt. Like there was something at his back, getting closer in the silence.

The kitchen is through there, he pointed, if you want a glass of water? Siwan looked confused, so he repeated himself. When she left the room, he found his mother studying him.

I knew, she said. I could tell yesterday evening.

Mack felt a tremor in his face. Tell what?

You weren't surprised to see her.

They heard the clink of glasses from the kitchen. A rush of water in the sink.

Do you know? Clara said, voice barely a whisper. I still pray for her mother, even now.

She made a series of statements as she drove, words even and rote, rehearsed to death in her head. She'd done all the reading, she said. The planning, the worrying over details. If anything seemed illogical or confusing it was designed to be that way. The time for thinking had long passed so he was not to ask questions. She'd tell him everything he needed to know.

If I ask you to do something, you do it, she said. If you don't want to do it, you go.

Mack watched the white lines of the road disappear between the wheels of the van.

All right, he said. But one small thing first. Why didn't you get Chris to help?

Chris? she asked.

Your boyfriend.

Oh, she said. Chris.

The road was still officially closed. They had the night to themselves.

Well? he pressed.

Well, what did I just say about questions?

The van went faster than he'd known. The suspension had a bounce to it. Their heads jounced in synchrony. Something slid around in the back as they turned a corner. She killed the headlights before turning onto her street and drove the rest of the way in the dark.

Outside, she pulled up and cut the engine but left her hands on the wheel.

My dad's at home.

Mack peered up at the house from the window.

So?

So we can't wake him up, all right?

Inside, she told him to wait a moment and disappeared upstairs. The door with no handle leered at him. He crept further down the hall to get away from it. At the entrance to the living room, he spied through the crack by the hinges. Saw the shape of the Doc asleep in his chair. An old man wearing a dressing gown and woolly slippers. Stockings to encourage the blood to his legs. The small table beside him bore dirty plates, an empty mug, a plastic case of coloured tablets partitioned by the days of the week. The television was set to coverage of the strike and the Passion. He wore a button on a string around his neck to be pressed in case of emergency.

When Siwan returned, she had a rag tied around her face and another in hand for him. An old T-shirt torn in half that she helped knot at the back of his neck. A swift pull, a pressure against the bridge of his nose. The fabric smelled like her.

She'd brought the handle for the door too. A knob with a metal spindle. She fed it through the hole.

The room had been stripped bare, covered in dust sheets and black bin liners and polythene wrap. The sacks Mack had helped load into the car were stacked against the far wall. More than he remembered. Three columns piled nearly as tall as his head. Plastic buckets and jugs and jam jars. A wooden trestle table holding a variety of tools. A hand saw, a Stanley knife, some kind of electric drill. Rolls of gaffer tape, superglue, assorted electronics. Chips and motherboards, a tangle of coloured wires. A smell on the air, chemical and cloying.

He felt dizzy on stepping through the door. There was something debased in the naked bulb, the creased sheeting, the rustle of the plastic on the walls. Something that belonged to murderers, guerrilla fighters, hostage-takers. Rudimentary and pragmatic. Siwan dug around, searching for an object among the clutter. A hurried action, almost panicked. The rag around her face kept slipping.

They'd take as many sacks as would fit in the back. There'd be no second trip.

Mack saw no reason to dally. Shouldered the first sack and made for the door. He put it in the van lengthways and returned for another. Siwan came out with him on the third run and rearranged everything.

He didn't ask questions, just moved. The same action repeated. Bend, lift, walk. Thirty-four steps from the room to the van, somehow thirty-three back again. He looked both ways down the street before stepping out the door. His nose began to run. The rag felt damp at his mouth. Every time he returned inside, the smell hit again. Something like sweat distilled, like a piss-soaked carpet. He grabbed a sack. He bent his knees. He lifted.

One of the sacks had a tear in the corner. Something he only noticed halfway to the van. A stream of tiny white prills trailing in his wake like polystyrene snow. Like insect eggs or ball bearings.

I'll sweep up later, she told him, close behind with cargo of her own. Don't stop, keep moving.

When the sacks were loaded, he carried other things. She'd piled everything they needed on one side of the room. Bales of sawdust wrapped in plastic. Unmarked jerrycans of what looked like apple juice. A cardboard box with the lid taped shut. A plywood board. A pair of shovels. An old plastic paint bucket he'd barely touched before Siwan called out in alarm.

She stood with her hand over her mouth, eyes upon the ceiling. It occurred to him she had no idea where her father was.

The bucket had a rock on the lid to weigh it down. The bottom wrapped in terrycloth to cradle it from disturbance. He stood over it, expecting some surprise. A jack-in-the-box, spring-loaded. A drip ran down the side from its previous life, the label sun-bleached halfway white. Siwan came over and eased him away by the back of his coat.

I'll get this one, she said, picking up the bucket gingerly. Just keep going.

She drove with the bucket in the footwell and her mouth half open, as though there was something important she was about to impart. She put on the wipers in an effort to clean the windscreen. Tried the spray, but it hadn't been refilled. The van felt weighted, front-loaded despite their cargo. Every time she shifted gear, the stick seemed to resist.

They did not see another car. What light there was came luminescent from the dash. Miles per hour, revs per minute. The needle rising. Clouds silent and drifting above. The moon just a smear. Mack felt cold after the exertion. Skin tender against his clothes. The pair of them with the rags around their necks now. Both sniffing and wiping at their noses with their hands. The road seemed to rush as they passed over it. After a while, Siwan dropped the headlights again and they became the night itself.

Would a person see them if they were to pass now? Or would they see nothing, feel only the speed and surge?

They pulled into the lane behind his grandparents' house. The road surface uneven with potholes and clumsy fixes. Siwan took it slow. When they parked up before the garage, she hesitated as if to catch her breath. Mack sat on his hands to warm them. Siwan exhaled through her nose. When they got out, he held the torch and she worked the keys. The moon struggled above like it wanted to help or else reveal them to the world. The paint from the door flaked off in black flecks and stuck to the damp of her palms. They were twitchy in their vigilance. If there was a sound, they froze.

The van ticked, the engine cooling. A black cat in the alley, a night-time wanderer, its eyes pure light.

They raised the door together. She had already moved in some supplies. Planks of wood, a set of metal drums. She disappeared back into the van and returned with a sheaf of notes, written in her careful hand. The contents of the sacks would be mixed with the sawdust, the fluid poured on top. The mixture would be turned over until combined then loaded into the drums. She knew the precise details. The amounts, the ratios, the maths.

There was twenty-five kilos in each sack and they were aiming for eight hundred. Twenty kilos of sawdust. Sixty litres of the fluid. She laid down a plywood board to stop the shovel sparking against the ground. Mack pulled the rag over his face again. Took a shovel from the back.

Siwan had the Stanley knife. She cut the sacks, he poured. She made tally marks on her sheet to keep a record of their progress. The wind picked up. The light swung on its wire. Their shadows met on the floor.

Grit hung on the air, particles ascending. The smell of the sawdust made him think of a pet shop, small creatures spinning in a wheel. His eyes watered, but he wasn't certain if it was the cold or the chemicals. He cut the mixture, turned it over. The shovel shuddered over the boards.

When the dry mixture was combined, she turned to the cans. Two types, labelled with permanent marker. Mack didn't ask what the fluid was, just waited as she measured it. She nodded her head as she counted.

Ten litres, twenty litres. Thirty.

She moved the cans with her feet towards him. He poured the fluid and it came out viscous. It smelled like gasoline.

He cut the mixture. He turned it over. The fumes of the slurry were overpowering. He tried to inhale through his nose to keep the taste out of his mouth. The hollow bodies of the drums thudded like distant thunder as Siwan rolled them in to be loaded. He took a new grip on the shovel, right up near the blade. He dug, he worked, he lifted. Every so often, he undid the rag on his face, then knotted it up again. He kept having to step out into the lane to breathe.

The slop hit the bottom of the drum like vomit. He kept his eyes on the ground, focused. Arms burning, shoulders straining, blisters forming on the meat between his finger and thumb. He repeated the same action over and over until thoughts slid right out of his head. The more he did it, the less he felt. It came to seem like prayer.

They filled five drums in all. When it was done, he removed his gloves to air his hands but didn't like what he found so put them back on again. It was only on getting the first drum to the back of the van that they realised it was too heavy to lift.

He watched as she flipped through her papers, frantic in her desperation.

We'll have to roll them, she decided quickly. Put them on their sides and find something to use as a ramp. I think the lids should hold.

Mack leaned with his hands on the barrel. He didn't like the uncertainty in her voice.

Yes, she decided. That's what we'll do.

He watched as she found a length of chipboard in the garage and balanced it at an incline into the back. The ramp

appeared a little steep to Mack's eye, but she seemed satis-
fied.

Hang on a sec, he said. Is this going to work?

It's fine.

You're sure?

We haven't got time, Mack.

Her shoulder bumped against his as she joined him at the
barrel. She made to tip it over, but he resisted.

Let's think about it a minute.

You don't trust me?

I didn't say that.

She pushed the drum. He pulled it back.

Mack, she said, voice low and seething. What else are we
going to do?

They eased it to the ground in front of the ramp.
Crouched, knees bent, as she counted down from three. On
one, he screwed his eyes and pushed and she followed. The
drum flopped over and rolled at an angle in the bed of the
van. The contents glugged. Siwan went scrambling in after it.

When the first was in position, they did the others. Five
barrels arranged in a quincunx. When all were loaded, she
retrieved the drill and screwed planks to the floor of the van
to stop the drums from sliding.

The wail of the bit almost killed him. In its aftermath,
they held their breath and waited.

The drums secured, she asked him to fill the gaps.
Whatever was left in the sacks, she said. Anything flammable
in the garage. While Mack did as he was told, Siwan went
into the front of the van to retrieve the final component.

She held the bucket as one might a baby. She'd saved a
place for it.

They stood at the back to admire their work. When Siwan closed the doors, she did so carefully. She got back into the front and turned the key. Mack flinched as the engine started. He held the garage open as she backed the van inside. White light on the wall, then red, then dark again. The engine coughed, then ceased.

He waited for her to get out, but she didn't get out, so he got in instead. The pair of them in the front seats, breathing the same air.

His palms burned, his back ached, he tasted chemicals in his mouth. He kept his gloves on so as not to see his blisters. His clothes felt heavy with sweat or condensation but he was afraid to ask her to put on the heat.

We're done, she said towards the windscreen. You can go.

But she didn't move, so neither did he. They sat together, facing forward, his arms trembling slightly in his lap, shocked in the wake of his effort. He wanted the taste out of his mouth. Would have killed a man for a glass of water. He tried not to think about what sat behind him.

What time on Sunday?

You don't need to worry about Sunday, she said.

He was already worrying about Sunday, but he didn't tell her that. He told her instead that he wanted to help. That he'd come this far.

Mack, she said. Don't make me repeat myself.

He felt the knotted rag around his neck as he nodded. Felt the tendons between his shoulders call out in complaint.

What about—

Go home, she said. Get some sleep.

He nodded again, eyes still set forward. The windscreen fogged with their breath. He thought of the sacks, the drums, the bucket. Questions he wanted to ask. The imagined sequence of events. The only thing he couldn't picture was how the whole thing might operate. Was there a fuse? A remote control?

His heart kicked. He chased the thought away.

What about your father? he asked instead.

Siwan swallowed before she answered.

My father will be all right.

But Siwan, what if—

He'll be fine.

Her voice flared in warning. He dropped the thought and looked forward, though saw nothing through the misted glass.

When will I see you next?

She considered the question. Or at least he thought she did.

Siwan?

We're tired, Mack. It's time to leave.

They sat together in the silence. He wasn't sure if he was delaying departure or afraid to open his door. She still had the mascara on her lashes, pink on her lips. When she moved beside him, he smelled the petrol coming off her clothes like perfume.

Siwan, he asked eventually, is there anything else you need from me?

Again she took a moment with the question.

There's just one more thing, she said softly. I need access. I need you to let me in.

XIV

Creeping into the bathroom, Mack closed the door and slid the latch before putting on the light. At the mirror, he undressed and examined himself. His body waxen in reflection, a man carved from soap. The bruise on his head had disappeared, but his hands were marked with blisters. Some of the scratches on his neck were deep enough to draw blood.

He put water on his face. Felt the cold of it. The sucked-breath shock. The bones of his ribs showed in the low light. The hollow of his clavicles. The notches at the base of his throat. His heart beat in his chest like something bewildered, and when he stopped to look close enough he could make out its hurried edges. A twitch beneath the skin he prayed might never stop.

He knew he would not sleep, so instead he got to his knees beside his bed and prayed. To St Michael, St Barbara, St Stephen. Prayed until his mind slowed and stiffness seized his limbs on the bare planks of his bedroom floor. When prayer left him, he repeated the words he'd been taught. When despair threatened, he put it to God directly.

Tell me, Father, have I understood?

Morning brought little light and no reprieve from the quiet. A great stillness engulfed the town and pinned the people to their beds. Mack peered from his window to find the street outside flooded with mist. Before leaving his room, he pressed his ear to the door, listening for his parents.

He pissed and washed his face. Could still smell petrol on his hands. Downstairs he opened the fridge but did not eat. Poured a glass of water. It was dark in the kitchen but the clock on the cooker, still an hour slow, suggested it was nine. He drank the water and refilled the glass. The fog seemed to be coming indoors.

He returned upstairs, showered and dressed himself. Beat the dust from his coat and wiped his shoes with a cloth over the sink. The blisters on his hands stung so he covered them with plasters. He put on his shoes again then went out to face the day.

Outside, the light struggled to penetrate the fog. Not a single person on the street. No breath of wind, no singing bird. An aftermath with not even a crow returned to pick clean the bones of the dead.

No patience for his morning walk, he headed straight for the church.

He knocked on the rectory door and waited. Tried the handle, found it open. Canon Sylvester was on the floor in the study. The once proud shelves now bare, the furniture covered in sheets. The old man on his knees on the thread-bare carpet, surrounded by books, cardboard boxes, a pair of scissors, parcel tape. Only the canon had become distracted.

He flipped through a text and turned to another. He had not heard Mack come in.

Books on St Paul, Job, St Thérèse of Lisieux. Hans Urs von Balthasar, Adrienne von Speyr. The gnostic gospel according to Judas Iscariot.

Heresy at this hour? Mack asked, squatting to his haunches.

The canon looked up. Squinted through his glasses as if to check it really was who he thought.

Just stopped in to see how you're doing. Noticed your cough during mass?

The canon dismissed the concern with a wave, but at that moment coughed again. He took a handkerchief from his pocket and covered his mouth, attention back on the books before him.

How long have you had it? Mack asked. Might be worth seeing a doc—

Canon Sylvester put the book down and peered up at his guest.

I'm old, Cormac. This is what happens.

Before Mack could question him further, the cough returned. Canon Sylvester excused himself and left the room, the hacking fading down the hall. The sound of the tap. Water moving through the pipes. When the canon reappeared, he was red in the face, a little out of breath. He put his glasses back on and settled again on the carpet.

I'm sorry, Mack said.

The canon looked at him. Sorry about what?

Mack didn't know what to say. The priest returned to his books. Any notion of packing appeared to have slipped from his mind. He read for a while before speaking.

Don't look so glum, he said. The end can go one of two ways yet. Redemption or damnation. The beauty of being a Catholic.

The room didn't look priestly. Too homely. Too lived in. Long bookshelves and big battered sofas. A Persian rug. Wooden cabinets, chests of drawers. Net curtains with a crimp in the end and a clock on the mantel that chirped on the hour. The marble of the hearthstone was green.

Mack wandered over to a stack of books and took one from the top. An illustrated version of the Canticle of the Sun. St Francis of Assisi. We praise you, Lord, for all your creatures. He flipped to the front and found a handwritten note on the inside cover. *To Canon Sylvester*, it read, *from Jasmine.*

Have you followed Judas's fate in the Apocrypha?

The canon's voice made Mack jump. He shut the book and put it back on the pile. Turned to find his old mentor brandishing another volume towards him.

It claims he suffered all manner of indignities, Canon Sylvester said. Disfigurement, bloating, his body infested with worms. He apparently grew so large he could barely pass between buildings. When he went away and hanged himself, he slipped from the noose and burst apart on the ground.

Mack had read it. The maggots, the pus, the genitals. The high stink. The plucked chicken rousing itself upon its stone in his kitchen.

They say the bursting might be a reference to a snake, the canon continued. The greedy constrictor who overestimates his own dimensions. Attempts to swallow a meal so large his midriff splits and guts come pouring out.

A blanket had been thrown over the television. The paper turned yellow on the walls. There was a broadsheet on the coffee table, creased and folded in half. A few days out of date now. Wars and rumours of wars.

I've always considered Judas misunderstood, Mack admitted.

The canon picked up another book and cracked it open.

And to think, he said, you accuse *me* of heresy.

But Mack was serious. Why would Judas be so public in his actions? Christ was conspicuous enough, never one to hide away. All that was achieved by the theatre of the kiss was Judas's own implication. He must have decided to act in such a manner, or else it was predetermined.

He continued his examination of the room as he spoke. There were marks on the wall where pictures had hung. A can of Mr Sheen on the mantel. A book on the telephone table from a garden centre out of town. A list of supplies and prices.

Stanley knife, electric drill, wood screws 4", superglue, cardboard boxes.

He revealed what he had done and thus condemned himself, Mack continued. Matthew in his Gospel. It would be better for Judas if he had never been born. But tell me, without his actions and what came after, what would have become of us?

Canon Sylvester closed the book and set it in a box. Removed his glasses to wipe them.

You heard Thursday's homily, he said, holding his glasses to the light. The crucifixion was essential.

Mack turned away again. Paced the room to match his internal movement. He stopped before a box and removed the top object. A framed embroidery. A prayer for hope in cross stitch.

He was a man who believed in the beauty of Christ so completely he forsook his own soul, he said. Everything was to fulfil scripture. Does that not make Judas the perfect disciple?

On returning home, he found the living room taken over. The apostles swollen in number now. Their clothes creased but mood bright, packed tight onto the settees to watch a report about the town on the lunchtime news. The men offered their own commentary as the crucifixion was beamed back to them. There were so many they'd had to carry chairs through from the dining room. Mack hesitated in the doorway, fearing he'd walked into an ambush, but the gang were too rapt with the television to notice his appearance. Someone was banging around in the kitchen. The air smelled of instant coffee, bacon grease, eggs poached in vinegar. The morning-after reek of stale smoke and beer as it evaporated through the pores of their skin.

A spokesman had said the Steel Company were monitoring developments in the town, the anchor explained. They were re-evaluating their vision. Amenable to fresh dialogue.

The gathered men cheered at the news. All the familiar faces, knee-to-knee on the furniture. Peggy, Curly, Dai and Bryn.

You didn't make it?

Mack turned as his father emerged from the kitchen, spatula in hand, Clara's pinny tied around his waist. His tone more consoling than angry or disappointed. Like he was genuinely sorry his son had missed a once-in-a-lifetime event.

The crucifixion? Mack asked. I was there.

We didn't see you.

I was there, Mack repeated. I just couldn't get down the front.

Jackie shook his head as though that was bad enough.

Do you want breakfast? he asked, gesturing with the utensil. All the sausages have gone, but I can make a bacon butty.

Mack said he wasn't hungry so his father offered coffee instead. Tea, orange juice, a hair-of-the-dog beer if he fancied it. Mack said he was fine and his father didn't press him. They turned back to the lounge instead and watched the gathering that had established itself there.

We didn't know what to do with ourselves today, Jackie chuckled fondly. Felt at a bit of a loose end.

The room looked smaller full of them. The curtains drawn, not so much as a lamp burning. An assembly called not out of purpose or principle but need. As though having spent the previous days together, they could no longer fathom life as they had previously lived it. An existence beyond one another's company.

Christ descended into hell, Mack said.

His father looked at him.

He what?

On the Saturday, Mack clarified. It's in the Apostles' Creed.

Jackie nodded slowly as though not quite following, the slightest concern nagging at his features.

And what was he doing down there?

Saving people, Mack said simply. What else would he be doing? For all we know, hell is empty by now.

When he finally made his way upstairs, he found the bathroom door open. The sink cleaned, the toilet ringed with bleach. His pile of clothes no longer in the bath.

I've washed them, his mother said, appearing behind him. They were filthy.

She seemed entirely unburdened by the migraine now. Her voice carried an edge of accusation he didn't like. He went to his room to escape, only on slipping inside and closing the door, his mother came barging in.

The state of the room halted her. No curtains at the windows, no sheets on the bed, the carpet torn up from the floor.

Cormac? was all she said.

He closed the door again and pressed his back to it. His mother paced in slow bewilderment across the room. What colour had returned to her cheeks in the wake of her illness appeared to be draining. When she turned back towards him, he saw her lips had begun to move.

Did you tell Dad about last night?

Tell him what?

You know what.

His mother looked at him. Face a picture of tired sympathy.

Do you want to tell me what's going on?

Mack felt the solidity of the door at his back. Tasted metal in his mouth. Saw a ripple in his vision. A cloud in the corner of the room. He didn't want to tell her. Or he did, but couldn't. He shook his head and looked at the floor.

Why did you used to take us to the Plaza? he asked suddenly.

Clara sat on the unmade bed and ran her hand over the

mattress. Looked at the bare room as she considered the question.

Her mother needed help, so I helped, she said simply. We were friends.

He waited for her to say more, but she was back to her silent prayer. The cloud pressed around them. His mother looked so discouraged on his stripped bed he could hardly bear it.

Siwan came to me, he said. At the seminary before I left. She wanted to tell me something. Had a confession to make.

His mother's lips stilled.

And?

I heard it for her.

And what did she say?

Her voice was quick and desperate. He wasn't sure if it was panic or hope. He leaned harder against the door, ensuring it was shut. The cloud thickened around them, a fog climbing the walls.

What did she say, Cormac?

His mother was on her feet now, eyes wide as she approached.

Mam, he said, you know I can't tell you that. There's a seal of silence I must keep. My vocation comes with rules.

His words stopped her in her tracks. Your vocation?

Yes, he said, taking her hands in his.

She looked up at him, suddenly calmed. Opened her mouth to speak but had nothing to say. The cloud was dispersing now, the room coming into focus. When her eyes met his, her smile broke forth like a light.

*

He spent the evening with the canon's books. Transcribed passages longhand, giddy with the pleasure of an old habit rekindled. He worked until his fingers cramped and the notebook was finished, its pages full front to back. When it was done, he put the books away and stored the box beneath his bed, then sat at his desk again and started reading what he had written. A stranger's words in his own hand.

Pause for a moment, you wretched weakling, he'd quoted, and take stock of yourself. Who are you, and what have you deserved, to be called like this by our Lord?

The admonishment struck him like a blow. He read on, wishing to be struck again.

At this stage, wretched man, you must keep an eye on your enemy. You must not think yourself any holier or better because of the worthiness of your calling, and because you live the solitary life . . . So go on, I beg you, with all speed. Look forward, not backward. See what you still lack, not what you have already.

He rose from his seat and dressed in his work clothes, then sat at the desk again.

When you first begin, he'd written, you find only darkness, as it were a cloud of unknowing. Reconcile yourself to wait in this darkness as long as is necessary, but still go on longing after Him whom you love.

He stood, retrieved his boots and laced them. He sat and turned the page.

You are to step over it resolutely and eagerly with a devout and kindling love, and try to penetrate the darkness above you. Strike that thick cloud of unknowing with the sharp dart of longing love, and on no account whatever think of giving up.

He got to his feet and went to the wardrobe. His vestments still hung inside. He took down the cassock and the alb from their hangers and put them on over his clothes, then turned to the Easter chasuble. A milk-white garment with a beige centre panel embroidered with the Lamb and the cross. He took it down from its hanger and raised it over his head. He returned to the desk and picked up the book.

> If you want this intention summed up in a word, to retain it more easily, take a short word . . . the shorter the word the better . . . a word like 'God' or 'Love' . . . Fix this word fast to your heart, so that it is always there come what may. It will be your shield and spear in peace and war alike. With this word you will hammer the cloud and the darkness above you.

He closed the notebook and opened the drawer beside him. Reached in blind and felt that familiar clank, a ring of teeth. He hoisted his vestments so he might get at his belt and attached the keys at the hip.

A handful of the apostles were still in the living room. Sleeping now, splayed on the sofas, cans left half drunk on the carpet. They'd spent the afternoon drinking in town and come back again. Mack had heard them through the floor of his room. Full of old songs and well-worn stories, familiar things repeated, connections reinforced. Their drinking had continued and the volume rose with it, but no neighbour knocked the door in complaint. These were the men, after all, who had committed to action, and now salvation was coming. Who could begrudge them a little festivity?

Before leaving the house, he stood before the Sacred Heart. Christ's expression soft and free of judgement. His hand raised as though in blessing, heart aflame, palms bearing wounds. Mack stood before Christ and crossed himself, a short word fastened to his heart.

He walked with his hands linked before his breast, his back straight, his eyes downcast. He headed through town towards the works but did not take the main entrance, instead followed the railway line along the perimeter, past the hot mill and the cold mill and the continuous annealing line. Beyond the wood plant, the BOC gas station, the crematorium. He walked down Longlands Lane into the dark industrial ground. A place for burning things, for burying strangers, a land of fly-tipped junk and coal piles, Portakabins painted blue and green and white.

The lights flashed on the crossing gates of the main rail line as he approached the entrance to the knuckle yard. He stopped as the barriers lowered and a hysterical alarm called out. Flowers had been tied to the railings there. Sun-bleached cards and stuffed animals matted with rain and filth. Memorials to those who had gone onto the tracks and never returned. Those unfortunate or determined now seated at the right hand of the Lord. The lines clittered electric when the train approached and his garments lifted with the force of it. The carriage windows looked like aquaria in the dark.

His chasuble was damask and stitched with silk. At the top of the cross at its centre flew a red banner. A symbol of divine victory.

The knuckle yard was weeded over. A forgotten place of rust and stone. Husks of train cars benighted in the scrub. Shunters and freighters and coil wagons emblazoned with graffitied names and indecipherable scrawl. Emblazoned too with the logos of companies. EWS, National Rail and Biomass. Germanic names of violent progress. DB Schenker, Drax.

He heard the drone of the wind. The sound of drip on tin. He knew the road led to the beach past the coal yard. Found the conveyor belt there motionless. No single light nor wisp of smoke. He heard the ocean before he saw it. Could tell by the smell that the tide was out.

Picking through helleborine and hawthorn and pennywort, he cut up through the marram and into the slacks. The climb took the wind out of him. Invited the pain back into his skull. When he reached the top, he shone his torch onto the beach and saw a figure halfway to the tideline. A man wrapped in red, supine on the sand. The sight brought the taste to Mack's tongue again. A shimmer in the corner of his eye. He scrambled for cover, struggling for footing on the loose silt, almost on all fours as he crouched amid the sea holly and shivering dune grass. The path towards the works across the top of the dunes was blocked by a tangle of brambles. He had no choice but to go along the beach.

He raised his head over the crest of the hill and peered down. The figure, it seemed, was dressed not as a monk but a Roman centurion. Leather tunic, burgundy cape and ivory breastplate, flat on his back like a defenestrated king. Another casualty of the Saturday night. A feller taken to the role offered to him, not quite ready to return to real life. Seeing no option than to pass the motionless figure, Mack rose and slid down the face of the dune as quietly as possible. He put one foot in front of the other. Kept his eyes on the path ahead.

The man made no sound as he crept by. Mack did not

check if he was breathing. The tide had furrowed the sand into intricate channels and a puckered brown scum lay in patches across the top. An iodine smell. A wrack line of cockle shells and razor clams, the woody heads of mason worms and ribboned lines of kelp. It occurred to Mack that everything was dead or in the process of dying. He heard a sound behind him. An upward clatter, a wooden puppet seized by its string.

It's dark, isn't it? a voice called. A rich timbre, baritone, chiselled clean.

Mack turned around. The man was on his feet now, not particularly tall but imposing nonetheless. His face familiar in a way he couldn't place. Features fit for a big screen.

Like the bottom of a pit, the man continued. What time is it?

Mack didn't answer. It was dark. No ships in the bay, no glow from the works, not even the red eyes of the obstruction lights atop the cranes on the docks. The man held out a hand and Mack shook it. The force of his grip matched his voice.

If he noticed Mack's attire, he offered no comment. His own costume was covered in fine sand, like he'd been buried in the dunes and had only now found reason to climb out. Mack put on the torch so he might see him better. Found the costume far more impressive than that worn by Pilate at the trial. The man rested one hand on the handle of his weapon; the other held a long robe stained with something dark. When he noticed Mack examining the attire, he drew his sword from its sheath.

Not historically accurate, he said, holding the weapon at arm's length.

The blade looked sharp. Mack took a step back, but the man followed him. His eyes were intense. Bright as a blade themselves. The colour of rock split down the centre. Grey-green with flecks of white.

The ripple blurred Mack's vision. A gauze before his eyes.

I won this in a game of dice, the man said, holding up the robe before him. He laughed bitterly at the object in his hands. I was delighted earlier in the evening, but now, so late at night, the prize has lost its appeal.

Waves broke sluggish in the distance. Wind moved sand across their feet.

Not that I'm the first to covet that which is not mine, the man said suddenly. I know that for sure. I've been reading a lot of history of late.

He put the sword back in its scabbard and gathered his cloak around him. A practised action, full of theatricality. If he was drunk, he did not slur. If he was lost, he didn't seem to mind. He spoke with a certain projection. The kind of voice you listened to.

The more I read about man, he continued, the more I realise he will never change. Our stupidity is immortal. The same mistakes, prejudices, injustices and lusts wheeling endlessly through the centuries.

The Roman's words gathered in rhythm as he spoke. The bark and purr of an engine warmed. The confidence of a practised script. Like a man so convinced by his own performance he'd found the urge to continue beyond the event. Adopt the persona in which he'd been cast. Seize the opportunity to become someone else.

Well? he said, as though expecting some response.

Mack's head pounded. He wanted to turn and run.

I try to not be so judgemental, he offered, wilting a little in the man's stare. What was it Christ the Saviour said? Father, forgive them, for they know not what they do?

God? the man asked, brow knotted. I want to believe in God, but I cannot. My intellect has grown too muscular. My imagination extends no further than the horizon. I've long held a suspicion that the last sound to be heard on this lovely planet will be that of a man screaming. I fear it might be me.

Mack glanced at his watch, then over his shoulder. Found the works moribund behind them, patiently awaiting its resurrection.

If there is a God, the man continued, turning to follow Mack's eye, then by all means let Him save us from death. Hell, let Him make a saint of me. Perhaps then I'll be more inclined to believe.

On reaching the plant, he went to the office. Unlocked the door by torchlight and locked it again behind him. It was dark inside save for the glow of the screens. The cameras still running, indifferent to the shutdown around them. He stopped to watch, looking for the centurion but finding only dormant stillness. His breath filled the quiet, the beating of his heart. When he made to move again, he startled himself with the manacle clank of the keys.

Monochrome images cycled by. He took a seat and watched. An eye on the entire plant, remote and all-seeing, god of his own small world. He wound the footage back and looked for himself in the pictures. A figure amid the teeming static and tumbling lines, wraithlike in the white flow of his alb. He wound further, through the hours and days. Saw everything happen in reverse. The stillness inverted, the birds flying backwards. The lights on the plant came on, smoke sucked down from the sky. He saw Dai's Mondeo reverse into the site and later pull out again. Saw himself and Denzil back up to the cameras and suddenly turn around. He might have gone back years if only he'd kept his finger on the button. Watched the workforce swell then recede again. The Chancellor of the Exchequer mend a ribbon with his scissors. Seen the plant itself dismantled beam by beam until all that was left was marshland. But he did not keep his finger on the button. He logged onto the computer and wiped every file from the drive.

He turned off the switch and pulled the plug from the wall. Filled a mug from the tap in the bathroom and poured it over the tower and in through the grille of the fan.

A small hiss. The sibilance of something suddenly cooled. He took the fire extinguisher from the wall and emptied its foam over the computer. Raised the can above his head and battered the tower to pieces.

He locked the door behind him and started his patrol. The circuit stretched tedious on foot, eerie in the quiet. He visited every gate and entranceway, every fast-secured door. He'd come to know the keys by now through diligent repetition. He was quick and he was quiet. Efficient in his work.

The vestments smelled of frankincense. He had sand in his shoes. The dizziness had returned but it was not unpleasant. Clouds played at the edges of his vision. He watched for intruders, for do-gooders, for Dai. When he came to a door, he barely needed to look to find the key he required. The teeth clicked as they went into the cylinder. The tension of the pins sang in the stillness of the night.

He passed the BOS plant and the concast. The slab yard

with its hulking Kress carriers. The refractory stores. The test house. The pensive eye of the looming furnaces. He was careful in his actions. Ran his torch along the railings to clear any unexpected life. Sometimes locked a door then unlocked it again, just to be sure. If there was a gate, he tied it open. If there was a padlock, he dropped it on the ground. He did not know what access she needed, so he gave her everything.

At the end of the patrol, he came upon the old abbey wall. Thought back to the monk of legend, that man of jinx and hexes. A Catholic man faced with the end of the only world he knew. A dark tunnel with but one direction remaining. He placed his palms on the stones. As damp as the earth, tarnished by lichen, some hewn stump of old history beset with climbing weeds and mosses. If he prised, he could almost get his fingers between the gaps. He pushed a little to test the structure. He leaned with the full weight of his body.

He walked his route in reverse. Back along the works, the rolling mills and furnaces. Through Margam and its echoing underpass. He thought of ringing her phone, going to her house, running to the centre of town and alerting the authorities. He could return home to tell his parents. Rouse the apostles. Break the seal, come clean. But instead, he followed the river in the still-dark morning until he reached its deepest point. He stopped to watch the surface, the water stretched so flat the firmament came back in reflection, then he removed the keys from the clip on his belt and with an overarm motion tossed them in.

His watch showed an hour until dawn. He pulled his vestments tight around himself and carried on walking.

Around the school and back again. Past St Joseph's and St Mary's. He did not once hesitate or err on his path. He knew where he was going.

The boards were still loose on the front of the Plaza, the wood slowly rotting. He pulled his sleeves over his hands and worked his way in. A struggle on his own, though he did not complain. He prised and yanked and tore. Got to the dirty floor and crawled on his hands and knees.

The dilapidation of the foyer struck him again. Felt like the dawn of something. Like the end of the world. He retrieved the torch from within his vestments and looked around the room. Put money on the counter and grabbed an empty popcorn box. Then he headed down the hall towards the main screen and shouldered through the heavy doors.

Twenty minutes until daybreak.

Inside the auditorium, he turned off the torch and imagined it was the beginning of a picture. The lights just lowered, the projector soon to whirr. The fizzle of an audience quieted.

The trailers would soon start. Promises for what was to come.

He climbed onto the stage and ran his hand over the red fabric of the drapes. If his palm came back soiled, he couldn't see it in the dark. The curtains threadbare but still bulky, thick with cobwebs and mummified bugs. He pushed through into the shadowed space beyond them. Used the light of his torch to find his way towards the controls.

The curtains opened on a pulley system, just like the one he'd once used in school.

Fifteen minutes until dawn.

He took the cord in his hands. Held tight to stop them shaking. The technique came back to him at once. The proper action he'd been taught. His own private ceremony. As the drapes parted, they made not a single sound.

Ten minutes.

He climbed down from the stage and into the audience. Took the same seat he'd always taken. Sat with his arms on the rests and closed his eyes. With five minutes to dawn, he waited in the quiet. Waited with a word fastened to his heart. Waited for what seemed like a lifetime, and when the waiting was done and morning broke and the silence gave way to sound, he opened his eyes and saw a blank screen before him, the naked face of God.

Acknowledgements

I would like to thank: the good people at Literature Wales, who provided invaluable support and assistance.

Tom Bullough for taking my work seriously at the beginning and helping me see what I was writing. Kasim Ali for spotting something and sticking his neck out, then going above and beyond the call of duty to crack open the door.

Emma Paterson for her belief, vision and trust – you pushed the book closer to the one I'd long envisioned – as well as everyone at Aitken Alexander for all the efforts unseen. James Roxburgh for his curiosity, good humour and perceptiveness – you undoubtedly made this novel stronger – plus everyone at Atlantic Books for bringing my work to the world with such care.

I'd also like to thank: everyone at Swansea University, particularly Alan Bilton for his patience and encouragement during the early days, and Elaine Canning for the unwavering optimism. Anthony Shapland for the help and reassurance. Eddie Matthews for the conversations about hometown messiahs long before I knew there was a novel in it. Matthew Greaves for the reliably cutting remarks on anything I sent him.

And, of course, I'd like to thank my family, especially my grandparents, my parents and Liam.

A Note on the Author

Jon Doyle is a writer based in Port Talbot, South Wales. He was part of Literature Wales' Representing Wales scheme in 2022/23, and won the Writers & Artists Working-Class Writers' Prize 2023. He holds a BSc and MRes in Zoology and MA in Creative Writing from Cardiff University, and a PhD in Creative Writing from Swansea University. His work has appeared in *Short Fiction*, *Hobart*, *Ploughshares Online*, *The Rumpus*, *3:AM Magazine* and *Critique: Studies in Contemporary Fiction* among other places. *Communion* is his first novel.